Push and Pull

The Vows of a Husband and Wife

Dedication

I dedicate this book to my family. If there was ever anyone who doubted me, it was never them.

I dedicate this book to the girl friends who walked with me while I built my world. My hype women who have earned the characters that represent them.

I dedicate this book to 6th grade me. It took us longer than we thought, but there's no stopping us now.

Disclaimer

Table of Contents

The Key

Concern	Pale Pink	Plums
Calm	Sky Blue	Lavender
Panic	Shock Yellow	Gasoline
Horror	Inky Black	Cinnamon
Disgust	Murky Green	Mildew
Anger	Red	Rusted Metal
Rage	Crimson	Burning Plastic
Lies	Oily Gray	Burnt Sugar
Uncertainty	Pale Yellow	Licorice
Confusion	Mute Rainbow	Cheap Perfume (citrus/musk)
Excitement	Sparkly Silver	Cotton Candy
Worry	Sunflower Yellow	Potting soil
Reluctance	Powder grey	Flour
Lust	Scarlet	Amber
Good Intentions	Bright Colored Kaleidoscope	Jasmine
Bad Intentions	Grey Matter Kaleidoscope	Melted Rubber
Sympathy	Powder blue	Apricot

Preface

Kaila

Incoming rabbit in three…two… I hear Kestien's velvety voice in my earpiece, the hint of sass that just comes with being him has been replaced with the militant tone that can only come from doing what we do. I whip my arm out to connect with my target's throat when he attempts to round the corner. Davon Draps. A low level Mafia Don who decided to get into some big level shit, about to meet the consequences of his actions. The disappointment at how easy this job has turned out to be is confirmed at this moment. I don't even feel it when the man practically flips over my arm from the force of his impromptu stop.

"Got him." I confirm aloud, my voice echoing sharply off of the cement walls of the parking garage. I grab the grown man by the ankle, shivering at the onslaught of his emotions seeping into my hand at a dull but still painful stream. I begin dragging him back through the shadows in the direction he came running from. "Rendezvous on the ground floor."

Copy. Copy. Kestien's reply is quick, and the frequency shift in our com system is subtle to my hypersensitive ears. It doesn't take long for the black SUV to pull up. The passenger door swings open to reveal Milo who jumps out with a huff to help hoist the dead weight into the back seat. Standing at 6'6" and big enough in the arms, shoulders, and chest to snap a neck by accident. You'd never tell by looking at him, but Milo is a man of many talents. Straight midnight hair cut shorter on the sides than on the top, painted nails, and the brightest smile I've ever seen on an Italian man. Let alone from anyone in his previous line of work, though I guess it could be considered an asset. There is an ease to the way Milo picks the unconscious Draps up by the collar and belt to hoist him into the back seat.

"Fuck, this guy is kinda heavy." Milo grunts before sliding Draps' body into the middle seat. Milo holds his hand out to

1

help me climb in, closing the door and making his way around to the other side as he checks over the surrounding area. Kairi sits relaxed in her happy place behind the wheel, peering at me from the rearview mirror as Milo gets in on his side with a soft grunt. Kiari's honey eyes narrow through the coily bangs that perpetually hang in her face when I catch her gaze. Her refusal to take the car out of park becomes more evident when her arms cross over her chest.

"You're in the wrong seat, Captain." she growls in her thick Brazilian accent. With a roll of my eyes I climb over the center console and into the front passenger seat. I let out a huff when I catch the way her shoulders bounce once with smug satisfaction. The van begins to move and she wastes no time running headfirst into the one thing I actually don't want to get into. "So are you going to talk about it yet?"

"Talk about what?" I ask, feigning oblivious.

"Don't play dumb. The order has been given. Spec-liu Black left this morning. You literally cannot hold this conversation off any longer." She has a point, and it's worse that she knows it. I know it, too. I'm just more willing to sit in the little bit of time I have left pretending everything is going exactly how I planned it.

"We are working." I hiss in a vain attempt to derail her for a little longer. I had better luck derailing a train last month.

"You aren't even trying anymore." Her face twists in absolute disgust, murky green smoke bleeding out around her. I chuckle, amused at the struggle I'm causing her. Small victory, short lived as it is. "I know the *plan*, but other than *that* you refuse to talk about *them*. I support you, I'm just having a hard time understanding why we have to jump through so many hoops."

"I guess we're talking about this." I grumble, gritting my teeth as the familiar pale pink color of concern fills the all too small space of the vehicle.

"We are. The three of us have talked it over only a million times. Complete and utter, bullshit." She leans forward,

2

pressing her breasts to the horn that doesn't make a sound under the pressure. The way her lean shoulders roll and her back straightens against the seat tells me we have a tail, and the speed demon has awoken in Kiari in response. With her extensive tactical driving record, accompanied by many street race wins, Kiari lays on the accelerator without dropping the conversation for even a beat, the sky blue of calm bleeding out of her at a tentative pace. "Tell her what you said Milo."

A groan comes from the middle seat behind me before Milo has the chance to answer, causing us all to go silent. When nothing else happens, he speaks up. "I told you not to drag me into your argument if you ever confronted her. I may have my personal thoughts and opinions on the matter but I trust the captain's choices."

"THANK YOU." I call out gratefully at the same time I unclip my seatbelt and drop my seat back as far as it will go. A quick spin on my ass has me facing the backseat to settle my back against the dashboard with a deep, steadying breath.

"However," Milo interjects, earning a loud groan of defeat from me. I should have known it wouldn't be that easy. "I have to agree. It's bullshit, and you deserve to be happy after everything you've been through. Though I will do my part without complaint, I just want to ask one more time. Are you sure that you don't want to try finding another way?"

"There is no other way. The circumstances are-"Kiari jerks the wheel to the right, sending us turning to the left at the last second before the light turns red, leaving our company behind us.

"Delicate! We know! I just don't think it should be this big of a fucking deal. What about when they see you at the walk through their first night? As First Captain you are supposed to give it to them." She makes a left quickly in an attempt to make sure there is no chance for them to catch up before a groan louder than the first escapes the captive's lips. His eyes flutter open to meet mine.

A smile spreads across my lips involuntarily along with relief for the reprieve from having to talk about the parts of the plan they think carry the biggest risk. If only.

"Black is going to do his part like we all are. Good Morning, bunny!" I sing out, exaggerating the tone of my voice to signal the end of this wretched conversation.

"No vas a pensar que terminamos con la conversación, cabrona. Don't even think we are done with this conversation, brat." Kiari bites, picking up speed at my que. Milo rolls his eyes when Draps makes a feeble attempt to get out of the vehicle, too disoriented to grasp that he's bound at the wrists and ankles. Screams turn into cries of realization for what exactly is happening to him as his shock yellow panic bursts through my vision. I shake my head. Leave it to a self-proclaimed alpha male to scream like a little girl.

"Shut the fuck up!" Milo shouts in a bored tone as he yanks Draps back to the middle with ease. The cries turn into angry sobs, though the man is trying his best to suppress himself. "Now listen, I'm going to hit you really, really hard, and you are going to take a little nap. But first, I need you to smile real big for me. I just need a quick little biometric scan here so the love of my life can drain the offshore and tie up the assets."

Milo holds up his biometric scanner, initiating the facial scan that was requested. The natural confusion that comes after just about anything that flies out of Milo's mouth is enough to stop the man in his struggle for long enough to allow Milo to finish the scan without any issue. "Got it, Cap'. I forwarded the requested copy to the client as well as to my sexy ass husband."

The guy's got a tracker on him, Captain. Kestian informs me just before his next words ring out through the car speaker for everyone to hear. *Ladies and gentlemen, we have four inbound vehicles approaching from the rear at just under one hundred miles per hour. Judging by my satellite imaging, you will find a grand total of four unfortunate souls in each. If my twin sister can manage the service exit on the far side of the highway, my darling husband can dispose of the device, then our lovely captain should have enough cover to play after a few miles.*

"If I can?" Kiari sucks her teeth at her brother's challenge before jerking the wheel without any warning at all. The hostage is thrown into the door, unceremoniously.

Milo, held in place by his seatbelt while I remain unmoved with my hands held together over my open knees. The vehicle skillfully slides through the oncoming traffic as instructed, darting down the dirt road that untrained eyes would have mistaken as nothing. The wall of trees that surrounds the service road opens up to untouched farmland on either side. Gotta love Nebraska, right? "Redirected and covered."

"On your mark, my love." Kestian quickly confirms the way he has hundreds of times. Milo takes his cue and slides the crying man closer to himself, giving me a quick wink.

"You know, I have to tell you that seeing you fall apart like this," He sucks in a dramatic breath through his teeth. "It does things to me."

I hold my snickers behind a stone mask. Milo has a *filthy* and non discriminant mouth and the man he's holding is visibly trying to vibrate out of his body. The look of disgust is quick before it's washed away by tears, but not fast enough that I don't see the murky green undertones within the inky black wisps of horror. "Now be a good boy and tell me where the tracker is."

The man shakes his head so hard I wouldn't be surprised if his neck snaps.

"Alright, but if I have to search you, my husband gets to fuck you when we get you back to base. Can't touch you if I don't share. Marital agreement and all, I'm sure you understand, I would have to be very thorough." Milo whispers the last words directly into his ear and goes to reach directly for the belt, causing the man to convulse violently, shaking his shoulders and trying to direct the attention to his neck. A simple chain sits on it, but I assume it's been embedded with some magic or another.

Milo unclips it, but not without allowing his fingers to tease the exposed skin on the man's neck and chest. I can't help the chuckle that rumbles low in my belly this time. The man's eyes squeeze shut so tight I feel they might slide right out the back like a soap bar in wet hands. The undeniable smell of human feces assaulting our noses when Milo's lips go to whisper a dangerous Italian growl right in the man's ear before pulling his fist back and knocking the target out just as promised. "Sveglia. L'unica che mio marito può toccare sono io. *Smart. The only one my husband is allowed to touch is me.*"

"Ah, seu filho da puta indecente! Acabei de limpar a merda dos assentos! *Oh you raunchy son of a bitch! I just got the shit out of the seats!*" Kiari shouts, reverting to Portuguese the moment she's angry. She slams open the skylight and stabs the buttons on the driver door to crack the windows. It offers absolutely no relief to our trained senses, but it does make an opening for what I'm about to have to do.

My eyes flick up to the back window, seeing one set of lights become four as the vehicles push into formation, gaining speed as they tear up the road after us. With my smile spread wide I exchange a glance with Milo before hoisting myself through the sunroof. I hear him call out to Kestien before I pull my focus. "Captain in position!"

Standing by for collar drop. Kestian states, in my earpiece once more. I plant my feet shoulder width apart while I watch the cars gain on us. I take a deep breath, and release it slowly. Once. Twice. I focus on forcing my surroundings to slip away to the farther reaches of my attention in preparation for the full weight of my Juggernaut ability.

"Alright Kes'," I say, my voice coming out in a dark growl. "Cut me loose."

The moment the metal collar around my neck separates into its four pieces, falling to the fading ground below, I allow

6

myself to step off the car still in motion. As I fall, time slows and my thoughts race with the barrage of emotions absorbing into me. Just before my feet are about to hit the floor in what I am sure would be a very gruesome death, I imagine a teapot opening and colors erupt all around me. Rage red, Black terror, and blue sadness as smoke that bleeds from my pores before I concentrate on pulling each color together to form three deep, dark, purple whips protruding like tails coming from the small of my back. At the snap of my will, my tails shoot forward to stop the earth itself and just as quickly as I fall, I land on my feet unharmed. I walk three full strides, allowing the hues to settle in their solidity. By the time my foot hits the ground at the end of the third stride, I am running at the vehicles that are now coming my way in slow motion.

Willing one tail to add force to my jump, I hurl my body into the air. Spinning mid flight as the first vehicle barrels over the spot I had just been standing.

I can never tell time when I am like this.

It should be unsettling, the imbalance of movement capable as opposed to the normal human.

I secretly enjoy it.

Taking my pistol in hand I allow one purple limb to grip the edge of the skylight, shattering the glass upon impact. The heels of my boots slam into the top edge of the trunk. I take aim, the two loose tails breaking through the back windshield below me, removing the obstacle in the way of their intended targets. I feel their necks snap like I've done it with my own hands, my thin whips growing in diameter as they do every time they take a life. There was a time when I would exhaust every last option before resorting to this level of violence, but I need to make a scene for the idiots who gave us this job. The thing about being forced (and I do say forced) to take in the emotions of absolutely-fucking everyone is that it's already a truly overwhelming experience to begin with even without adding my own issues into it. The feelings of the dead always cling to me harder than the living, and they waste no time intermixing with my own emotions, muddling the world around me. My drive is no longer my own, not entirely. Not completely.

I try to focus on the task at hand, but my body is on autopilot as I leap from one vehicle to the next, forcing them one by one careening off and out of my way. *I just want them out of my way.* Desperate shots zip out of windows to ultimately find an unintended target somewhere off in the distance, and I'm at least conscious enough to be grateful to Kestien. I know he will have checked for collateral damage, it's the reason he cut me loose here. The thoughts that cloud my mental focus buzz through my head as three more souls join the afterlife leaving two more cars. A blink and I'm on one of them, alarm bells start to go off in my brain, and the whispering begins its demand to be heard. I've reached my limit, probably beyond it as my vision begins to cloud with the colors.

I feel my tails untangling but I shake my head, pulling the reserves of my focus and allowing myself to sink into instinct. My attacks are precise, as they should be for all the work I've put in. Muscle memory and something deeper that I just haven't been able to figure out continue to fight my control, and somewhere along the line I don't realize it slips entirely.

Milo says you're looking a little savage, Captain. Warning one's been missed.

Kestien's voice snaps me back to just enough of reality to realize I have somehow made it to the final car, my back pressing against the steering wheel while my tails keep the vehicle from careening off the road. The blare of the car horn is enough to pause me for the amount of time it takes to see the man I am straddling holding my gaze with blank horror, and I realize then that I am laughing to myself as I hold my hand inside this stranger's chest. His heart still beating in my hand coming to a slow stop between my fingers.

Damn it.

8

Captain. Kestian says my title roughly, giving me the signal for my final chance to answer before the choice is taken from me. I shake my head again, harder this time before releasing the heart that pumps one final time between my fingers. While I ungracefully throw myself off the body, I desperately will my tails to stop the car. It takes all the strength I can muster. The reality of what I have done falls on me as it always does when I am finally aware that I am losing my grip. I throw myself from the vehicle just as the three tendrils that have now grown tenfold begin to untether into a barrage of colored smoke. I try every trick I've been taught to reign it in, but it becomes quickly apparent that I won't get the lid back on without help. I sink to my knees under the weight of the insanity beating against my mind, squeezing my palms to my ears like it will help, even when I know it won't. Too many emotions. Too many feelings. I feel them all, and just like always, I can't fucking handle it.

"SEND IT!" I scream, redundant as it is. I missed my window to answer in my struggle. The last thing I see through the bright shadows in my vision is the collar coming at me at full speed from the four cardinal directions. I force myself up so my neck is exposed without letting go of my head before the device latches itself onto my neck once again. I'm only able to gasp, and then I'm pulled into a stasis just before unconsciousness.

Milo must pick me up to bring me back to the car, and I can hear him whisper to me softly. "If you keep ending up like this, you're going to force my hand, Kaila."

My body is completely immobile. The precipice I'm riding allows me enough awareness to listen in on my team while they speak freely thinking I can't hear them, a commotion beginning that I can't feel nor quite understand.

"Vitals, Kes'." Milo's voice is even, a testament to his craft. Yet no matter how dull I'll always be able to feel the shock yellow seeping as slowly as molasses into my skin, especially when it's coming from all of them. Kestien's are duller, but my time with him is its own advantage, and its own curse.

*All over the damn place, honey. Her heart rate is in the sky, her pulse is climbing, and if she doesn't have a seizure soon I'll be-" He's cut off suddenly by what sounds to me like distant but heavy thudding.

"Impressed?" I hear Milo spit through clenched teeth, the struggle in his tone evident. "Were you about to say 'impressed'?"

His sudden anger would choke me if I wasn't wearing the inhibitor collar around my neck, but it still doesn't stop me from feeling the weight of it entirely. The device itself was originally used for darker purposes, but with Kestien's technical background and the help of a few friends, it now assists in making sure my juggernaut ability doesn't drive me insane. Kestien doesn't respond. It's best not to when Milo gets what we call "medically irritated". I still can't feel anything, but I can hear Milo grunting against my apparent struggle, which is funny in theory, but ultimately concerning. I have no doubt that he is trying his best to hold me down so I don't hurt myself, but I also know that he's having a hard time with it, he always does. I don't overpower him in terms of strength until I blackout. The only reason he's even able to hold me now is with the help of the collar and the fact that I am essentially incapacitated. Time passes, though I don't know how much before I hear them release a collective sigh of relief.

"FUCK!" Milo is fed up with me, but I can't help it, which he knows and it irritates him all the more. I hear what can only be Kiari beating the shit out of her steering wheel with an open palm. "Vitals."

They bottomed out for a second. They're stabilizing now. Kestien breaths. *I had to turn the collar up.*

More muffled curses fill the vehicle as I slip a little deeper into the void. Kestien really must have turned it up, because the emotions are fighting to enter. Like molasses trying to get through cheesecloth now. The quick sound of Kiari sucking her teeth at this development is loud and clear even though when she speaks again, her voice is even more muffled. "Again?"

"What's the output at now?" Milo asks, reluctantly.

7.5 Kestien's confirmation sparks fear of my own. The collar is only capable of giving an output of nine. Anything more and they overload. It may not be a secret that my struggle to keep sane is rough, but I made Kes' promise to keep my last two frequencies a secret. I should have known he wouldn't keep anything from his sister, and more so his husband.

"She's not going to survive much more of this damn it." Milo's voice is somewhere in the distance now, making that the last thing I hear.

I can't help but think about what happens if he's right.

I can't help but feel like I already know.

Chapter One
Augustine

The sun surrounds me but I don't feel its heat like I did then. I know this isn't real. I'm just remembering, no matter how bad I wish I could forget. I walk onto the plane with my arms full of crates full of the only detail I can't remember about that fucking day that I set down with the others. I never did need to look very hard for her, so when I turn to find my definition of beauty hunched over her laptop, I do everything in my power to take in the sight. Her face is slightly scrunched at the nose in an almost mouse-like manner. Pencil eraser between her teeth, tension that has been growing for days on her brow, and the single dark brown curl hanging over matching narrow eyes. I had figured she would tell me when she was ready, there were never secrets between us but the look in her eyes became too much for me to wait.

"Porque tan seria, mi amor? Why so serious, my love?"

She looks at me from where she sits with a smile that melts my soul. She never gets the chance to answer, the world dissipates too quickly.

The memory changes.

She's standing right in front of me now, face contorted in emotions like fear, panic, and realization. "Augustine!"

Her screams will forever ring through every fiber of my being.

***

My eyes snap open, my hands reaching for what logic knows won't ever be there again. Back in my cell. Back in my hellscape reality.

Have you ever been or done something so incredibly stupid, that no matter what you do to justify it, it just can't be justified? Until a few months ago, neither had I. That's about the same time I found myself locked up in this fancy ass maximum security military prison. Most people know about the Hague, but this place doesn't even have a name. We inmates just call it Limbo while the guards call it 'the end'.

It's not like I've ever tried to run, but knowing the rest of my unit is still outside this shithole seems to be enough for the government to want to drop me in a dark place. Little do they know, I already gave the order not to come after me even if the boys do know where I am. Which is why I'm not expecting to be dragged out of my cell at this god forsaken hour by a few girl scouts in full tactical gear. I don't fight them. It isn't worth it to me. The bastards herd me through the concrete halls to the shower room. A place usually full of a prisoner per shower head that is now filled with three perverts and a chance to clean myself up. I do so, hurriedly, before I'm escorted to a conference room somewhere in the prison. The halls and doors look too similar to know exactly. The prison is underground, so the exact time is hard to tell, but the lack of guards lets me know it is definitely sometime after midnight by the time we make it to our final destination.

I have a very clear memory of the old man that put me in here. Judge Jackass, I dubbed him in the beginning. I never learned his name, it was never important because he hated me as much as I needed him to. The crease of his brow, the gray in his buzz cut, and the wrinkles that pulled his face down to the level of his hopes and dreams led me to believe that the man I picture inside the toilet bowl when I piss was an old geezer. It seems to be that I've been very wrong, apparently. The man sitting in front of me now has hard features. Bright blue eyes, chest length salt and pepper hair, and all the wrinkles gone to reveal the well aged man with tattoos all over his arms that must have been covered by the robe. The demeanor as he leans that gives off an old school rocker vibe is what really throws me off. Not because he's wearing it, but because it fucking suits him.

Including he and I, there are now a total of ten people in the room. I ignore eight of them as his blue eyes lock on me for a moment, studying me with his intent unwritten on his face. I'm trying to focus on the bastard before me but the sudden and sharp scent of rust starting to overtake my breathing is making it hard. I don't exactly know how I do it, or why it happens. I know it's a bitch to ignore when it keeps you safe and all you want to do is fucking die. I keep my eyes locked with the "judge" while he finishes his silent assessment. While I do my damndest to ignore the itch at the center of my chest urging me to eliminate the threat in the room. There's nothing I know better than the scent of anger.

As far as I've gathered, it's like someone went and turned the dial on certain senses all the way up. My nose in particular, my sense of smell taking on a mind of its own. A few things I've managed to work out the meaning of by pure luck, but not much else about it makes sense other than that.

"Don't worry too much about me boys. My friend here is planning on minding his manners like the good soldier he is. Aren't you, Augustine?" He raises an eyebrow when I don't answer him right away. It's hard to focus with the smells clogging my nose, so I nod once in place of searching out the source of the scent. Eight men filter out of the room in what I know to be practiced formation, but not without some of them giving me a quick size up. I would scoff, but the salty sting of a liar's air all the way up my nose as one of them shoulder checks me has me holding back a laugh. The move itself is an attempt to assert some kind of dominance, but all it really does is let me know it wouldn't be worth it to teach any of them one thing let alone two. I don't drop my eyes from my obvious problem. The man I now find myself alone with as his demeanor slackens and he leans back to prop his boots up on the table.

"Relax." He begins, motioning to the chair across the table from his own. I just stand there at attention, my gaze unmoving from him. Unbothered, he starts talking again. "You sir, have caused quite the commotion in my world. The stunt you pulled with those friends of yours has my bosses extremely interested."

I shrug. "Tell your 'boss' I said I'm flattered, but my friends had nothing to do with it."

He studies me for a moment before rolling his eyes with a 'tisk'.

"Cut the shit and understand that I've known you were bullshitting from the beginning of your trial. We both know that job could have never even gotten started with just one person. Hell! By my calculations, it should have taken no less than fifty to make that happen." I know he is right, but I stand my ground. Remaining silent before a sigh leaves his lips along with something else I don't expect. "What you four did was the single most impressive thing I've seen from an unauthorized unit in at least five years. The government might be too afraid of the embarrassment to admit they got screwed out of a shining moment, but I'm not."

The scent of lavender calm emanates from him, which throws me because it isn't a scent I catch often from people around the prison. It's clear he isn't here to hurt me, but I remain stoic. I study the man further instead, breathing one, slow, lung filling breath at a time. The sudden twitch of the curiosity in his eye is subtle, but the impish grin is knowing as he leans forward, dropping his feet from the table.

"It's the face, isn't it? I'm trying really hard not to be offended that you haven't asked about it. Allow me to re-introduce myself, as I am sure the image you have of me is just a bit different from the handsome mug you see now." He offers a grin. "My name is Special Lieutenant Andrew Black. You've never been briefed on my kind specifically, but they tell our campfire stories during basic training."

Memories of stories I'd heard as a grunt soldier spurt through my mind. Stories of a special class of the military. Ghost units with skills godlike in nature, tall tales used to scare recruits and keep them entertained. I, like many others, put no stock into the reality of rumors, but the way the man before me seems so relaxed in a place full of war criminals and murderers let me know that at least in him there has to be some kind of truth. "What I'm offering you now is an opportunity. Keeping in mind that what I'm about to offer-if refused-will ensure your ass back in your cell in fifteen minutes. Along with Max, Vince, and that Marco Polo kid by nightfall tomorrow."

Any fight in me just died.

Not because of his threat, but the fact that he's bringing Marco into it at all. The anger accompanying the thought of how much trouble Max went through to keep Marco as far away as possible is only going to rival Max's when he finds out. However, the anger is quickly replaced with the full impact of his words, and panic sets in. A feeling that only grows heavier with each word as the special lieutenant continues without asking for permission. "I want the four of you to come with me. I can't give you any more than that for now. Flies are everywhere."

He wants to get me out of here? Where are we going? Who is this guy? I am smart enough to know when I'm beat, even if I only admit it to myself for now. This guy has me by the balls, and he knows my answer already or he wouldn't be here giving me a bogus ultimatum.

"What's the catch? It isn't like they would let you just walk out of here with me." I grit through my clenched teeth.

"A...precaution." He says matter-of-factly. "Think of it as your team's preliminary entrance exam."

Before he goes any further the Special lieutenant hands me a cellphone with a strange green screen illuminated as he holds it out to me, pulling it back just before I can actually grab it. "You get one message. This phone is only encrypted for the next two minutes and the prison tracks everything with more than ten characters. Make them Count! I'm curious to see what your team can do unsupervised on your word."

I take the phone with a cringe. I know he has no idea what he's asking, so I mull over his challenge for just a second. I need to be direct with them or my boys will take it too far. Then again, it sounds like that's exactly what he wants. I take a deep breath and shrug, typing quickly as I allow a devious grin to spread across my face. The smile quickly fades when the soldiers return to the room, filling it fast in an attempt to overwhelm me. I let them, taking note of the fact that not a single one of them is employed by the prison. They drag me back to my cell, while I stick to the guise that their tactics work. As we exit the room, I watch the Special Lieutenant who stays behind. A curious smile twists into a grin of excitement as he reads the words I sent.

Raise Hell

It doesn't take long to get me back to my prison cell. The moment the door closes, I begin keeping time. After an hour of steady pace I find my mind drifting slightly to the past. Back to the day I got arrested.

***

I run into the house from the back door with my shirt torn and jeans ripped at the knees. Vince slams the door behind me, setting all six locks and barring it. We're out of breath, and the fear and realization in Vince's eyes when he turns to me is bright, and the scent wafting off of him screams last ditch effort that only I can seem to smell. The sound of heavy footsteps running down the stairs lets me know that Max and Marco are on their way to convince me not to do what I'm about to do.

I won't listen.

I can't.

Someone needs to answer for this, and I refuse to let it be them.

With that decided, I strip down to my boxers, tossing the bloody clothes in the trash and making my way to my bedroom door off to the right of the kitchen. The others follow, only silent until they see me hang up my dog tags.

"You can't do this!" Marco growls, breathing through his hands the way his sister taught him. Once I'm dressed, I make my way over to him, quickly gripping the back of his neck to force his eyes on mine.

"We talked about this. Listen to Vince and stay out of trouble." I say, pleading with my eyes for him to understand before letting him go so I can slip on my tennis shoes.

"No! This is bullshit, and you know it!" Vince roars with panic I've only ever seen in him once. I've known this guy for most of my life, and to see him this way again shifts something inside of me I'm not ready nor willing to address.

"Max, you know what you have to do. Keep enough of a trail to be believable but keep him out of it. Heat stays on me and that's an order." I say, glancing at Marco.

"She would never let-" Vince tries to hit me with the only reason I've ever needed to breathe, but the situation prompts a visceral reaction. I pick up the small, empty Urn with the mangled dog tag wrapped around the neck and launch it as hard as I can at the wall in front of me.

"SHE ISN'T HERE ANYMORE!" I cry as it shatters. My chest heaves. My voice breaks. *"And that's the fucking problem."*

***

I shake my mind back to the present, only to realize I've lost track of the time. Rolling my eyes, I decide to sit on the single bed, my elbows resting on my knees while I stare at the floor. If not for the light bar outside my cell door, I would be sitting in complete silence. Other than the constant buzzing sound it emits, I find no need to strain to listen to the hallway it illuminates. The usual number of guards line the cell block from what I can make out. In my time here I have learned the names of each guard on rotation. Kordova and Andres at the farthest end of the hall, Alida and Madison at the center of the hall, and Adams and Pinto on the end closest to my cell. Time seems to be standing still, as is the point of this facility. No windows, with solid doors, and no way to really tell what day it is becomes the reason for a lot of prisoners losing their minds. I however, will take so much more effort than the lack of a few clocks.

I never got a cellmate. Most don't on account of violent tendencies, but I have never been one for unnecessary violence. Funny stance to take, being a marine and all. I just see no use for senseless fighting.

Necessary violence, though?

That shit is fun.

As if the thought itself somehow prompts them, the lights cut at the same time as two heavy thuds and the sounds of firearms hitting the ground pull me from the edge of another flashback, but it's the voices that bring on the sigh of relief as the dark lights turn on.

"How the hell did you-"

"How the hell did you get in here?" The mocking voice is childish, and can only be one person I know. There's gunfire, followed by struggling and more bodies dropping. I count the thuds.

Three.

Four.

Five.

One left, but I don't hear the thud of a body. I only hear the clatter of an M16 meeting the earth.

"Buenas Tardes. Good evening." Marco's business voice isn't one I would ever describe as light, there's too much power behind it. His sweet face makes people underestimate him as a soldier, but the proof is in the gruffness that laces his words. I would describe it as a warning, possibly chill inducing. It's the reason I know exactly what the scene is outside the door.

Max is off in the control room somewhere, making a mess of their entire system but making sure not to let the other prisoners out.

Vince is behind Adams, the only jackass with an M16 and no intention of using it, with his own pistol trained at the back of the guard's head. While Marco holds his pistol ready at his side as he speaks. "We just want one. All you gotta do is point, and take a nice little nap. Collect a little worker's comp after and talk about this with your buddies over too much to drink. How's that sound?"

"I...I can't.." Adams is the guard I've been dying to fucking destroy. His standing scent is cat piss, a smell I've come to associate with cowardice. A scent I have determined sticks with someone who naturally is just a piece of shit. It neither dissipates nor grows to my strange senses yet I know it's something only I am privy to.

"Of course you can." Marco's venomous smile is clear in his words, and pride blossoms in my chest. "Because we still need an example...and if we have to find our brother ourselves, you're it."

I don't wait even a heartbeat before I run to my door like my ass is on fire. I knock on the cell door with two distinct taps, followed by the slam of my fist against it.

"Damn, did you hear how fast that was?" Max's cool tone grows closer as he speaks. "He doesn't like you at all."

The sounds of Adams getting the piss beat out of him brings me a joy that should make me feel like a bad person, but it doesn't. I am a little sad it doesn't last long before three familiar faces stumble over one another into the now open cell door. Relieved grins on each of their faces as they straightened up in front of me. "Told you he'd miss us."

"As glad as I am to see you fuckers, I'm assuming we're on a time crunch for some reason or another." I rush, smiling so wide my face hurts.

"Oh, absolutely." Max's amusement is forced but the urgency is still confirmed with a quick glance to his hazel eyes. We embrace quickly before walking out into the hallway and making our way toward the front door of the prison. As we hurry through, my eyes trail over the soldiers strewn about along the hallway floor. I know they aren't dead, purely because I can see a few of their chests still moving. I also notice how some of them are pretty banged up though, no doubt Vince's handywork. While others lay with non-life threatening stab wounds that are like Marco's call sign. I can't ignore the relief from the fact that they understood the assignment. If I had wanted anyone dead, I'd have said that.

We make our way past an open control room and I peer in to confirm that the guards have been taken care of. What I find instead, I don't think anybody could've guessed. In the center of the room there are four guards knocked out and flat on their bellies, wrapped from head to toe in every wire and cord Max felt the need to remove from the nine server towers at the back of the room. More cords have been disconnected and reconnected in a way I am positive is going to make some wannabe tech genius cry. While the real reason Max is the definition of a problem child is on full display on all six of the screens in the room. File after file of all the inmates is being scrubbed from the main server. I only know this because it's a program I've only ever seen him use when he's doing illegal shit. A program birthed entirely from the darker parts of his mind.

A low chuckle manages its way into the air through my lips before I breathe a single word of praise. "Jesus."

"You'll never be able to say we aren't thorough." shrugs Max as he reopens the first checkpoint gate with the swipe of a few keys on his tablet.

"I would never. Overachievers with a taste for theatrics maybe, but never not thorough." They all beam with pride in their own way.

A smile from Max.

A lazy two finger salute from Vince.

And a murmured "Thanks,' from Marco.

A few more feet down the hall we are in and we are in the stairwell leading up to the ground level floors. Most inmates are brought here unconscious as a precaution, but I had been preparing to end up here for years now and knew the entire compound better than anyone. As if aware of that thought, Vince stops me with a big hand on my chest before turning to face me.

"Hold up." He begins, the others facing me now. "Spit it out Cap'. We know you didn't suddenly decide you missed us and wanted to come home."

"I know what was said-"

"Not what was said. Who said it." Marco corrects, moving away from us to check the corner we are about to round and waving for us to follow again.

"Exactly. I mean, don't get me wrong, we were planning to come get you regardless, but let's not pretend like you just decided to nullify your own orders." Vince is right. We all know how bad I want to rot in here. Plus, I have always been the kind of captain that gives an order once and sticks with it, making this the first time I have ever gone back on an order I've given. The order to leave me to take the fall and carry on in peace was no different, though I had known they would eventually make an attempt to get me out, or at least have figured out a way to come see me. The air between us grows uncomfortable as my hesitation to answer seems to stretch long enough to become my answer. "That bad?"

"Bad enough." I sigh.

I know they won't ask anything more on the matter until we are clear of this place, so without a word we all continue down the last corridor coming up on the prison exit to the lobby. Once inside, I am immediately blinded by the single set of headlights bleeding through the windows so bright I can't help let out an audible hiss. Light is a cruel joke in Limbo, so the sudden impact of them makes my eyes water instantly.

"Shit," I hissed. "you idiots left the headlights on?"

My response is three guns clicking out of safety behind me before cold steel touches the exposed skin of my arm. I look down to see my favorite pistol as Vince holds it out for me to take before whispering in warning. "We didn't bring a car."

I tense ever so slightly. My guys aren't stupid. Even if they did bring a car, they wouldn't leave the car on this block let alone with the lights on. My spine steels before taking my weapon. The all too familiar steel in hand is cold to the touch, but emanates a warmth I always feel when I hold it. As if the lives I have claimed offer their own temperature. With the safety off, we slowly make our way through the door with our guns trained on the potential threat. Once in the open, we come face to face with a small, unmarked van, and a cigarette smoking Special Lieutenant Black leaning against the hood. He watches as we approach, but seems way too unbothered by the four firearms trained at his head. I hesitate as he begins to nod, a smile spreading across his lips.

"August?" Vince growls when the Lieutenant begins to chuckle. I roll my eyes and reluctantly lower my weapon.

"Stand down, guys." I mumble. They comply hesitantly, but I know them well enough to know their guard won't go down. I want it to stay that way.

"Not the most impressive." Black calls from where he stands. "But your team definitely earned spot number two. Deleting inmate files was a nice touch."

"It's cute you think that's all I did." Max calls back quickly before he whispers to me. "Is that judge jackass' son or something?"

"Or something. Fellas, this is Special Lieutenant Andrew Black." I answer when we stand in front of the man surrounded by questions. "The Lieutenant here is 'bad enough'. So, now what?"

"Now? If you wouldn't mind getting in. I would like to get back before curfew." He muses, making his way to the driver's side door after snuffing out his cigarette bud under the heel of his boot. I don't need to look to see the identical faces of confusion burning a hole in the back of my head. I would have liked to have time to explain, but this is neither the time nor the place for that. In any case, I really don't have any answers to give them.

"Choice?" Max grumbled behind me, seeming to sense my inner struggle.

"Not this time." I sighed, making my way to the passenger side door. I had always been aware of the trust they had in me, but for them to follow without much question made the guilt of the situation heavier in my chest. They don't even hesitate to follow, exchanging a hard glance among them. "Vamonos a una aventura, hermanos. Let's go on an adventure, brothers."

***

We've managed to ride in comfortable silence for two extremely uncomfortable hours. Though we have been taking as many unmarked roads as we can, I have come to several conclusions so far. First, that we are somewhere in the state of Arizona. The second, is that the man who calls himself a Special Lieutenant may have a lot of power, but he has no intentions of being a threat to us.

Until now, the four of us have only been exchanging check-in glances through the mirrors. Marco and Max, in true fashion, fell asleep about thirty minutes ago after we piled back into the van. The Lieutenant pulled into a gas station/truck stop about fifteen minutes ago so we could all change into a uniform that reminds me of the ones we wear during basic training, without the coat. Tight black shirt, black camo cargo pants, and if I am being completely honest, the best damn combat boots I've ever put on. We piled back into the van right after, deciding to let Max and Marco take up the back since the two of them are the definition of 'sleep when you can', while Vince and I sat in the middle two seats.

The final conclusion I have drawn is that Special Lieutenant Andrew Black might actually be insane enough to rival Vince's crazy. That alone is saying something. The radio station that has been playing nothing but Latin music is now playing its third Vicente Fernandez song. The Lieutenant, to our surprise, seems to know every word and begins to sing proudly at the top of his lungs once again. Completely unbothered by the fact that he is the color of milk and his pronunciation of each word is a crime against my culture. Judging by the look of agonizing pain Vince is giving me, I am guessing he feels the same way. Although I must admit, the way the Special Lieutenant seems to understand and convey the correct emotions of the song is almost impressive.

When the song finally comes to an end, the radio is shut off and the sound of his laughter fills the car. "You should see your faces."

"What?! "Vince shouts, feigning deaf. "I can't hear you because my EARS ARE FUCKING BLEEDING!"

I slap his chest, jutting my thumb toward the back seat. You would think that being in a car with a man who went all out and basically kidnapped us would have us all drowning in tension, but they must've picked up on Black's lack of hostility just as fast as I did.

"Shut up, you're gonna wake the boys." I say, stifling a laugh. The boys suck their teeth in unison, adjusting to lean against their respective windows. Eyes still shut.

"I've slept through air raids quieter than this motherfucker." Max growls, crossing his arms over his chest.

"That's Special Lieutenant Motherfucker to you." he calls over his shoulder.

"HAHA!" Marco bellows making Max jump, his eyes flying open. "Oh you're 'special' alright. NO TAN-GO TROH-NO NEE-RAY-NAH-"

My eyes roll at Marcos near perfect impression, only to completely lose my battle with laughter when Max's arms fly out in a dramatic fashion.

"NEE-NAW-DEN K-MEY KUM-PRAYN-DUH!"

My smile grows wider when I look at Vince's pained expression. We can't help but throw one hand out and slap one to our chest prompting us to shout together in an ungodly key.

"PEH-ROW   SEE-GO   SEE-ENDOH   EL RAAAAAAAAAAAAAAAAY!"

We erupt into fits of laughter that if not for the current circumstances would have calmed the tension in the car completely. However when the laughing dies out, the underlying tension returns, along with the silence. We keep on driving for another thirty minutes before pulling into what looks like an abandoned convenience store. Special Lieutenant Black exits the vehicle, pulling his phone out to make a call. We watch him, stirring uncomfortably in our seats. My ass is beginning to go numb, I think to myself when he finally makes his way back toward the car. Only instead of getting back in like I expect, he moves to open the back passenger door. "Alright, gentlemen. We're here."

"Where the fuck is 'here'?" Vince groans, asking the question we all have on our faces as we climb out of the van with a symphony of moans and popping bones. Without answering, the Special Lieutenant walks lazily to the front door, stopping just short of it to turn back to us.

"I am going to ask you this one last time. Are you sure you want to come with me? My other option still stands." I scoff loudly, knowing I don't need to confirm anything for my boys to follow me. "Just checking. Now listen up. When you step through this door, you will never be allowed to walk as you are in the land of the living. Life, along with the truth of the world as you know it will end. From here on out, you four are Dead Soldiers. Understood?"

He is met with confused nods, but must see that we are as all in as we can be, because in the next breath, he pushes the door open.

Chapter Two
Augustine

When the door closes behind us, the smell of mold and dingy air fill my nose along with the consistent subtle smell of burnt fucking sugar. After much trial and error I have come to know this as the scent of lies. At least, that's what I say in my mind after testing the theory with my brothers who already can't hide anything from me. A single table sits in the corner and several chairs lay strewn about the empty room of the hollowed out convenience store. We stand tentatively with our backs to the now barred door, watching as Special Lieutenant Black slumps down into a backward chair.

"Take a seat boys, we have a few things to discuss before we get to where we are going, and not a lot of time or permission to discuss them."

With raised eyebrows, the boys each pull up a seat. Marco has been holding his questions for an impressive amount of time, so when he finally speaks, none of us bother to stop him. "Am I allowed to ask what we are doing here? Where are we going, maybe? You are aware that this is kidnaping right? DO you know where we are, *Special Lieutenant Andrew Black*? Or is this one of those times when you try to make us feel safe then poison us?"

"Slow down, kid." Black snorts, shaking his head. "Truth be told, I can't answer those questions on this side of the street. You see, as we speak my associate is solidifying our entryway to the deadlands." he answers, pointing to a hand sketched map on the open wall to his left. I study it, but even with my extensive geographical background, I am having a hard time figuring out exactly where this is a map of. I am also having a hard time with what he is saying entirely. "You won't recognize it. We make it a point to keep the location a complete secret, and maps have never been digitally copied. This here is just somewhat of a precaution. We won't be able to get where we're going any other way but a jump point."

"Jump point?" We all question in various tones of confusion.

"Well…" Black lets out a frustrated sigh, and I can scent the war within him. Licorice uncertainty mixed with the cheap citrusy perfume of confusion. Suddenly his arms fly up in exacerbation and the tinge of rusted metal anger filters through. "I usually have a whole speech planned out, but if I am being quite honest the circumstances of your team's activation are unprecedented."

"How so?" I asked, dragging my eyes back to him from the map.

"How about the fact that I can't tell you that." he deadpans.

"Excuse me?" Vince growls for me. "So you just brought us out to the middle of nowhere talking nonsense and you just expected us to follow you?"

"No…I expected you to follow him." The Lieutenant points to me and Vince shrugs as if that was a reason enough. For Vince I suppose it might be, we have been through too much not to trust each other. "I have orders, kids. Bring you in. Tell you basically nothing. Even the things I can tell you, I won't until we are in Deadman's land."

The resignation in his voice is upsetting to say the least. Max, Vince, and I exchange a look, but Marco doesn't meet our gaze. Instead he chews the inside of his cheek before decidedly speaking up. His words snap our attention to him, everyone seeming surprised but the Special Lieutenant.

"Does this have anything to do with the No Fly Territory passing the Andes Mountains?"

"So you *are* a pilot. " The Special Lieutenant states, raising an eyebrow.

"The best." We all answer. Marco beams at our confirmation of his skill. Marco is the best pilot anyone has ever seen. Something about him behind the wheel of any aircraft is like watching a masterpiece come alive.

"This has everything to do with the No Fly Zone. Though you will come to know it by its given name of Deadman's

Land." As he speaks, a blond haired woman trudges into the room from the back somewhere.

"What's the no fly zone?" I ask Marco who squirms. A hint of licorice and plums wafting from him, and I know nobody else can smell his uncertainty or concern like I can.

"Something they teach us when we're sworn in. They kind of beat it into us that a certain flight path heading through the Andes Mountains is an absolute no fly zone. We get flight warnings about getting shot down if we get too close." I watch his chest while he speaks, just in case his breathing gets too fast. Being the one of us with active panic attacks and acute asthma.

"Special Lieutenant Black." She salutes respectfully, though I have never seen a salute quite like it before. Her right fist hit her chest as if she was stabbing her heart with a dagger. Her left arm resting behind her back, head bowed at an angle away from her fist with her eyes closed. The motion is quick but precise before she continues. My team stands to our feet, respectful in the presence of a female soldier. "I've fixed the jump point, though you will all have to go quick. We've been given orders to shut down all entry points in preparation. There's a storm coming in so we've been called back to man supply points."

"Thank you, agent. Boys, this is Special Agent Aurora Donovan. If you follow her instructions, we can all get a little closer to the informative part of our journey." He stands finally, following closely behind us while we follow her into what clearly used to be the back storage area. Now it's just an empty room with a door painted black at the far end. Special Agent Donovan walks right up beside it, turning on her heels to face us.

"I don't need you to close your eyes, but I do need you to keep walking until you feel the temperature shift. Don't turn around, it makes it annoying to maintain if you stop moving at any given point in my tunnel. Got it?" The irritation in her voice is unmistakable, though I am unaware of what we've done to cause it. Probably something to do with the plum concern I scent from her. There's a tinge of cotton candy that sprinkles my breathing every time she slightly looks at us, but she avoids us all the same. I don't touch on the subject, mostly because of how absolutely insane it sounds to even myself.

"Yes, Ma'am." We all bark, simultaneously opting to focus on the parts of her instructions that make any sense which aren't very many. She seems rather startled at our reply, or more so maybe our lack of push back, before she peers over my shoulder to look at Special Lieutenant Black.

"Can I keep them?" She asks, her words and tone relaying what she is saying, but the spike of burnt sugar in the air tells me that her words are full of other meanings and lies. He laughs, shaking his head, but for the first time since he re-entered my life, the faintest whiff of burnt sugar begins to bleed through his words as well.

"I doubt their First Captain will allow that." Black's reply has us all looking at him with matching raised eyebrows. Cotton candy comes from him too, but it's the slight brightening of his eyes that catches my attention.

"Are they ranking low?" She waves her hand in the air in dismissal before turning back to the door. She can hide her face, but she can't hide the way her shoulders relax to a degree.

"I doubt that too, considering the mess they made of their Pre-entry." You can hear the smile in his voice, but I glance back to see that as I suspect, it doesn't quite reach his eyes. The mask he's been wearing cracking just a bit before it returns in its full glory.

"I see." She replies, her tone flat and void of the interest she had been trying to convey, the salty smell changing into a low lavender wafting off her for just a second. Aurora tears the door open and begins walking through, shoulders square while her form seems to ripple somehow. We all follow as instructed, willing ourselves to keep going in spite of how wrong it feels to do so. Instead of walking out the back of the convenience store, we find ourselves inside the halls of a library. The bookshelves on either side of the corridor we now find ourselves in stretches the entire halfway down before stopping at a gap, and beginning again until it reaches the wall on the other side.

The energy as we walk only helps to aid in our collective confusion. If I had to describe it, I would use the word suffocating. I can breathe, but it's as if the atmosphere around us is constricted. I take seven steps through the door before the feeling breaks and the lukewarm air hits my skin, forcing me to suck in a breath.

"What the fuck just happened!?" Vince shivers in a way that would be dramatic if I didn't want to do the same thing.

"SH!" The harsh whispers seem to be coming from everywhere, echoing off the vaulted ceiling from every direction. We turn to Special Lieutenant Black when Special Agent Donovan goes jogging off without another word in our direction. Black holds a finger to his lips before motioning for us to continue to follow him, leading us all out of the building.

The crisp mountain air is the first thing to alert me to our change in location. We aren't just in a different building, we are in a different country entirely judging by the bright sun bleeding through the tall picture windows. My heart rate picks up speed, and we all start looking around as if the answer to the obvious question can be found in our surroundings. Spoiler alert, we're still confused. We step into blazing heat and the moment we clear the steps and touch down on the gravel drive I spin hard on my heels to see the shining building that sits in place of where the convenience store should be. Instead, I am overcome by the glasslike structure that towers in front of me. Columns and stairs that are Cathedral like in model, but the art of the outside puts any building I've ever seen to shame with architecture and beauty alone. Turning back with need to take stock of the others, I see Vince touching his face and checking his arms for track marks. "He drugged us. I don't know how, but this is the trippiest fucking thing I've ever been through! How the fuck did we get here?!" "Where the fuck IS here?!" Max rubs at the back of his neck, a grimace on his face. Marco looks absolutely green, the words falling out of his mouth in a childlike groan and the subtle scent of plums. I check to see if anyone else can smell it, but nobody says anything. This one must be 'concern', it's the emotion I'm catching in Marco's eyes.

"We're inside the No Fly Zone." He whines. Special Lieutenant Black lets loose an amused snort, pulling our attention back to him.

"Well done." He walks through the rest of us to a black jeep parked in a reserved parking spot. "Hop in boys, we only have a short drive ahead of us. I'll be able to give you some answers to a few of those questions you got written on your faces."

"Fucking finally!" Vince growls. We all climb in, reluctant to be cramped in another vehicle so quickly. With myself in the front passenger while the others squeeze into the back seat, their collective looks of discomfort mirroring my own as we pull out of the parking lot and onto the gravel road.

We wait for a few moments, and I am doing everything in my power not to gag with the intermixing scents all collecting in the car. Lavender, burnt sugar, plums, gasoline, and the hint of licorice that I just know isn't coming from the car.

"The Library we just left is the only entrance hub we have that is known to all units. It was built shortly after Heart Center, the building we are headed to now. Which makes it the second building created here in our town of the undead." I lock eyes with Vince in the rearview, speaking to each other through facial expressions, but it's Marco once again who asks out loud.

"Created?"

Without acknowledging Marco's question, the Special Lieutenant continues. "This facility was commissioned three days after the end of the Holocaust. The United Nations realized that if something like that happened again not only were we unprepared, but horribly outgunned."

As he explains, the gravel road changes into the mountain terrain. Though covered by trees that seem to vine their branches to fit with the various buildings, and each seems to shine like the first. It is impossible to tell where the trees begin and the strange material ends. The beauty of the land around us is distracting to say the least, making it hard to pay attention, but I pull my focus because I have to. Absolutely nothing coming out of this man's mouth makes sense, but the smell of lies has dissipated for now so there is nothing but truth to his story, and what he says next has me enthralled even more. "To be clear, every bad thing you have ever been informed of as a soldier in the land of the living, is basically surface level recon, clean up, or a blatant cover up to what really goes on when we get our hands on it."

"In the land of the living, all the textbooks say Hitler offed himself on April 30th, 1945 after he realized he was losing. However, the snake tongued bastard met no such mercy. The history books-surprise. Surprise.-have been wiped of the facts entirely on the order of our Council. Truths rewritten, to hide the realities and separate us from the real world."

"You're not making any sense." I breathe when the others take this as their que to all start talking at once.

"What the fuck does that even mean? En que mierda nos metistes, Augustine!? What the fuck did you get us into, Augustine?!" Vince bellows.

"You've said five different things! How are we supposed to follow any of it!" Marco calls.

"What kind of cult shit are you running here? You sound like a fucking psycho!" Max's barks.

"Woah!" We silence out of habit. "It never makes sense at first. That's the point. If the lies were easy to untangle, every conspiracy theorist would be a lot more dead, and maybe a little less crazy. Tell me, have you boys ever heard whispers of last resort units?" Black asks, curiosity brimming in his eyes again. I look at the boys, curious to know if they are even reading the same book as me, let alone on the same page.

"The Ghost Units? They tell us the stories at Basic. Units they send in to dismantle terrorist organizations. We just assume they mean the Green Beret and the Black Ops boys." Max answers with a shrug.

"HA! Those Black Ops boys *WISH* they had our, um...*jurisdictional advantages*." he chortles. "Not that they would survive if they had it. Despite what you *THINK* you believe, the stories are very true. Only, the versions they tell you are watered down to PG-13."

"What does this have to do with Hitler?" Marco sounds more confused than anyone.

"What's this got to do with *reality*?" Max says it so low at the same time I almost miss it.

"Because Hitler, was what we call a Juggernaut." a crackle of confusion is only interrupted by Marco and Max's snickers.

"A...Juggernaut?" I asked. "Like in the superhero movie?"

"While Stan Lee is one of the most famous and historically worthy Juggernaut, the character was more of an embodiment of what we are, not a depiction. Think superheroes but with a lot more blood between our fingers. Juggernauts are true born soldiers. Individuals that have been gifted with abilities that are beyond regular human comprehension. Every single person you meet here is a Juggernaut capable of some pretty bad ass things." he glances at me, chuckling more. "Your eyes cannot get any bigger."

I can't laugh, and paying attention to my surroundings is the furthest thing from my mind. All any of us can do is stare. He glances once. Then once again before shaking his head with a sigh, pulling over to the side of the road. "Everything we are taught in schools growing up. The way you knew the world before this moment, is what we call The Land of the Living. Regular people, doing regular shit, in their regular everyday life. The human-humans."

Vince throws his hands up, the most fed up as always. I settle him with a look that says to give it a chance. He is obliging me, but I'm in for it later and I can tell by the glare he shoots me.

"Regular nurses, doctors, soldiers. *Heroes* fighting wars at home and on other people's soil and la-di-da-di-da. NOW! From the moment you sent your boys that message, the four of you entered into a whole different ball game. The Land of the Dead. Here, we have different rules. Practically none, but the rules we have are binding. Our secrets keep a whole lot of people safe on both sides." By this point I'm fascinated, but something else has me remaining silent. "Juggernauts on the other hand, while still technically classified as human for your primary species, are not technically nor entirely human."

"How?" We all throw out at once.

"Nobody knows. All we know for certain is that once a juggernaut is activated, they are volatile if they aren't trained right. Here, we train in units, after we test you a little and run you through the ringer to figure out what you can do, how well you can survive, and if you can even be an asset to the cause." In this small amount of information, everything he says starts to ring truer to me. My own "special ability" should be proof enough, though I have always suspected a brain tumor. That explanation doesn't have a clear scan proving it wrong.

"Why the distinction? What makes them alive and us dead?" Marco asked, trying once again to move Vince over but failing.

"Because we can't do what we do in the Land of the Living. So we die. Every single thing about you four, has been erased or redacted. You were all determined killed or dead in some way."

"WHAT?!" we all shout.

The jeep falls completely silent and I can't even process the influx of concern taking up the confined space.

My eyes slide slowly to Vince who meets my gaze with a mask of pure stone before all three of us drag our eyes reluctantly over to Marco. The tears brimming his eyes are ones I've seen many times, but these feel different. They *smell* different. His anger the scent of rusted metal, sharp in the air enough to force my hand over my nose for a moment. We all know. Vince will be feeling the same way as his anger grows to mix with his little brothers as he puts the pieces together. I, however, am suddenly horrified with this reality. The Special Lieutenant's statement has just made an impact that hits me square in the chest like a bullet. The destruction that now forces guilt to take hold of my heart and a single face enters my mind.

She's sitting on her favorite chair in the backyard smoking a Marlboro Menthol cigarette. Her long dark hair pulled over her shoulder as she speaks into the phone. The wisdom pulling at the corners of her eyes while she swings the glasses she's meant to be wearing wildly around as she speaks. My heart breaks even more at the thought of two men in uniform and cold expressions coming to tell her that I have broken my promise once again.

"Ma-" His name catches in my throat when his hand goes up. Marco shakes his head quickly, a warning before he stumbles out of the vehicle. Vince and I lock eyes for half a second before we're both flying out of the vehicle after him. Max hot on our heels with the Special Lieutenant following leisurely behind.

Chapter Three
Marco

I have to get out of this vehicle before I start swinging, and it doesn't help that I know they will all be right behind me. I consider myself a gentle person, and surely the most gentle of the four of us, but there is no feeling other than rage in my chest. My gentle nature is about to call it quits entirely.

When my sister was taken, it almost killed me and my brothers. We almost killed each other, but we kept each other together. We had someone there to look after one another. My mom on the other hand, barely survived losing one child and she had to grieve alone. The images in my head of my mom hearing the news that my sister Kaila had been taken begins to assault my mind. Her screams will echo in my mind, and I know they are burnt into all of theirs, too.

What I wouldn't give to be in a cockpit at this very moment.

It's the captain's voice that pulls me out of my panic. But, at this moment it isn't my captain I am seeing.

This isn't the man whose orders I will follow into hell and out of high waters.

No no.

This is my brother in law.

What's the difference? Well, you don't put hands on your Captain.

My brother in law, however, is a free game.

"Marco I-" The crack of my knuckled against his jaw stops whatever Augustine is about to say with force. He takes it, as well as the second punch I thrust into his gut before Vince pulls me off.

"!Calmate, Marco! Calm down, Marco!" he growls through a locked jaw. I try to yank free, but my brother has a vice hold on me. "You have to calm down."

"How can you tell me to be calm?!" My voice breaks a little and I turn on Vince. I don't know what else to do. We're halfway around the world, in territory I don't have pounded into my brain like the Captain and his obsession with fucking land maps. Even now we are in a wide open space on the ground yet I have never felt more trapped in my life. I'm breathing, but it's coming in short gasps. I tear my arm away one last time and Vince finally lets me go. "Get the fuck off me, Vince!"

Another gasp and I turned back to my Captain speaking in sections. "What about...mom...August?"

"You have to breathe, Marco!" He barks. In the back of my mind I know he isn't ignoring me, but I can't think straight enough to remember that. I slap Augustine's hand away when he tries to reach for me. I know exactly what he's trying to do and I just can't bring myself to let it happen. But he pushes through my protest, easily yanking me to him. He shakes me violently once in an attempt to shake me out of the haze and I quit fighting. My chest keeps heaving, but I don't have any fight left in me right now. When he finally gets me to look him in the eyes, I see my pain reflected back at me tenfold. The break in my brother in law's voice is a confirmation of it when he half whispers, half pleads with me. "Do it."

"I look...fucking stupid man." My head shakes and I push at him again but none of the force from before is there. My limbs have started to feel weird, and the breaths are coming in a bit more shallow now.

"Marco!" Max barks, the warning louder in his tone than in the others. I roll my eyes and let out the best sound of aggravation I can muster. Then I cup both hands over my nose and mouth. Fingertips to tear ducts. Palms to chin. Then I close my eyes the way my sister taught me to do when we were little.

My sister...the smartest person I have ever known. The purpose of the trick is to force my brain into thinking I'm wearing an oxygen mask like I do when I fly a jet. I never could figure out how my sister made the connection, but she was the first to notice that my asthma seems to disappear when I fly. I've never lost my cool, even though sitting in a cockpit always messes with my claustrophobia, it was always more tolerable than being on the ground.

After a few deep breaths into my hands, the panic begins to subside and the breathing comes easier the longer I do it. In through my mouth, out through my nose. My sister called it breathing in reverse.

When I can breathe without additional effort, I drop my hands to my sides before turning back to the captain with an accusatory finger. "Did you know about this, Augustine?"

"I would never do that to Ava." The guilt thickening his voice makes my chest ache. I know better than to think he would do something like this on purpose. Especially if it involves my mother in any way. With that thought in mind, I turn hard on my heels, already storming toward the so-called "Special" Lieutenant. I'm not the only one who comes to the same conclusion, because before I can close the distance, Vince has the man's shirt wrapped up in his white knuckled fists.

"Give me one good reason why my brothers and I shouldn't tear you apart and find a way back home our-fucking-selves?" Vince spits. There's a fury in his blown pupils coupled with the full body shake is a tell tale sign that my big brother is about to get very violent, very quickly. The thing about my brother and I is that we have never been very alike. I've always been rather attached to my mom, but my brother took up after our father, and had no issue imitating him after his passing. He has always been stronger than me, both physically and emotionally, while I however got the lion's share of the mental fortitude. Vince is a block head, and I have had to keep him from beating his head against a wall more than a few times. He isn't stupid, he just isn't exactly a people person. A fighter though? Never seen a better one, and he isn't the type to ask questions. How my brother is managing to keep his cool even this much is beyond me because I am losing mine.

"I can give you three." retorts the Special Lieutenant as he holds both hands in the air like a show of surrender. "One, because first and foremost your mother will be taken care of. Abundantly well, might I add. Two, because if we didn't feel like she would be taken care of well enough, you wouldn't be here. You would be there with her. And three, because as good as you four may be, you wouldn't make it very far even if you did manage to get me on my ass long enough to try."

He points with his chin somewhere behind us, encouraging us to look. I turn to see several different groups of people huddled together in batches. Each one my eyes glide over makes my stomach drop a little more. I've had enough time in the service to know what a unit looks like from anywhere. We are ridiculously outnumbered, and while I am not entirely opposed to taking a few of them with me to make a point, I know this just isn't the time or place.

I squeeze my brother's arm twice and he lets go slowly. Looking around now, Vince's eyebrows furrow but he nods once, backing up a few steps to stand beside Augustine.

"Look, I could tell you all the cute civilian shit like 'I'm sorry' or 'there was no other way', but I most certainly am not sorry. As far as there being no other way? You could go back at any time you please, but the moment you step foot outside our borders they will be on everyone you love faster than it takes Junior here to get his hands on a bird. Even if you could somehow manage to make it to defend your mother, without training you'd be dead before you ever managed to fire a weapon."

"Who is 'they'?" Captain asks, a venom in his voice I've heard many times before. Looking over to him, I realize he's pale and looks like he is about to pass out. Instinctively I move to his right, opposite to Vince. Neither of us make a move to touch him, because even though we've seen him like this before, none of us ever can figure out why or what to do when it happens. So instead we stand ready, with Max having taken notice at this point and putting himself to stand close enough to get in the middle if necessary.

"Short answer? Hitler." he explains with a shrug, making me groan. "They look like us, they walk like us, they talk like us, but they are nothing like us. They are an army of soldiers who have completely given themselves over to their abilities. Like I told you earlier, Hitler was a dark juggernaut. Someone whose ability was born from bad intentions."

"This is absolutely insane." Vince is bewildered to say the least. I wish I could say that I am afraid. Maybe then I could feel a bit better about the anger. I just keep seething when Captain's hand finds my shoulder. I nod, not needing to look at him to know he is making sure I am okay. My focus may be on him, but my eyes won't leave Special Lieutenant Black's face. None of ours will.

"Call it what you want. The proof is in the pudding so to speak. Although, the pudding is not bad at all. Now, can we get back in the Jeep, please. I have orders to walk you through Heart Center."

"You keep telling us about these orders of yours. Yet, I haven't heard you mention anything about who is giving them to you. Now I am all about the chain of command, but let's not pretend we volunteered to be here." Much like myself, it's clear that August has had enough. He's finally in the Special Lieutenant's face. Chest to chest with the man's back pressed against the Jeep. "The cryptic bullshit might work with the civi's and basic soldiers, but you seem to have NO idea what is going on outside of this little game you're playing. You get one chance to tell me something that makes us *WANT* to stay, because your '*have to*' is getting thinner and thinner by the second."

I watch Black's face as he contemplates his next words. There is no fear in his eyes where there probably should be. The Captain doesn't look like the strongest of us, but he is our captain for a very good reason.

"Do you need to see oxygen to breathe it?"

I suck in a breath that is echoed by the others. My eyes draw to August just in time for the phrase to register with him like a slap in the face. He stumbles back like his feet stopped working, clutching his chest as if it will somehow relieve the pain we will all be feeling right now. Stunned. Frozen at the memories. Everyone else may be too dumbfounded to speak, but I've never had that problem. "What did you say?"

Vince reaches out to me to steady himself, but we all look at the Special Lieutenant with a new sense of disbelief. "I said, do you need to see oxygen to breathe it?"

The way he asks the question tells me it isn't his words he's speaking. Rather that he's relaying a message. A message that hits each one of us like a brick to the teeth. We've all heard it before, the phrase sprinkled over our childhood like well seasoned food. She always used it to rope us into one of her schemes. The ones that never had a chance of working, but somehow she always found a way to pull off. She would use it when we were little and I wanted to be brave like Vince, then again as I got older when I wanted to follow Augustine.

"Being brave is kind of like breathing." she'd said to me once when I asked why she always spoke the same phrase. *"You can't see oxygen, you just know it's there. You believe it is, and you inhale."* I look at Max and we lock eyes. There's agony in his, and just the slightest shimmer of hope. Then, still remaining silent, Max nods slowly, as if the same realization hit him. The same voice playing back in his mind the way it is in mine. Which leaves us all in a dilemma. There are so many questions that we should be asking right now, and although I don't know where my brothers are with needing the answers for them, I know where I stand. A deep breath fills my lungs, along with a new found resolve when I turn my eyes back to our captain. I know before I look at him what I am about to see.

Dead, far away eyes. Agony on his face, and a rapid rise and fall to his chest.

A quick look shared between Max, Vince and I confirms our next move. Even more so when Max turns on his heels and walks back to the car, Vince growling deep in his chest as he follows. Closing the small distance to Augustine, I snap my attention to the Special Lieutenant, there's a look of confusion on his face, sure. But it doesn't reach his eyes, prompting a snarl to rip from my throat. It startles him, because it startles everyone. I'm the sweet boy, but I'm still a marine.

"You got our attention, but let me make one thing clear. Don't play with the wrong matches, *Lieutenant.*" Turning my back to him, I place my left hand on Augustine's right shoulder, bracing my forearm across his chest and under his left arm. I know the moment Black's attention settles on the Captain's face by the shock in his quick intake of breath. "You don't understand the fires we've seen, or what they left behind."

With light pressure on his chest, I guide the captain toward the car, making sure he has good enough footing to turn him around. Vince is waiting for me by the front passenger door, but I shake my head and he moves to help me put the captain in the back seat. He isn't here right now, and we won't get him back for fuck knows how long. For now, we split duties as a team. The Special Lieutenant climbs back into the driver's side, all jokes bled away from his features while Max pulls August's seatbelt on and I stand outside the car in front of Vince once again. We still haven't uttered a word, and the silence isn't a comfortable one anymore. All of us are fighting demons we swore we had buried with our sister now. Vince and I turn to one another with a fist out. We pump them three times, then throw.

Vince holds his hand open palm down for paper. I hold out two fingers for scissors. I win and I've never been happier about it. If what Black is insinuating has any kind of truth, if it holds any kind of water at all…we are going to find out. The captain won't be able to do it on his own, because while we all lost a sister, that man lost the love of his life, and he was never the same after that day. So now, we do our part until he can come back and do his.

Then we get answers.

Chapter Four

Kaila

"Ela vai arrancar a porra da cabeça dele. She's going to rip his fucking head off." Kestian's voice is distant the way sound always is when I come out of an episode. I lost control again, and I don't need the burning pain at the small of my back to remind me. I listen as my surroundings become clearer. My team seems to be discussing softly, more than likely in an attempt not to disturb me, but my ears are better than most. "This is a huge deviation from the plan."

"It didn't look like he had much of a choice." Milo sighs. "Should we be worried about the kid? Or...*him*? Those freakouts don't look like something that screams combat ready. More like they need a psych evaluation."

"Foda-se insensível. Imagine perder meu irmão. Você estaria andando por aí? Insensitive fuck. Imagine losing my brother. Would you be out walking around?" Kiari whispers in a harsh tone. Her native tongue rolls out of her mouth like rats scurrying across the floor. They only speak in Portuguese in front of me because they think I don't understand. I didn't initially, but I never did like to be kept out of a loop.

"No. I would be an absolute mess." Milo states. "Kind of like these guys, only I wouldn't be out here still playing soldier."

"Ela sempre dizia que a gente não iria entender eles de imediato. She always said we wouldn't understand them right away." Kestien interjects with a shrug in his tone evident as the last bits of the universe settle into their place around my senses. The conversation ceases suddenly and I know it's because of me. The collar stops me from feeling the full weight of the emotions I take in, but it doesn't stop my own from shifting the energy around me, and right now it's beginning to spill into the air in the room.

"I would like to remind our captain that I do have a date with my husband tonight and I would like to look my best." Milo says slowly as he moves closer.

"I," Kestian says with what I'm sure is a sly smile, "would like to remind my husband that I think he looks ruggedly handsome every time his mouth gets him into trouble with our merciful captain."

I can't help but laugh, propping myself up on my elbows and letting my head hang back. The sounds that permeate the room are a symphony of blissful cracks and pops as my bones slide back into their respective places. Kiari stands to bring me a glass of water that was sitting on the desk beside her. "Can we talk about this now?"

"Like you ever have to ask?" I mumble in reply, swinging my legs over Kestian's bed. I grunt at the ache in my bones.

"They all seem to have…some issues. Are you even sure they can make it?" Milo rubs at his neck. It's never been hard to talk about anything between the four of us, but this particular subject is touchy. None of them want to overstep, but they all want to protect me as much as they can.

"You aren't watching close enough." I sigh, resting my elbows on my knees. The three of them turn to me eager to hear my explanation, sure, but the concern for my well being is written in their eyes just as well as it surrounds them. "You're watching the one that's freaking out. Not the rest of them. Besides, I haven't given you a briefing on them yet. I know how chaotic they look to the naked eye but now that they're within borders I can let you in on some of our secrets."

I know they will follow when I make my way to our family room, so I don't look back to check. The layout of the room is similar to that of the rest of the units on this floor but we've added our personal touches over the years.

I don't want to waste anymore time. My plan is very specific. The meticulousness is not without its reasons.

"We'll start from the odd ball out. Maxwell St. James." They each take their respective seats in front of the wall to wall monitors. Milo is leaning against the armrest of the couch with Kestian fitted into his side. The tablet in Kestian hands is controlling the briefing slides I've been preparing for years as I speak. Kiari sits with her legs crossed at the ankles on the opposite end of the couch, all of them listening intently as I begin to dive into details. "A twenty-nine year old white boy who doesn't even identify as such. Born in California to the late Carson and Maxine St. James, two drug addicts who overdosed within twenty-four hours of one another. Max found them when he was four years old. They had been holed up in a house that was about to be repossessed by the bank and had no other family to check on them, until a neighbor heard Max crying on the porch two days after his father died. From then on he bounced around from foster home to group home until one day, as the story goes, some of the older boys in the group home he was staying in at the time noticed that Max had an affinity for technology. He kept stealing the remotes to turn them into signal disruptors after they would bully him. Needless to say, boys being boys, the other kids questioned his abilities. You can do a lot to Max, he's almost as passive as Marco, but the one thing you'll never get away with is insulting his craft. So, one night after they beat his ass real good, Max had had enough and turned the house wireless router into a satellite disruptor.

"Why would he do that?" Kiari laughs.

"Because he could." I smile, remembering the reason I was given so long ago. "Naturally, the Pentagon caught wind of what he was doing, but only after he had started sending the president emails of cat videos along with the address to the group home attached to the file. Equip with turn by turn directions, rest stops, and highly rated food stops from the white house, to the front door of the group home in Texas."

"What a fucking menace." Milo snorts, impressed.

"That stunt landed him in a Juvenile detention center where he met none other than the blockhead himself, Vincent Arrio." I force myself to take a steadying breath, the memories

I hadn't allowed myself to remember in a long time clashing with my clear vision of the present. "When Vince and Marco were in elementary school, there was this shit eater by the name of Xavier Cannon. Rotten little piss ant who tormented Marco for years before Vince found out. The thing about my big brother is that he was born with an extremely short fuse. By the time he even got to the sixth grade, he had racked up seventeen in school suspension, and three out of school suspensions for fighting. Vince and Xavier had fought several times, until right before Christmas break Vince's freshman year when I transferred into 8th grade at their school from an all girls catholic school."

"That's not real." Milo cackles.

"My mom had a plan. We ruined it." It was my turn to chuckle now. "Xavier zeroed in on me on my first day of school. Cut my hair with a pair of scissors in the middle of a school assembly. To this day, I don't even think the poor kid knew who my brothers were, but he probably couldn't remember it after the beating he got from my brother. It took five grown officers to pull Vince off of Xavier, and I remember the paramedic saying that he would probably never look the same."

"Fired." Kestien and Milo gasp in unison. Kiari and I giggle and roll our eyes.

"Vince went into juvie alone at twelve years old, and came back out at fifteen with Max following right behind him. The way I remember it, Vince kept Max from being used as a mop in Juvie, and Max has spent every moment after trying to make it up to him. Vince, being the hot head that he is, has the most obvious set of abilities. After watching how he handled my death I would call it a blind rage, but he was always meant to be our heaviest hitter. Most people get weaker the more punches they take, but not him. From what I can tell, his hits just get harder. It's going to take some serious training for him, but I doubt anyone will get him down once he learns to actually use his abilities correctly."

"While Vince was doing his time, I got to watch something really fucking cool happen with Marco. Marco Arrio. Call sign Marco Polo." I continue with a smile. "After the fight with Vince, people pretty much left us alone in high school. Marco had made Vince a promise, and Marco always hung on the word of our older brother after our father died. He made a promise to step up, and never let anybody step on us. The summer after Vince went in, Marco spent every single day running and training. He was never going to be as big as Vince, considering Vince was bigger than his entire class by the third grade. Marco got into sports, became the people person I always knew he could be, and eventually had the entire school wired in his favor. By the time Vince and Max came back, nobody had messed with us at all. Now, Marco is a conundrum. After following the boys into the Marines, we quickly found out that the little shit was the best fighter pilot in the corp. On the ground? Practically useless, even he'll tell you that, a fighter who'd rather not. He's quick, and can fight as well as anyone, sure, but he isn't the best on the field. Off the ground? Davinci. The freakout you witnessed when he got overwhelmed is just a side effect of his anxiety and asthma. I have more than enough reason to believe that his Juggernaut manifested earlier this year. My theory is that his lungs aren't meant for the ground entirely, but the air. My hope is that by him being up here on the mountain it will help the process a bit."

"Which," I force myself to pause when images of him lit up the screen. His short black hair, eyes the color of dark chocolate, and smooth golden brown skin on a body women fantasize about. I can't help remembering the day this picture was taken. The tuxedo adorning his skin, jaw set like stone. This was also the last photograph I allowed myself to have of my husband. It was taken the day of my 'funeral'. Feelings I've been forcing myself to hide well up in my eyes only for a moment before the tears bleed into the purple that I know swirl in them ever so lightly. I clear my throat before pushing through. "Brings us to Augustin Juan Petras...my husband and your soon-to-be Second Captain. Augustine came into our lives with his ass on fire. Driven, kind, and gutsy as all hell. My brothers and I had managed to find ourselves in summer school. Vince and Max because of the time they spent out of school, and Marco and I for reasons that escape me to this day."

"Always the rebel, aren't you?" Kiari snorts but I don't respond. She already knows the answer to that.

"Augustine, as we would come to learn, had just moved to the district from a prestigious military school. His mother had passed away that year, and his uncle couldn't afford to keep him in the private school sector, so he ended up at our public school. I don't exactly know how we all ended up clicking, or what we bonded over at first. All I know is that we left that summer school session inseparable. August is the one who got Vince and Max's heads on straight enough to go into the military. He convinced all of us. I know for a fact his ability manifested when I left the Land of the Living, but I haven't been able to explain what it is. I don't need anyone else finding out first, but with everything going on, it wouldn't surprise me if things begin to escalate soon. The blackouts he has are an indication that his ability isn't going to be within a norm."

"Which is where we come in." Both boys smile wide and exchange a sly glance. I was to be left unaware of this particular part. There are certain levels of plausible deniability required for this plan to work. There are ways things are done here. The first week of our life among the dead is called The Choosing Game. The first full day is filled with a battery of physicals, mental evaluations, and the longest speech from the High General before the first years are gassed and moved to their spots on "the board". Though the rules change every year, something in my gut tells me this year's game is going to be an absolute shit show. "Don't worry captain, we'll get it done."

"I have taken the liberty of reactivating the listening devices I had placed during our time in The Game. I managed to get into the database months ago and it looks like they were expecting it considering there is absolutely nothing in here on this year's game, stark contrast to the last few years. However, from what I've managed to gather from various communications across campus, the lower ranking agents are talking about plans we aren't privy to in some kind of code." Kestian informs me. Kiara uncrosses her legs and rises in a dramatic fashion, taking her a stand next to me. Her brother tossed her the remote and she bumped her hip against mine lazily.

"This is why Captain sends me in for gossip. You two have yet to come up with more than me." She clicks the remote and a slew of text messages and agent files splay wildly across all screens. Drawing in a deep breath she takes a moment to warn. "You aren't going to like any of this, Captain."

"I already don't fucking like this, Kiari." I grumble.

"Whoever is pulling the strings on this year's game has it in for your boys. Someone let slip through the wire that they are of interest, but I haven't been able to figure out who the mole is. I have my suspicions. There's also talk of a big player behind the scenes but nobody's giving hard information."

Something in my eyes must've made her snap her mouth shut. "The location they're using is Galla The Wild Island. Ironic?"

There is nothing Ironic about it at all.

"It will require some adjustment to our plan, for which I have already briefed my dear sweet brother. However, it will be better in some big ways. I only have to ask one question...do you trust us, Captain?"

"In life and in death." I say firmly. Kiari nods and takes her leave. Without another word, I leave the boys to contemplate the information they've been given while I go to my room to think.

Galla The Wild Island.

Four years ago, I entered that Island afraid.
I left that Island feared. The carefully cultivated plan I have been working on from the moment I stepped foot into this strange world is already beginning to take its own shape. I don't like it, but it is the way things have to be. The generals are making moves for their own sets of discourse, while I am working under the demands of a different form of leadership. My orders are absolute, and if all goes well, everything about the world will change for the better. I just hope my boys are up for the fight like I know they can be.

Chapter Five
Augustine

My sight returns first, followed by the distinct smell of coffee and Vince's cooking. As my senses return, so too does the reason for my black out, followed immediately by the realization that I have absolutely no idea where I am. Special Lieutenant Black's words were like salt rock bullets to the face. Disorienting and Painful. I barely remember walking through the halls of what will now be our home.

With my senses now returned, I look around me and begin to take stock of my surroundings. Bookshelves full of encyclopedias and various charts line the wall directly in front of my bed. Cork and dry erase boards fill the space around three large monitors. A bathroom door wedged between the wall and the bed to my left, and a nightstand sits to the right of the bed. Bookshelves fill the rest off the wall space. Four floor to ceiling shelves covering the empty wall on the right of the room, while a three paned window sits with its curtains shut on the left. As I familiarize myself with the books, I realize one of the shelves is stocked full of world encyclopedias and various atlas' that bring me a deep sense of mental joy. Whoever put this room together did their research. I notice the faint smell of Vince's huevos rancheros starting to get heavier the closer I get to the farthest bookshelf from my bed, and my stomach practically leaps from my body to seek it out. Curious, I jostle the shelf itself and to my surprise, it pulls inward.

When I pull it open all the way, I walk into a small hallway with four doors. Each with a name plate for one of the boys, and I don't bother checking to see if mine has the same, instead I make my way down the hallway and toward the smell of food. I hear the boys and the worry I feel when I leave them unattended lessens.

"No fair! You got a secret door!" Marco whines from the couch while he tries his best to annoy Max by touching random buttons on the tablet. "What about this one?"

"If you don't quit touching my shit I'm gonna to taze you." Max growls his hands behind the very wide-screen television. I know that whatever he's doing to it, he's having the time of his life even while Marco has taken to trying to ruin his focus. It's Marco's favorite pastime, because while Max does have some anxiety issues, focus is not one of his issues. Vince, being the big brother he is, has fitted the breakfast bar with his famous something's-eating-him-so-we're-eating-everything spread. He's done this since we were in high school. Every time we had a big exam, a shit relationship, or a bad day, Vince would tear the kitchen apart making whatever he could with whatever he could. It was always his way of balancing whatever he thought he was responsible for solving at the time. Most people think he's stupid and his penchant for raging out makes him seem unfeeling at times, but I know better.

Vince motions for me to take a seat on one of the stools at the bar, then goes back to washing dishes. I trudge to a stool and look up to see him loading a plate full of food. Eggs, bacon, some chorizo and tortillas. It's only now that I realize I haven't even seen real food in almost a year.

Is it going to slow me down? No.

Is it going to hurt later? Absolutely. Now ask me if I care.

I groan when Vince places the full plate in front of me. A barrage of smells hitting my nose that only just mask the scent of lavender coming from Vince, but nothing ever masks the burnt sugar scent of somebody lying to me. I table it for now, listening to the boys argue while Vince continues to clean up the mess he made. But their banter doesn't last long before they join me at the table. Marco takes the plate Vince holds out. When Max tries to refuse Vince and Marco let out very fed up sighs. "Take it or I'm gonna tell August how long it's been since you had anything to eat other than bacon mac and cheese."

I drop my fork and whip my head to my left to look Max dead in the eyes, fighting against the overwhelming scent of guilt coming off of him now. Last time he went on a bender, it was weeks. I can only imagine how bad it was this time. He opens his mouth like he's going to argue, but a raised eyebrow from me has him rethinking his options. So instead he shuts it, shoulders dropping as he takes the plate and begins loading it up with enough to where we won't bitch about. Satisfied, I turn back to my meal and we all eat in silence. Metal utensils clunking and scraping across glass plates. Chewing and swallowing. I feel Vince's eyes on me while we eat, and I am fully aware of the conversation that needs to be had. A conversation I'm not fucking ready for. He won't press the matter until we are all finished eating, so I take this time to try and sort through my thoughts.

Do you need to see oxygen to breathe it?

Such a simple phrase. Yet, I fixate on what they could mean.

Did he know her? Does he know something? What if he knows what really happened to my wife? The questions just keep rolling and rolling in my brain and before I know it I've dissociated into my mind. I only notice when Vince barks my name like a dad.

"Augustine!" My attention comes back like a snapped rubber band and my eyes find him instantly. There's worry on his face, but there is hope in his eyes I haven't seen in a long time. It's difficult to look at it head on, so I look away. Big mistake, apparently. "No! We're too deep in the shit to start closing up now. You owe us an explanation and then we need to fill you in on what we heard while you were in lala land."

I take a deep breath and let it out slowly, glancing at them. Everyone's plates have been cleared and washed, and mine sits empty in front of me. I feel like there are rocks in my stomach, so I pick it up and move to wash it. Max stops me by getting up first and grabbing my plate.

"I ate. You talk." he says simply before continuing to wash the plate at the sink quickly and returning to his seat. Vince is leaned against the prep counter, and Marco sits to my right. They've grown in the time I've been gone. Max is growing out his hair and beard, Marco seems to have filled out in the chest and shoulders, and Vince's facial hair is much shorter and well kept than before. Slowly I begin.

"I don't know what is actually going on. What I do know is that Black came to me telling me I had two options. Come with him, or have all of us locked up."

"No evidence, no case." Max snorts. I brace for what's about to happen, and I'm suddenly happy he ate already.

"He had all your names, Max. All three of you."

"Bullshit. I scrubbed that shit better than the toilets at basic training." Max is standing now, pacing back and forth as he is undoubtedly running through every single program he put in place to keep it all under wraps. I know the moment he figures out where the hole in his fire wall is because he stops abruptly to curse under his breath.

"Let's get to the important stuff!" Marco whines. "What's up with the Special shit bag that brought us here anyway?"

"Well, if it looks like a fuck…" I wait for them to understand, and they all give me different levels of disbelief.

"There is no fucking way that scraggly ass motherfucker and this hippie biker wanna-be are the same person." Vince's disbelief is shown in his face screwing up in disgust.

"No. Gotta be a son. At the very least, the guy is a cousin or something. As much as dude pissed me off, he was pretty cool. No way it's the guy with the stick shoved so far up his ass you could smell it on his breath." Marco shakes his head, making me snort at his comment. Max remains silent, rewriting programs in his head too hard to add to the conversation.

"I don't know how he did it, but clearly there's a whole world of possibilities to consider. He mentioned the trial, and the fact that he was playing a role to maintain appearances. I don't think he's lying, but I do think it's something to keep a lookout for." I shrug, standing to head into the open living room. Without being prompted, the boys follow and take a respective seat. We form a circle around the coffee table in the center of all the couches. "How long was I out this time?"

"Hours, August." Vince answers. I grimace at this bit of knowledge. I have been blacking out since my wife died, and we never could get a straight answer from anyone as to why it happens. The longest I've been out before was three days, and that was the very first time. From then on it was never longer than one hour. I haven't fully blacked out since being locked up, but with all of the pressure of the situation, everything is weighing on me. There are too many unanswered questions. For a long moment nobody speaks, because none of us ever got the chance to figure out how to address it. "We learned a lot about this place while you were out."

"I took notes." Marco nods, pulling out the notepad he always carries and hands it off to me.

"I did some digging." Max leans over to grab a brand new laptop and plugs his master key into it, prompting a smile.

"I did my best to make a map of the places and directions we went. I left it on your swanky ass desk." Vince jokes.

"Great job guys." I praise. They just shrug and nod once, ready to fill me in completely.

"As the story goes, a scientist by the name of Yvonne Dastrov went to President Truman not long after Hitler was actually captured and killed with a proposal. Yvonne and another man named Adam Lester-Kane said they had planted seven seeds across the globe. Seeds that would only sprout if a treaty was signed promising complete and total anonymity. At the time, Juggernauts were still theories scientists and soldiers talked about but nobody had actually been able to come up with feasible evidence to support such theories, so they were written off as delusions." Max rattles off from memory as he types. "As a show of faith, and as a way of preemptively confirming the existence of their people, President Truman was invited to...awe fuck- where was it again?"

"Philippines." Vince grunts.

"Right! Right! So, they had the president meet them in the Philippines, covertly of course, because there is not one single record of this meeting. Believe me, I checked." Max continues. "In order to help the president understand what they are, they hatched one of the seeds. There are seven places like this around the world, August. Seven different, as Black called them, pocket dimensions full of people like them. Truman signed the treaty, barring the amendment where in case of absolute dire need, the sitting president would be able to call on them for aid."

"Did you learn anything more about Juggernauts?" I ask.

"Somewhat." Marco answers. "Black says there are technical terms and classifications but most juggernauts are unique to a person."

"Are they a species?"

"Sorta. The way he's making it out to be is that Juggernauts are humans that have gone through some kind of traumatic event, horrible crime, or intense situation that causes them to evolve in the moment. Humans with stronger wills and good intentions." Max's answer doesn't satisfy me enough but I table that bit for the time being.

"So he thinks we're one of them?" I press.

"He does, but in order to maintain the natural process of it all he said he has to keep certain parts of information to himself." Max finishes speaking and moves to stand beside the large television in the living room. "One thing he also said is that apparently we are supposed to learn how to fight the sins of humanity."

"Sins of humanity?" I draw out each word slowly. After everything I have heard so far, that seems like the biggest crock of bullshit so far. "Like 'Thou shalt not' and all that?"

Vince holds his hand out to his baby brother who reluctantly slips him what I can only assume is cash. A bet won at my expense being paid out. I chuckle and shake my head. "Seems like I really did miss a lot."

"You've been checked out for hours. The longest I've seen since.." Max trailed off. None of us speak of her out loud to one another really, least of all Max. "Anyway, I narrowed down the main points of the briefing. Sporadic as it was, there was a ton of information and a heavy inflow of 'fun facts' I have personally been dying to fill you in on."

"Fun facts?" My voice is strained, exhausted from the trip and post-black out fatigue.

"Yes. Fun-facts. For instance, did you notice how the buildings when we got here were made out of some shiny material?"

"I did." I answer with a raised eyebrow.

"That is because when Adam Lester-Kane hatched the seeds, they grew trees and vines, but when Yvonne worked his magic, we are pretty much using that word literally at this point, he created diamond buildings."

"Bull-" Before I can finish the curse, Marco has a knife hilt extended out to me.

"The window sill above the stove." He jerks his chin toward the kitchen, rolling his eyes and pressing it into my palm before dragging me to the window himself. "If it was bullshit, we would be able to mark it. A dent, a chunk, fuck-even a damn scratch."

The aggravation dripping in his voice keeps me quiet. We have all been jerked around mentally and emotionally today, and it's clear he needs me to be done with my skepticism. I flip the hilt of the blade, swiping the windowsill with the tip which seems to only deflect off the surface. My eyes go wide as I examine the place a mark should be, but there's nothing to see. Not a fucking scratch. I return to the couch, giving Marco his blade back by the hilt with a nod. "Alright then. What's next?"

"I suppose the main point is what we should expect in the coming days." Max clears his throat, seemingly eager to get to it as images come onto the screen of the research he's done. "Tomorrow we will all be going through what Special Lieutenant Black called 'The Battery'. We'll go in, fill out some paperwork, then we are subjected to extensive tests. Blood Tests, Physicals, Cardiac assessments."

"Black says they call it 'The Battery' because they basically throw every machine plus the batteries at us." Vince interjects. I look at him with an eyebrow raised. "No me mires con esse cara, cabrón. Es lo que dijo el gringo. Do not look at me with that face, jackass. It's what the white boy said. Don't look at me like I just shit on the floor."

I hold up my hands in surrender. Tensions are higher than has ever been normal for us as a team. Of that I am painfully aware of, their scents light but still come off of them in waves. They're hurt, worried, and maybe even a little afraid. I know I am, but I can't show it. "Once they are done bleeding us dry, we will have dinner here to be allowed a debrief. From there we are to be given further instruction for the rest of the week. Which is basically the biggest shady shit the man has said thus far."

"How so?"

"The only thing Black could tell us is that we should figure out a safe word. We already have one of course but he made it seem like we were going to be separated at some point. All he could say at the time was that I should be prepared." The roll of his eyes is quick, but my curiosity has reached a new peak.

"You specifically?" I ask, and he just nods in reply. I let out a heavy, exaggerated breath. "Well, did you tell him you're always prepared?"

"Of course I did." He boasts. "I started my bots on a file chase trying to see if we can get a leg up before we set out tomorrow but it's going to need a few hours before I get results if any. Though something tells me secrets are earned here."

We sit silently for a few moments while they allow me to take it all in. As tired as I am, my brain is a cacophony of contingency plans. Clapping my hands together and plaster on a brave face in an attempt to shift the focus. "I'm tired as fuck. Let's call it a night and regroup. We'll wake up early and hit the day with a clear head."

A sigh of relief from all three of them has their shoulders dropping simultaneously. A pang of guilt for each one makes me stand on my feet. "I got breakfast in the morning."

"Awe Captain." Vince yawns, slightly amused. "If you touch my kitchen for anything other than to wash your plate, we will box in this nice ass living room."

"Been here less than a day and you've already claimed the kitchen?" I banter.

"You're surprised?" he asks, rhetorically. I'm not but I shrug anyway. We all break into somewhat lighthearted laughter before saying our goodnights and returning to our respective rooms. Before they disburse, I hear them whispering amongst themselves before Vince shuts it down. "Not tonight guys."

I slide my back down the closed shelf of my bedroom. The silence is deafening here. I sit there for a moment just to allow myself the crushing weight of everything all at once. Deep breaths. Tears in my closed eyes. I feel a sense of calm wash over me after a minute or two. Ebbing and flowing just enough to bring me to my feet. Trudging to the bed I don't even bother to get undressed before I'm asleep. Mentally diving headfirst into the nightmares I think I'll have. However on this night I am met with something I would have never expected.

A woman whose face should be the same as it always is when I dream of her, is changed. Older now, and a pain to the

61

brown eyes that only just outmatch the hints of purple with which I am unfamiliar. Two full strides would be more than enough to close the fog filled gap between us but I stand frozen. Gawking at an image that in spite of the dreaming state I find myself in, looks so very real.

She stands so still. Watching my soul constrict behind my eyes as I watch her chest rise and fall with a beating heart. So steady I feel envy in my chest as it moves at twice the speed. I could stay forever simply in her presence alone. But this isn't real. It can't be.

Even now as she moves slow enough for a sloth to feel some sort of jealousy, a smile spreads across my face. She is as beautiful as ever, arms now crossed over her chest with an attitude in her stance that long ago took hold as my conscience. It's only when she sucks her teeth and rolls her eyes that I truly realize this feels like no dream I've ever had. The smile falls from my face with a snap of her fingers and I am taken aback by the edge in her tone. "I need you to stay focused, Augustine."

My eyes fly open, her name escaping my lips like my breath is being chased out of my body. I'm on my feet in an instant. Pacing in parallel to the foot of the bed, my hands in my hair all but tearing it out at the roots. I need to breathe. It was just a dream. It wasn't- SHE isn't real. I need to...*stay focused, Augustine.*

I stop pacing, spinning hard on my feet to face the wall of boards. My eyes settled on what looks like a pamphlet pinned dead center where it wasn't before. Upon closer inspection I realize it's a map, but one I have never seen before. On the outside there are three small letters.

B.A.R

Burn After Reading.

Her words drift through my mind once again and I get to work committing the map to memory. Though I have no clue where it came from or where this is a map of, I know that someone is watching out for us. For now, I refuse to admit the possibility of who it could be. For now I just have to make sure not to let it go to waste.

Chapter Six
Vince

I don't dream.

So when I see the woman standing in the center of ominous smoke, I know it isn't that.

It can't be real though…can it? Tears threaten my eyes instantly, and when I clear my throat to speak my voice is foreign to my ears.

"Kaila." I attempt, but my voice breaks so I try again. "Kaila…are you-"

"Real?" She guesses and her voice makes my heart constrict. I shake my head warily. "Alive?"

I nod absentmindedly, stunned. She offers a heavy sigh, the kind she lets out when she's reluctant to make a choice. "Wake up and find out for yourself."

I'm fully conscious and on my feet instantaneously, my feet tangling in the blanket for a second causing anxious panic. I search the dark room wildly, but before her name has the chance to make it out of my mouth, I find myself falling. At least, that's what I think, until my back hits the ground. The air evacuates my lungs as quickly as I find myself on my stomach with an unmistakable weight pinning me down.

I'm not one to lose my cool over nothing. Even less the one to be bested. It takes quite a bit of weight to pin me. The realization has panic ripping through me while I thrash about, unable to shake the mass enough to stand. I'm so frantic I almost miss the voice that stops everything.

"Cool it, hothead!" The panic evolves into a pain that takes hold of my chest. Tears prick my eyes now with emotions too big to hold back. If this is a joke, it's cruel. Which is why I hold my breath in the hope that I'll hear it again. When I do, I can't breathe, and it isn't because of whatever is on top of me anymore. "I'm going to let you up now. You gonna keep it aces?"

I'm in shock, unable to answer as words escape me. Seeming to take the silence as a suitable response, the weight lifts. I test my limbs quickly before I shoot to my feet, turning to have my eyes land on the origin of the tears that now blur my vision. A strangled sob leaves me, and just like that, I'm not a soldier. Right now, I'm just a big brother, looking at the little sister he thought he'd never get the chance to see again. "Oh my god...Kai-Kaila? Kaila Jane, is that you?"

"You better hope it's me. Somebody else would have shot you dead while you were snoring like a fat ass." Her quip doesn't even offend me. It validates the one thing I have been holding onto for the past four years. The world comes back at the speed of mach Jesus and before I even realize it, I'm screaming desperately.

"Guys! August! Marc-"

"Shut up! The room is soundproof, brick head! It was made for interrogation!" she calls over me, aggravation dripping from every word. I move to the door, but in a blink she's in my way, eyes blazing with a challenge I haven't seen matched in all the years she's been gone. I stagger back a few steps, baffled by her speed. "I can't let you do that, Vince."

"You can't WHAT?!" Before I realize what I'm doing, I have her by the shoulders, needing to know she is really here. Needing to feel it in all its truth. My hands come up to cup her head between my hands, running them down her face to her upper arms before she shrugs me off. I take a slight step back, offended. "Kaila? Kaila, how is this possible?"

"I can't tell you that yet." I roll my eyes and attempt to get past her only to fail once more. "Make one more move toward the door, and I will drop you big brother."

Her threat lingers in the air while I can just feel confusion and bewilderment fighting for dominance in my expression. My skin feels like it's vibrating and the air in the room is somehow thick. Anger making my throat close up but still desperate to tell everyone else hurting and in the dark. "What the hell are you saying? Let me go get August, Kai."

"No." With one word, the atmosphere becomes thicker. My chest feels constricted suddenly and panic begins to rise even further. "I'm putting enough risk on you by talking to you at all. Now sit down and pay attention."

After a moment, I nod and make my way on wobbly legs to the workout bench, not allowing her out of my sight as I do so. She plops down beside me with a sigh that screams equal parts exasperation and exhaustion. Her care not to touch me is obvious as she sits but keeps her distance.

"You boys kicked up all kinds of dust in Texas." she begins. My eyebrow rises in shock. How the hell does she know about Texas? "You think for one second I haven't been keeping tabs on you four idiots then you've lost more brain cells than I thought."

Anxiety and anger peak within me. "Stop giving me shit like I didn't just find out the baby sister I've mourned for four years has been alive all this time! Joke like I haven't been holding two little brothers and your HUSBAND together because you DIED!"

She doesn't jump at my outburst. She doesn't even flinch. Guilt hits me for yelling, only slightly overshadowed by relief and rage. At this moment I see her. I really see her. Her hair is black instead of its natural brown. Her eyes somehow swim with hues of purple that are visible beyond the dark chocolate. Though there isn't much light offered around us, her proximity allows my eyes to adjust enough to drag over the scars that etch her forearms like tiger skin. My eyes narrow on the ones on her upper arms, noting the way they have scarred ugly. As if having been reopened more than once. My stomach continues to fall with my eyes when it bottoms out at the horror of her wrists. The scars are so deep, blending into her skin with the time that has faded them. The reality of them screaming in my brain.

I slide from the bench and shatter at her feet. Overwhelmed now by the horrors she must have been through to have her skin so marred. "I'm sorry. I'm so sorry.

We tried. I tried to get to you but they ambushed us. We searched for you for *months*. When you were declared legally dead we held out for as long as we could. We tried to find you. We tried to bring you home. I was supposed to bring you home. How did this happen? How is this real?"

"Sh. Sh. Calm down, Vince." There's a softness to her voice now as she begins patting my hair the way she used to when we were kids. My head is in her lap now and I'm squeezing her so tight I might be hurting her, but she doesn't complain. "You don't have anything to apologize for. I know you have questions, and I want nothing more than to give you all the answers. I just can't yet."

I sit up to look her in the eyes again as she says, "The answer's aren't important right now."

"Not important?" My voice comes out in a breath of defeat.

"Listen," she hisses. "Outside of this moment, you do not under any circumstances speak to anyone about this interaction. You saw nothing. You say nothing. I don't care what you have to do. Nobody can know you four have any connection to me in the Light of the Living. My team and I have our own job to do and we cannot do it unless you and the boys stay as in the dark about me as possible."

"I don't understand." I groan.

"I know." She whispers, but I can hear the pain behind it. "Most recruits come here knowing what their gifts are and having some semblance of what we are and what we do. You all have no such advantage. You have to trust me. Believe me," she moves to place a hand on mine. There's a roughness to it that wasn't there before we lost her. Like my own, only from years of beating against hard surfaces are these callouses allowed to form. "I know what I'm asking. I can't tell you much, but I can tell you that we will all be together again. But it can't be before the time is right or it will blow everything I have been working toward."

"Please, just let me tell them you're alive. You can't ask me to hold onto this. Not from them." My voice is raw from crying. "Not from August."

"Something is happening to him, Vince. You can't tell me you haven't noticed. The blackouts are getting worse and you know it. His Juggernaut is manifesting, and I can't let anybody find out what it is until *we* know exactly what it is." she pauses, her eyes falling to the window before she speaks again. "Tomorrow, you four will go through The Battery. It's invasive, and it's designed to weed out the duds. But it's cake compared to what comes after."

"What comes after?" I ask, my training forcing me to focus solely on her intel.

"We call it the Choosing Game." She answers, definitively. "You will be drugged, and dispersed throughout an island. Officially it's name is Galla, but anyone who survives it knows it unofficially as the Wild Island. From the time you wake up you will have three days to not only find each other, but find your way to the end."

"How are we supposed to do that?"

"Max will bring you all back together." She waves a hand in the air as if the answer was obvious. In hindsight I guess it is, but I can't focus past her. "As long as you boys can find each other again, Augustine will take the lead. My people will handle the rest."

"Blind?" I'm growing irrationally angry, losing my grip on the small semblance of cool I've got left.

"I would never send you in blind." There is something about the way she says it, hinting at a silent knowledge. "I need you to keep him focused. You all need to keep focused. The mountains and forest are completely overrun with predators of every kind. On top of that, the island is criminal land. Angry Juggernauts looking for fresh meat to play with."

"Is that why it's called The Choosing Game?"

"No, big brother. We call it the Choosing Game because this is the final step to decide who becomes one of the Living

Dead and who ends up just…dead." I don't know what my face looks like at this point as she watches me before shaking her head and standing to her feet. As she speaks her final words, she moves to the window. In my room. "You're new pieces in a game that's about to change the way you look at the world. Embrace it. All of it. Pretending it isn't real is going to get you all killed."

She swings the window out wide before shooting me one last look. I call out to her with one last question. "Why is it called the Wild Island?"

"Because. Only the wild survive." She winks, then falls backward out the window. Yet, even as I watch her do it, something tells me there is no danger in her action. The high pitched howl that will play on the soundtrack of my childhood rings through the night, and I know it's her simple way of telling me she is just fine.

When I finally get myself put together enough to sleep, I only manage a few hours before I just decide to pull myself up out of bed. A new motivation holding my spine straight and my head high as I begin breakfast quietly so as not to wake the others. Unfortunately, the sounds coming from the hall of doors lets me know that nobody is sleeping.

For the slightest moment, I almost decided to throw her warning to the wind. But as I take a few steps to reach the captain's door, the image of the scars that paint my sister's body overload me, forcing me to pause. No matter how bad I want to ignore her request, I need to trust that the reasoning for keeping this silent is sound. Because what would I say? How can I even begin to describe what I saw, to break the near porcelain memory they all have will shake them more than we need right now. As angry as the truth of the matter makes me, I do understand why I would be the one she would come to first. I'm the only one who can keep August in check. Nothing makes much sense at all. But she's alive. And that can be enough for me. For now.

Chapter Seven
Augustine

Vince is up early. Sounds like the others are too. Restless nights are a thing for Vince and I, but I've watched the boys sleep through heavy artillery fire, so they have to be struggling mentally. I've managed to commit the entire map to memory. After the transcendent kick in the ass, I spent the better part of the night looking through my books and devising plan after plan with the sporadic information I'd found.

When I've finished going over my notes for the last time, I swing the shelf door to the living room open. Marco stands just outside the doorway with his hands buried in his pockets and a curious gleam in his eyes.

"Good Morning, Captain." he chirps, peering over my shoulder into the room behind me. "Vince made me wait until you were up before I bothered you."

"Marcito's eager." Max calls from behind his laptop once again, unsurprisingly.

"I've seen the other three, and Mr. Mom didn't let me see it last night. You can't tell me you don't want to see what kind of mind-fuck room he's got." Marco whines. It's then that I realize he's talking about my bedroom, so I move to one side and allow him access. Marco saunters inside while Max ditches his current activities to shuffle in behind him. As they 'ooh' and 'aah' around, I take the time to quell my own curiosity, as well as balance myself mentally.

I decide to start in Vince's room, the door directly across from me in the hall. I notice right away the theme is personality on paper. His room is perfectly tailored to his role on the team. Each wall is designated differently. Unlike in my room, which is lined with bookshelves and tactical boards, his room is neat in an entirely different way.

The room is clear of a single desk or protruding piece of furniture aside from the two loveseats in the corner in front of the single window separated by a coffee table. Like the window is a television. Aside from that, it's basically a personal gym. A treadmill, heavy bag, full wall of just weights, and a sparring matt in the middle of it all. To the left side of the door, there is a blank wall with a ladder protruding through the floor. Walking over to the weight bench at the end of the bed, I take a seat allowing a full view of the room and give him a look of concern. Vince, who is leaning casually against the doorframe with a rag slung over his shoulder and flour splattered along the belly of his T-shirt. I snicker at the sight before asking cautiously. "Do I want to know about the ladder?"

"Oh, you mean this ladder?" He says, pointing directly to it. A boyish smile spreads from ear to ear now as he pushes off the doorframe. I nod slowly. Vince steps onto the ladder and begins lowering himself down, but before he disappears from sight he calls out over his shoulder. "Zaglyani v moyu komnatu razvlecheniy. Step into my fun room."

Vince is nothing if not a warm blooded Latino, but he learned Russian for one reason and one reason only. The one reason that makes this room I'm lowering myself into, a necessity for him. Extraction of information and in his words, *"Torture in Russian just hits different."* Pun completely intended. I turn to get a full view of this room, and then my jaw hits the floor. The Comic book level of devices and tools perfectly lining the walls is enough to make any normal human being wet themselves. Surgical tools from every era. Vince is not a doctor...but he is a sick individual when he needs to be.

"Overkill much?" I say when I gather enough sense to speak.

"Dude. No. Check it out." He dramatically slides closer to the center of the room. Clearing his throat he begins speaking in his best impression of a realtor. "Now if you don't like the open floor plan. If it's just not working for what you need at the time."

He presses a button on the remote he pulls out of his pocket, prompting the floorboards in the center of the room beside him to sink and slide open. "We also offer this lovely island option. Great for entertaining the particularly unruly guests."

The surgical table comes up from under the floor and my eyes go wide. I am both impressed and horrified. Once the bed is raised completely, the floor closes around it as if it's been there all along. A few more button presses move the table into different positions and each one prompts an amused chuckle from Vince. He's got the wild look in his eyes we try to keep at bay. "You're twisted."

"Don't tell Marco." he says firmly, suddenly very serious. Being the youngest, we try our best to keep the full extent of certain things hidden as best we can. Vince's sadism is one of those things we try to keep under a tight lock and key. He knows it's bad, but Marco doesn't know how bad it really is.

We laugh at the thought for a moment before we find ourselves in Max's room. I can only describe his room as our own personal war room. Every screen has something on it. Pictures, maps, redacted documents in several languages. It reminds me of a different time. A garage, burned down by the stupidity of boys. The setup is almost identical to the memory.

"No puede ser. It can't be." I breathe when I notice the fridge in the left corner.

"I said the same thing when I noticed." Max smiles solemnly. "Some things are different, but it's basically an upgrade of the old garage."

"Add that to the list of things that shouldn't be possible." Vince calls, the scent of deception spiking when he does, raising my hackles slightly. "Come and eat, it's almost time!"

Without another word, Max zips past me and I turn to look over his screens once more before joining them. But before I can inspect further all screens go white with bold black letters.

Food.
***

72

Once the kitchen is clean after a quick breakfast and showers all around, the four of us gather in Max's room for a briefing before we make our way to meet the Special Lieutenant. "Alright Max. Hit me with it."

"So, like we were saying last night, The Battery begins today. They'll start with extensive tests. I didn't find much, but I did find some information that pretty much confirms what Black said about the origin of this place. Pretty heavy read, I already sent it to your computer. I'm still trying to decrypt their firewalls, but once I make it into their system I should be able to find all our answers."

"What comes after the doctor's visit?" I scoff, knowing my history with doctors isn't the best. I'll lie on the paperwork like I always do. When you have a psychological genius for a wife, you pick up a few things.

"I couldn't dig anything else up. All we have to go on is what we were told by the Special Lieutenant. He said we would have time to come back here to have dinner before we are asked to gather for an orientation." Max informs us. There is a slight pause in his words, and the cinnamon spice of concern enters my nose.

"What's bothering you?" I press.

"It's just the way he told me to be ready. I'm assuming Black knew I would go searching, which means he knew I wouldn't find anything to give me a leg up on what's going on here. So, it's right to assume that he isn't talking about me being ready with information. If I'm not supposed to hack into anything, then why would he single me out?" Max's answer makes me remember the map.

"I might have something to answer that." I say, pulling the map from my back pocket and handing it to him. "I found it in my room last night. I don't know how or when it got there, but whoever put it there clearly wasn't a threat, so they must've had a reason."

Before I pass it over I flip it so the three letter code is face up. Max's face lights up once again with curiosity as he unfolds it and places it in his scanner. After a few seconds the map's image pulls up on the monitors, spanning across every screen. Plopping back into his desk chair he starts at his keyboard. The language of the click and clack of key he seems to understand, filling our ears. "Alright, let's see what we have here."

"Obviously it's a map, but I have no previous knowledge as to where. I have forty-two books of maps in my room and not one of them has even a partial image." I add quickly. From the corner of my vision I can see Marco nodding off in the corner of the room to my left. Vince at the scanner, studying the now refolded map in his hands. Drawing my full attention back to the map on the screens I lean forward with one hand on the desk and the other on the back of Max's chair. "See if you can figure out where in the country it is. Maybe it's wrong."

"It's not in-country. My system searches automatically so I don't have to ask. To be more specific, it's not in-system. If it's a map of a real place, it's not documented in any database, including textbooks." He sounded as puzzled as I felt, though I knew better than to ask if his system made a mistake. "What are these cluster points all over the mountains?"

"They remind me of drop points." Vince added, getting closer. After starting to snore and waking himself up, Marco looks up and rises with renewed interest.

"Blue is bad." He throws us all for a loop with the statement. We all turn slowly to him, prompting him to suck his teeth and scowl. "You guys can't see the words? Then I'm assuming you also can't see the "x"s scattered all over the place."

I lock eyes with Vince then Max before he proceeds to zoom in on the spots Marco points out. Sure enough, scattered across the map are clustered x's. On the mountain are the four in black. The others are blue. Scrawled in the bottom corner were the exact words Marco had spoken before. "How the fuck did you see that?"

"You know I have good eyes. Not like it's anything new." He shrugs, but the scent of deception is thicker in the air. Marco walks out of the room. I look at Max again who looks between Vince and I wide eyed.

"Nobody's eyes are that good. I've never even seen print this small. He saw something that basically isn't even there. Pilot's by design have to have perfect far vision but if it was that simple, the Captain should've seen them too as a certified sniper." We all shift uncomfortably, our gazes falling to the door Marco left out of. "His vision is great...but that's new."

"Let's keep an eye on him." I said, rubbing my own eyes from straining. "We need to burn this and get down to meet the Special Lieutenant."

"Captain," Vince piped up suddenly. "Assume the black x's are our drop points. Where would you have us meet up?"

"I wouldn't have us dropped so far apart. Especially in a region we aren't familiar with. What are you thinking?" I ask.

"I know you're planning for it anyway. Humor me." he says, the bitter sweet scent lingering making my eyes narrow.

I mull it over for a moment, choosing to continue ignoring the warning scent of plums. Instead I turn to Max's screens again. "Zoom out all the way."

Max complies. "Assuming, the blue are insurgents based on the message. The real problem will be getting down the mountain. I don't know where the end goal would be, but I would make our rendezvous point with this body of water here. Under the mountain's bridge."

Vince's gaze was far away suddenly, like he was remembering something important. After a couple seconds he nods, and follows Marco out.

"What's with him?" I wonder aloud.

"I don't know. He's been acting weird all morning." Max grumbled under his breath.

"Well, I'll keep an eye on Marco. You see if you can figure out what's putting Vince off. We have to burn the original copy of the map." Max concludes before the boys rejoin us. We all take a moment to watch the flame burn out before I give my final orders.

"Alright. Let's get this done. Stick together as best we can. Gather as much information as possible."

"Can we make friends?" Marco smiles, earning a soft chuckle from the rest of us.

"Hell, at this point let's just try not to make any enemies. Figure out as much as we can about life on the land and try to get some decent answers to what the hell is going to happen tonight. I would like to keep the surprises as small as possible." I add.

"Copy." They bark back in unison.

Chapter Eight

Vince

"Hey kid, are you feeling okay?" I ask my younger brother as I walk out of Max's room.

"I'm fine. Just thinking, " He replies cryptically. My brother and I aren't the touchy feely kind of siblings. But after yesterday, he's been acting noticeably strange. Distant, and not his usual childish self. My sister used to say that he is the best of us. She's wrong of course, because that crown belongs to her and she would never know it.

"Alright well, I'm telling you right now, I notice. Do with that what you will." I offer. He nods, his shoulders relaxing ever so slightly like he was bracing for me to push the subject. As bad as I want to, he isn't the only one keeping secrets right now, so I leave it. "Look. If we get separated, meet by the river under the mountain pass."

"Are we going to get separated?" His eyebrow raises at my sudden shift in tone.

"We might. Judging by what Black said yesterday, and this map that popped up out of nowhere. I just want us prepared for anything. The river. Under the mountain pass." I reiterate more sternly this time. He nods again, his eyes narrowing. I know he memorized the way down the mountain. It's a trick we learned thanks to Augustine. If you can't remember all of it, at least remember the way out.

"Oye. Listen." He calls out. I lock eyes with him again, noticing a difference in them. I am taken aback for a moment before the thick black bleeds back into his natural brown, then back to concern. "Yo me doy cuenta también. I notice, too."

Before I can reply, we re-enter Max's room to see him holding a lighter and the map. We all gather around, standing shoulder to shoulder to watch it burn. I watch as my sister's words go up in smoke while a myriad of thoughts panging through my skull.

"I would never send you in blind."

At that moment I assumed she was going to find a way to keep me informed or something. Now I feel like I'm seeing a bigger picture. What the hell has she been through?

She sent us the map.

She knows how good the Captain is when it comes to cartography.

Blue is bad.

If she's talking about the color of the x's on the map, then it's safe to assume that they are who we will need to watch out for. Though I am curious to know if she knew Marco would see them, or if she was counting on Max's computers to pick up her message. It really irritates me to continue to be reminded of how little I actually know. If she got us this, I am going to do whatever I can to follow up on the task she's entrusted me with. Though August seems focused for now, I am going to have to do my damndest to keep an extra eye on him. Truthfully, his focus has been fractured since the day she disappeared. We all left one another to our own devices a little, and I'm guilty of letting him go too far when he got locked up. It's time to correct that.

"Alright. Let's get this done. Stick together as best we can. Gather as much information as possible." Captain begins again once the map is nothing but ashes in the bathroom sink.

"Can we make friends?" Marco plasters a smile on his face, unable to hide the slight strain in the corners of his eyes. Though we know full well he will manage to find at least one friend by the time the day is over.

"Hell, at this point let's just try not to make any enemies. Figure out as much as we can about life on the land and try to get some decent answers to what the hell is going to happen tonight. I would like to keep the surprises as small as possible." The Captain adds to his final remarks.

"Copy." We bark back, breaking apart from our circle and making our way through the family room and out the door. The hallway is full of soldiers now. All dressed in the same black camouflage pants and tight gray shirts. For a short moment we all stand outside our room to watch the different units hustling in one direction or another. The sight reminds me a little bit of basic training camps. Watching the different races and genders all trying to make it to the right place before the wrong time.

August steps away from the door, then stops once he realizes that he still has no memory of how we got to our room the night before. Even with the half assed map I drew up, the way the halls were built into the mountain is mazelike. I place a silent hand on August's shoulder and lightly pull him behind me, knowing they will all take to the formation change. The last thing you want to do is sneak up on me. I shoot, fuck questioning a corpse. I start walking in the opposite direction that August was just about to lead us. With my hands in my pockets, I turned the corner at the end of our hall, while doing my best to keep a shoulder to the wall. Ignoring the growing panic in my chest. I've never been one for crowds, that's always been Marco's gift. My sister's too. I was always too big for the space I was in, so I've always done my best to make myself as small as I possibly can. I can hear the whispers as we all walk. Only a few emerge from behind me. The halls seem longer than before but I chalk it up to lack of sleep. Continuing to follow the paintings at the end of each corridor, I begin to notice more and more the looks we are getting. I would like to focus on the smiles and waves from the many attractive female soldiers, but the smiles only slightly overshadow the glares. The challenging gazes behind them are the problem. At the end of the hall we turn into, I see one set of eyes that stop me so hard the others ram into my back with an oof.

"Yo!"

"Sorry! Uh, Cap?" The confusion is thick in my voice but I keep my eyes locked on this stranger's. You would assume that the gray-ish paleness, snow white buzz cut, and sharp features are the things throwing me off. It's not. It's the eyes.

Slivers.

White slivers with deep black pools behind them. They're cold. Expressionless. Snakelike. August sucks in a breath beside me and curses under it. I press my back against the wall, allowing the others to openly gawk with me. We must look for too long, and I know we aren't subtle, because in an instant the guy is walking toward us with two others in tow. August's body goes rigid, muscles taut. He's always had a sense for things we didn't, but it's like the sense has been heightened somehow by the loss of our girl. August squares his shoulder, and I instinctively turn my shoulder away from the wall to shield Marco behind me.

When they finally reach us, I am able to see the eyes of the other two. Similar in shape, the colors are different. Black slivers on gray backing for the ashy blond beanpole, red slivers on white backing for the redhead with the unfortunate face. Chills draw up my spine when I feel Marco's fingers pressing into my lower back to signal me. One finger presses quickly twice to signal combatants to the left of me, followed by the single simultaneous press of five fingers signaling five bodies. I repeat the gesture on August's back as the captains of both groups exchange banter that quickly gets unfriendlier by the second.

"You boys got staring problem?" the stranger sneers in choppy English.

"You'll have to forgive us. We've never seen eyes like yours." August replies, extending a hand, unbeknownst to them, the only attempt at diplomacy he will offer. A sound fills the air, starting at the stranger's chest as his face contorts in disgust at the appendage. The sound seems to echo off the walls of my brain making my hairs stand on end.

"I don't believe I *have* to do anything." The fucker's voice is grating, like heels on unfinished marble, but it deepens only just when he speaks again in Russian. "Oni deystvitel'no prosto khodyachie misheni. They really are just walking targets."

Their laughs are hollow and deep like the act itself is unnatural to them. The flashes of High School memories and the unmistakable deja vu rattle around in my brain forcing me to roll my eyes. Creepy as they might be, disrespect is not something we take very lightly as a team anyway. The captain, however, has no patience for it.

"Vizhu, u kogo-to net maner. I see someone has no manners." August's easy transition to their language seems to take them by surprise, though they recover quickly enough.

"Vizhu, ty govorish' po-russki. I see you speak Russian." Their leader sneers with a flat tone before turning to his buddies. "No yemu ne pomeshala by praktika. Though he could use some more practice."

They laugh again in that strange way, harder now like what they're saying is actually funny. Augustine doesn't wait for them to finish. Speaking in a tone so passive you would think the rest of him matched. Spoiler alert. It doesn't. "Ya dumayu, ty obnaruzhish', chto moy russkiy v polnom poryadke. A chto kasaetsya tvoikh maner? Chto zh, ty mog by rabotat' nad nimi godami, i vse ravno ne smozhesh' izbavit'sya ot pozora, kotoriy ty prinosish' sebe, kogda otkryvayesh' rot. I think you'll come to find that my Russian is just fine. As far as your manners? Well, you could work on those for years and never pull yourself out of the disgrace you bring to yourself when you open your mouth."

There's that sound again, but this time there's no mistaking it. This time, the three in front of us stiffen and let out a rattling hiss that sounds less snakelike and more…inhuman. An evil smile spreads across their leader's lips. When his smile peaks, I feel Marco's back press against my own. Something is happening behind me, but all I can see is Max moving out of my field of vision. No doubt to place himself between Marco and someone or something else. The man closes the gap ever so slightly, a feeble show for dominance. "Ya dolzhen vyrvat' tvoy yazyk pryam zdes' i seychas za to, chto ty osmelilsya govorit' so mnoy takim obrazom. I should rip out your tongue here and now for daring to speak to me in such a way."

"Ne mogu skazat', chto mne nravitsya byt' ugrozhayemym kem-to, kogo ya ne znayu po imeni. Can't say I appreciate being threatened by someone I don't have a name for."

"Zachem tebe moje imya? What use would you have for my name?" The leader pauses for a moment to glance over our shoulders. Neither of us give way to his bait, so he puts the nail right in the coffin of any diplomacy Augustine might have been holding on to. "Nikto iz vas ne perezhit dostatochno dolgo, chtoby eto bylo vazhno. None of you will be alive long enough for it to matter."

They laugh, like it's a good idea to do that. It's in that instance I hear the hissing again. Low and far enough out of audible range to not be too close behind us, but they are broken, like the sounds of snakes chuckling.

That's when something changes.

Augustine's body goes rigid and his head lolls forward a bit for a split second. His hands enter his pockets slowly and he stands straighter. The air in the room begins to grow cold around August. Marco begins to shiver behind me and I have to clench my jaw shut to keep my teeth from clacking together too. Without moving my head much I search my peripheral vision only to realize we are being HEAVILY watched by the other soldiers in the hallway. Though conversations carry on, there are breaks in focus where most are taking the time to look toward the growing tension between our two groups. I am beginning to wonder if the cold is actually coming from Augustine, or something else all together. However, I'm trained better than to expose my throat in an attempt to look up and check for a vent, so the lack of air current will have to suffice for me.

I need you to keep him focused. Her words roll into my mind again and I know it's time to get him out of here.

I notice the way Marco's back lightens its press against my own just a breath before the three men in front of us back down, all with varying degrees of confusion and anger written on their faces.

"Pomni, v t'eme vsegda bol'she zmei. Just remember there are always more snakes in a den." Their leader hisses through gritted teeth before they turn on their heels and walk away. The farther they get, the warmer the air gets around us once again. I place a hand on August's shoulder and he jumps ever so slightly.

"What was that about making enemies?" I ask in a low tone. He doesn't answer, just nods as we all watch them walk away.

"Snake eyed asshole probably just needs his ass beat." August finally states way too casually.

"Captain, come on…" I press, trying to get him to cop to it on his own. He won't though, because that's who he is.

"What? Forget which way we're going?" August's obliviousness, while fake as all fuck, will be all I'll get for now. He's with us and isn't blacking out. I can work with that.

"Forget it. I think we go this way." I shrug, relief settling in my gut.

Short lived as it is.

"You fuckers get lost or something?!" Special Lieutenant Black's voice booms through the hallway better than any Drill Sergeant I've ever met. All movement in the hallway ceases, all heads whipping to give him undivided attention. "I know more than one of you've got somewhere to be sooner than the time it'll take you to get there! I suggest doing like my daddy when my momma starts cleaning and MOVE YOUR ASSES!"

All at once the hall erupts into a full on rat race. We all press our backs against the wall quickly to make way for the stampede of people. Making the jabs to the gut we keep getting as they pass nothing but intentional. Before we can join in on the fray, the Special Lieutenant reaches our spot in the hallway. "Not you four."

Instinctively we stand at attention, receiving a chuckle from him that instantly annoys me. Something about what he says next makes Augustine stiffen, stopping his breathing the way he does now. "Relax. I've been informed of a slight change in location for your physicals. Nothing to be alarmed about, just a few overscheduling problems we are working through in our main clinic. As a result you will go through The Battery in Building 9. I've been sent to take you there now."

August hesitates, eyeing the Special Lieutenant warily before schooling his expression again. "On your lead."

Black's eyebrow raises, much like the rest of ours, but then he starts off down the hall again. August follows, but the rest of us stick behind.

"Something's happening to him." Marco says under his breath to Max and I. There are practically no more people in this hallway now, but he speaks low enough so only we hear. We don't respond but the agreement is in the air between us. I recall the warning my sister gave me. I want nothing more than to at least share the news of her return with my brother. Marco deserves to know. However, I refuse to break her trust. Things are clearly complicated and the need for everyone's absolute focus in this moment is the priority.

I turn my head to check the hallway out of habit when I spot the girl staring at us. She's unassuming, and the sight of her throws me. She can't be older than her early twenties at best. My face screws up in shock, prompting her to take off like her ass is on fire. I shake my head to clear it. I can't deal with her right now. So instead I follow after the captain like I always do.

Chapter Nine
Marco

I know better than to keep secrets from my older brother. Although with everything happening right now, I don't have time to really figure out what this is that I need to tell him. Yeah, something is clearly going on with the captain, but I know things are starting to get weird for me too. It started after I had gone to sleep. My dream started the same as it always does. The last happy memory I have with my sister, coupled with the nightmare that is the last memory I have of her, period.

***

It was late August. I only remember because it was one of the hotter days in Okinawa. A fun fact courtesy of my brainy sister. My memory isn't the best, one too many times being thrown around by Vince and Augustine, but this memory was the one that remained at the forefront of my mind on a constant basis. The way she wore her hair on top of her head as high as it would go so as to keep it both off of her neck and out of her eyes. I remember sitting at the airstrip, waiting for the last of our takeoff checks to be conducted. I can't quite remember why I wasn't in the cockpit for this mission. I do know it was the last time anybody but me was in it for us.

Although it's supposed to be a dream I can always recall the nervous feeling about not being the one flying the plane. I always flew the plane. The dream flashes and my sister sits beside me now, hair down. She was relaxed as we made our unplanned descent. She always had a way of being calm in situations she had absolutely no business being calm in. She looked at me with concern in her eyes the way she always did when we were on foreign soil. At the time I found it annoying, big sister hovering over the baby like a second mom even if I am older. Looking back after having time to miss her, there are things I notice in the moments I have with her in my dreams.

The vision flashes again. This time landing me dead center of the beginning of the worst time of my life. I recall the scent of rusted metal and gasoline. Fumes from the fuel that had been leaking out since our departure. Why didn't the censor warn us sooner about fuel loss? In the days after, this thought would take up an ungodly space in my mind. We were surrounded from the very beginning. As soon as the hatch door opened for us to "stretch our legs" we were outnumbered, and horribly outgunned. I reached for my gun in what would have been the saddest attempt to defend myself, but Kaila's hand reached out to grab my wrist. Eyes wide I looked at her and I can distinctly remember the realization and fear in her eyes. Before that moment I had always looked to her as a guiding force for bravery and valor, but in it I saw something I had never seen in her eyes. The little girl that just wanted to keep her brother safe. That was when she pulled me behind her, guns had been pointed at me with intent, and she put her body between us.

Flash

The men closed in on us.

Flash

We try to fight, but there's too many of them.

Flash

My body hits the dirt by force. I can hear my sister screaming, pleading for help. Where were the others? Why are they doing this? I thought as I craned my neck as best I can, desperately thrashing against the hands that were trying to bind me.

Flash

The pain at the back of my head from the butt of the gun. My vision going blurry, fading in and out as images become flashes of brief moments of consciousness.

Flash.

Augustine's screaming, fighting with every ounce of strength against his bindings. The muscles and tendons pulled away from his neck as if attempting to dislodge themselves in his fury.

Flash. Max is unconscious, laying in a pile bound in the same way we all were.

Flash, Vince, bleeding from the chest.

Flash…my sister being taken away forever.

Then I woke up. I always wake up the moment I fall into unconsciousness. So many "if"s attached to every minor detail that bombards my mind. I sat up with a sharp breath. I was drenched in sweat and my breathing was coming in ragged. Rolling my eyes I brought my hands up to my face to cup them over my mouth and nose. Closing my eyes I tried to take in a deep breath through my nose but instead of the soothing I had come to expect in my chest, I was met with a sharp pain right behind my eyes. I squeezed my eyes shut as tight as I could, slamming my hands on either side of my head. I tried to scream but the sound caught in my chest. I tried to breathe in but it was so much harder than usual.

The attempt to focus through the pain was ill spent as the pain ebbed away and shot through me again. In a seconds worth of eternity the pain became too much, panic overtook me as I kept trying desperately to inhale. I dropped out of my bed at some point, too focused on the pain to notice as I lay there clutching my head. It was at this moment I heard my sister's voice. "Your mouth. Breath through your mouth."

Not a whisper from memory.

Not a scream from nightmares.

Like an instinct manifesting itself from the depth of necessity.

Air forced its way through my lungs so hard it forced my back as straight as it would go before I exhaled in a pained sound. I continued taking breaths through my mouth until the pain subsided and my lungs had fully recovered from the lack of oxygen. With one hand on the bed to steady myself I stood shakily to my feet. When I opened my eyes everything was clearer.

Sharper.

I hobbled over to the window, rubbing at my eyes before looking out. I drew in a quick breath, shock rendering me still. Everything was magnified. The rocks in the mountain, the dips and jagged edges of its peaks were now being outlined by my line of sight. Every divot and crevice seemed miles deep. The clarity and precision of it all was overwhelming. I closed my eyes once again, shaking my head quickly before looking once more. The clarity continued and I turned on my heel to look around the room. Things remained the same, however in a way, it was almost even now. More normal.

I let out a breath through my nose. How was I supposed to sleep if I could only breathe in through my mouth? As the thought crossed my mind I realized once again why my brother is always hounding me about my priorities. Sucking my teeth, I made my way to my small desk in the corner. My room isn't really like the others, it's simple. I like it better this way.

"I should make a list." I said aloud, echoing another of one of my sister's many pieces of advice. But when I opened the drawer where I had previously placed my notebook, what I found instead was a brand new set of bright orange earplugs and a note.

Gotta do what you gotta do. Practice makes precision.

I thought for a moment, analyzing the handwriting but couldn't place the familiarity. Instead I look at the note, then the foamy plugs. After a moment I realized that they aren't meant for my ears and a reluctant groan passed my lips. "Ah fuck."

***

We all sit in the waiting room of the testing center in building nine. As it turns out, the jump points are all set up differently. According to the Lieutenant, the buildings connected inside the mountain are smoother because those outside are connected both ways, while each on the inside is connected one way at different points. No single doorway leads to the same building twice. I don't understand the logistics of it all. All I know is that the jump points are only possible because of trained Juggernauts.

I stare at the second page of the intake form. To summarize, a long list of "Have you ever" but the farther I go on the page, the weirder the questions get. It's more like a psych test on drugs, I can't help but answer no to all of them. Doesn't everybody lie at the doctors office? I hear Vince's harsh whisper beside me as I come to the last question on the page. "Hijo de la puta madre. Son of a bitch. Yo, I thought there were just more intake sheets for other people."

I chew the end of my pen, contemplating if I should say yes on the last question just to throw a wrench in the game. I lean over slightly, not really giving him much mind while I read. "What do you mean?"

"There's twenty three pages of questions on this motherfucker, man." Vince whispers to me, disgusted with the fact. I sit straighter shooting him a look of disbelief, gathering a few of the pages between my fingers.

"No fuckin' way." I look at the bottom center of the very last page in the stack, bewildered at the sight of the number twenty three printed on it. We meet each other's eyes before all turning to look at our captain at the end of our row of seats, waiting for him to come to the same realization as the rest of us. My new eyes watch him check the final box "no" as I knew he would before he proceeds to pull the first two pages out of the clipboard. I watch the hope die in his eyes when he looks down to see a full page of more questions like the one before it, then we watch him flip to the last page with a small groan. We all break into a series of poorly muffled laughter, dropping our heads when he looks at us wide eyed.

"Are we supposed to answer all of these?" August whispers, sinking into his seat and putting the pages at the back of the stack with a roll of his eyes.

"I would say so." The tone of the woman's voice has us all sitting nice and straight. "We dinnae just hand out paperwork tae help strengthen yer shootin' hand."

The woman has the soft touches of Scotland in her voice. Soft enough to be understood, but still unmistakable. The woman looks warm and kind, her scrubs black to match our uniforms which gives her a bad ass appeal. The short, bright red hair laid down perfectly with gel. The subtle red in her dark green eyes is not nearly as shocking to see on our second day in this place. "Nor dae we hand them out for ye tae lie. Hand them over."

"Ma'am?" I attempt to stare stupidly while we most likely are all hoping she isn't asking what she's asking. She lets loose an "ack" in annoyance and holds her hand out.

"The first two pages. If ye've made it past, ye can hand those pages over as well."

We comply, swallowing our laughter and chasing it with reluctance. This gives me a vague reminder of junior high. The four of us sat up in the principal's office for some bone head thing we'd done. The woman hands over fresh first and second pages to each of us. "Ye can just take them with ye, but I'll expect ye to return the writing utensils the moment ye've finished."

"Yes, Ma'am." we confirm. She waves for us to follow her back to a hall of exam rooms. Most of the buildings, we had learned, are set up mostly the same. Due to the original creator having simple luxury in mind. Opting for practicality rather than difference. All the walls are made from the same Diamond material, the vines that intermix adding an earthy look to the unnatural look of the buildings themselves.

"Start frae the youngest, all the doors on the left side o' the hallway. Yer nurse will be in tae speak wi' ye in a moment. Now, ye young lads might be a wee bit curious as tae what mysteries lie beyond the door ye see when ye walk in." The way she says it tells me she's speaking from the experience of years. No nonsense in her face or words. "Don't. Ye'll do damage to the poor thing holding it open."

"What's it for?" I asked before thinking, a problem I may never be rid of.

"It is for emergency purposes ONLY." she starts, giving us a stern look individually. She must've noticed something in my face because she softens a bit before answering with "There is a room, like a clothing press that has been closed off and emptied. Inside there is a lad or lass with some form of teleportation Juggernaut. Much like our Miss Aurora, these people have been trained to open jump points. However they take their shifts in order to ensure that any of the active duty teams who need medical attention can have it in a moment's notice. Anywhere in the world, they open the second half of the door to get the victim here as fast as possible."

"Has anyone ever opened the door against your warning?" I ask, knowing the answer before she gives it in the form of a sorrowful tip of her chin. "May I ask what happened?"

"The poor lass never woke up. Passed away the moment the door separated from the frame." The woman's sadness at the memory does something in my chest. The way she looks at her hands lets me know she's remembering her attempts to revive the one she speaks of.

"I'm so sorry." I place a hand in hers and squeeze once. "No te preocupes. Don't you worry. I may know how to ask a stupid question, but I try to keep the stupid decisions to a minimum. May I ask your name?"

The others listen intently to our exchange, knowing what I'm doing. I make friends that turn into allies. It's my specialty other than flying jets.

"Helena. My name is Helena, sweet lad." She softens, offering a small smile. I smile back and turn to enter the room she instructed. The minute I enter I notice the door Helena spoke of. Without question I slide a chair as far away from it as I can get. Not out of fear, but more out of respect. I feel a chill roll up my back just before the forbidden door opens.

Instinct causes me to flip the pen so the point is facing the potential threat. We were instructed not to bring any weapons today, but I'm very willing to use what I've got. Even if it's only what's attached to me.

I'm definitely not expecting anything close to the woman who walks through. Dressed in the shortest jean shorts I've ever seen and a tank top that my sister used to call a bra cover, I drop the pen and grip the clipboard holding my intake packet against the teenage tent in my cargo pants. The woman is a wet dream. Coffee colored skin and wild curly hair. The way she stops in front of me, arms crossed and pushing her boobs together in a way that makes me actively look somewhere...literally anywhere else. Unfortunately, it's not enough for me to miss that fucking smile. I almost choke on the groan I have to hold back at the sight of it. At this point, I'm positive that she knows I'm basically gawking.

"Viu algo de que gostou, querido. See something you like, sweetheart?" Her gravelly voice and perfect Portuguese have me sitting straighter in my seat. Something about a Brazilian woman that is just unmatched. So much so that the only other language I know aside from English and Spanish, is Portuguese. I let my own cocky smile settle on my face, leaning back like I just started a good poker game.

"Acho que você já sabe a resposta para isso, menina. I think you already know the answer to that, baby girl." Her surprise is subtle but it's just enough to catch only because I'm holding eye contact. Just as fast as it was there, it's gone. She's definitely a soldier with great training, even the best have trouble schooling their expressions that fast. I know because I have that issue. She doesn't take the bait though. Instead she pulls a lollipop from the jar sitting on the exam counter next to a jar of cotton balls, pops it in her mouth, and walks over to me while holding her hand out.

"Give it here." she says around the candy, eying the intake forms in my hands. I pass it over obediently, leaning forward and staying right fucking there. She takes it with a wink, moving the stick from the left corner to the right corner of her mouth with her tongue. Not in any kind of hurry, she walks over to the counter and props her elbow on it. She pulls a cellphone from her pocket, taps a few times, then she starts filling out the paperwork in silence. I watch her, careful to keep my eyes above her…assets. I may be a man, she may be a gift from God, but I am a gentleman through and through. She scribbles, every page swiping the screen of her phone. The moment I notice, I perk up again in an attempt to see what she's writing but I'm not at a good enough angle to see anything. Eventually my curiosity wins out.

"What are you doing?"

"My job." She replies without looking up.

"And your job would be?" I push, but she doesn't answer right away. Instead she finishes the entire packet while I sit there. My eyes wander a little much, but with the way she's leaning over the counter by the end of the stack of pages has me making sure there isn't really drool on my chin. When she finally finishes, she returns the phone to her pockets and disposes of the lollipop before grabbing another and handing me the clipboard once more.

"O que quer que o meu capitão me peça. Whatever my captain asks of me." She looks me dead in the eyes when she finally gives me the answer to my question. Not a joke to be read in the honey color of her eyes. She makes her way back to the forbidden door, rapping out some predetermined code then reaching for the handle.

"Do I get to know your name, menina?" I call out, just before she walks through thick black smoke.

"Kiari." She winks at me again then slips away before the door swings shut behind her. I drop back in my chair, releasing a long cool breath. I don't have time to process what she did with the paperwork she filled out before Helena walks in.

"Have ye finished the forms?" Helena smiles, warmer now after our earlier conversation. Reluctantly I hand over the clipboard and pen, and she leaves once more. I start fidgeting, I don't like not knowing what she did on that form. Or who she is beyond her name. Once the doctor comes in, I push it all to the back of my mind. It'll have to be something I address later. Even though that list is getting pretty freaking long.

Chapter Ten

Kaila

"Caaaaaptain?" I hear Kestien's reluctant groan over the sound of the blow dryer before I switch it off. I toss my curls in a bun at the top of my head before I make my way through the living room and down the winding stairs. As soon as we were given our maiden mission as a team all those years before now, we decided it would be best to have our own base of operations. Somewhere away from prying eyes and nosey council. The island we built our home is large and relatively uninhabited by tourists which makes this the ideal spot for our own little "no man's land".

The Special General's are less than pleased with the way our latest job was done, as they usually are. However, I can only work with the intelligence I am given, and lately, it hasn't exactly been accurate. When I walk into our library/computer room, the three of them are just about exactly where I left them. Milo is still behind a stack of books while Kiari is sat scrolling through our latest acquisition's phone, and Kestien is in his computer chair running surveillance.

"Feeling better?" Milo asks without looking up from the page he's on.

"Much." I admit. "Did you find anything interesting there, Kiari?"

"I had Kes' print out the nitty gritty and incriminating stuff and went ahead and left it on your desk to review. Now I'm just looking for a connection to Dion Salvatorenia." She sighs, readjusting herself in her seat. "Dude takes more selfies than my brother. It should be a crime."

I chuckle while walking up behind Kestien who is waiting to show me what he has paused on his screen. I can already tell from the yellow strands of worry coming from him that I won't like what I am about to see. "Before I show you this, I took the liberty of searching faces and getting some files put together for you. Figure you'll want one of us to keep an eye on them."

When the video on the screen comes to life, I can feel my blood begin to simmer just like I feel the others come up behind me. Curious about the exchange unfolding before us. I listen intently while trying to maintain my rage. When I hear German, I motion for Kestien to raise the volume, knowing I am the only one who fully understands German of the four of us. Although it doesn't take a genius to understand the point of the exchange. "Captain, what's that thing Marco's doing with his hand when he's got his back to Vince?"

"Signaling for blind spots." I answer absentmindedly, leaning one hand on the table to get a closer look at the screen. "Give me a visual?"

With a single key press, the image inverts and we are able to see everything from the opposite side of the hallway, giving us the perfect angle to see Marco and Max signal the same. Quick and barely visible I watch five fingers press first, immediately I count the stack of profiles in my hand, frowning when the numbers don't match. "Where's the last one?"

"One?" Kestien raises an eyebrow at me, clearly confused. With a quick glance I see that the others haven't spotted it either. I'm almost disappointed, but a bigger part of me is just proud of the fact that my brother's and I still hold some things sacred.

"They signal using all five fingers. They're signaling five hostiles that Augustine and Vince can't see. But there's three in front of them. I only have five faces here."

Looking at the faces once more, I noticed one face stands out above the others. "Motherfucker."

"I figured you would recognize him, I just wanted to be sure before jumping to conclusions considering I've only ever seen him the one time. Though I can't find his brothers on screen, I did take the liberty of gathering the little information I could on them, too. I assume they're the ones we are looking for."

Kestien hands me the last page and pulls them all up side by side on the top corner screen before us.

"Those are Special General Short Shaft's kids." Milo grumbles.

"Why do you guys call him that again?" Kiari's face wrinkles as she quickly rethinks her statement. " Na verdade, não me diga, filho da puta. Matter of fact don't tell me, motherfucker. You like going into unnecessary detail and shit."

I mean to smile, but I'm stuck watching the surveillance footage as it loops back again. I can't help watching them. My boys. The way Vince moves in front of Marco. The way Max makes moves to protect August's back. They've always been a great team. So good I based my own team standards by their example.

My boys follow Special Lieutenant Black through the halls, each one looking around simultaneously in different directions. I take notice of the fact that my brothers are becoming aware of my husband's awakening, which is good. It should help them to not ignore their own.

In truth I was forced to stop my personal surveillance on the boys months before now, but they've still grown so much even in that time. The way they have all decided to keep Marco safely between them makes me chuckle to myself. Knowing this works best to keep him out of trouble as well as keep Marco safe is one thing. Knowing how much he loathes it is another. I almost miss the days I took place right next to him. Of course, in those days I was someone who deliberately needed protection. Now as it so happens I would sooner see the leash burned to the ground before I ever see myself on it again. I'm so focused on them and the way Augustine's head lolls forward that I finally see a single blur flit across the screen. Completely admissible for dust if I hadn't been paying attention to my husband so hard, only confirmed by Kiari's pale pink concern flashing before she speaks.

"Captain-" Kiari calls out, attempting to warn me to what her eyes can undoubtedly see clear as day.

"I see it." I cut her off, stepping out of the way for Kestien to slide his tablet to his sister. "Find me an angle and make him look real pretty for me."

She taps the screen a few times before taking two fingers and sliding the image onto the screen with the others of his group. "There he is."

"That would be the brother." I say matter of factly.

"May I, Captain?" Milo's lips split into a grin that could scare children. I contemplate the permission he's requesting. As it so happens, even if Kestien specializes in online surveillance, Milo has a gift all his own. If I gave him the go ahead, he would bring me back their baby teeth and every last detail about them all. The only problem would be the time it would take him to acquire it. In his time among the living, Milo was a spy for the Italian Military. His specialty was intelligence and asset retrieval as well as espionage. The man is a demented fucker, and being the brains behind a few of my teams more sinister jobs, I can attest to his talents. Even more so when you realize that even though his skills are unreal, they have nothing to do with his actual Juggernaut ability.

"How long do you need?" I ask. He mulls it over silently for a moment before locking eyes with his husband as they deliberate in the silent language of lovers.

"Now that depends on the briefing my husband is about to give us." He smiles softly now, pulling out the notepad he keeps in his breast pocket at all times and flipping to a fresh page. "And how deep you want me to go."

"Special General Short Shit." Kestien begins swiftly. "Better known as Special General Artur Mikhailov, in the land of the living he was one of the top war tactic specialists of the Russian Special Forces for his time. Married to one Mia Mikhailov-formerly Mia Zelenkova- and father to the two walking terroristic threats, Damien and Ascher Mikhailov.

Because Artur and Mia met here in the Land of the Dead, those boys were raised here and know the ins and outs of the whole structure. Rumor has it they both have manipulated Juggernauts."

"Courtesy of their psycho fucking father I bet." Kiari shivers. "Mia ain't exactly got all her marbles in a row either."

"Ducks." Milo corrects with the same pestering tone he always uses to correct her. Kiari takes him literally, dropping slightly. Just a simple motion that sends Milo and I choking on our laughter.

Kestien drops his head in disappointment, groaning before he explains. "Not 'duck', pendeja. Dumbass. Ducks. The ducks are in a row."

"Então onde estão as bolinhas de gude? Then where are the marbles?" she asks, her accent thick with confusion on all fronts, making my smile bleed into a pained cringe. I know Kiari struggles with English more than her twin, but at times her language barrier makes her seem more aloof than she comes off already. We all roll our eyes, leaving her to her confusion when they turn to me again.

"I'll tell you what, Captain. I will be here in time for you to have your magical meeting with your boys in one week. Lord knows I am dying to meet *him*." He wiggles his eyebrows dramatically, taking the palm up hands I'm holding out to him and promptly turning both our wrists until the backs of my hands face the sky.

"I want the dirty but don't bring any dirt into this house. You got me?" The room is suddenly serious as the twins begin zipping out of the library. Our moments such as these always happen so quickly, and I know it's always been this way. Milo and I remain with our eyes locked and he mirrors my look of no nonsense with a confident expression. This small ritual became a habit for our little bonus family from our inception. When the others walk back into the room with gear and their own scolding advice at the ready, I make my own remark quickly. "I don't care how deep the rabbit hole goes, I do not give you permission to pull an Alice Mission. Use an alias you can burn after and burn it so he can't come back. I want to know exactly what that bastard is planning."

"Copy. Copy." He sighs. There was a whole lifetime where this guy lived down the rabbit hole, and the disappointment in not getting to visit it again is palpable. I drop his hands, allowing him to, as we have come to call it, hit the stations. Kiari goes first, as she often will in order to give her brothers the respect of their final goodbyes. I slip from the room, still listening in on a moment that isn't mine just yet.

"Aurora is going to fix your jump point to Kirishi, in the northwest region of Leningrad Oblast. Low density so you should be able to slip in and around fairly undetected."

I go to what we call our "middle door." The jump point we have set up in my bedroom closet back at Deadman's land that leads to the home we had built far, far, away from the mountain. The top brass know nothing of this place, and only a handful even know it exists.

The way the door works is that it will only open correctly if one of us goes through it first. "Us" includes the person who set up the pathways. Though nobody knows who that really is except for my team. Passing through my closet I shake off the molecule splitting feeling that always comes in different intensities when walking through a jump point door. The magic behind it is often described as uncomfortable the first few times someone passes. After a while, the feelings of discomfort slip into understanding when realizing your molecular structure is untethering and retethering within a fraction of a second. Or so we have come to scientifically describe for the sake of an answer.

Aurora will be waiting in the main hallway outside Kestien's front door, as we've dubbed his room useless even in our aesthetics and turned it into a makeshift front room. Making it look like we still live on the mountain alongside everyone else means that we sleep there the majority of the week, but ever since we began our sole mission we have moved anything of true importance. Agreeing that at some point we would have to make a break for a place nobody will be able to follow. We named it "The hatch" after some movie Kestien liked as a kid. When I open the door, Aurora wears a sour expression while she stands scanning the hall around her.

"Thank fuck!" she exhales, pushing through me and into space. "You have some explaining to do."

"Can it wait?" I don't wait for a response. She huffs her annoyance at my dry remark as I flit in and out of Milo's room with various clothing for the week to come. Making sure to pack light, but for any weather he may encounter I pack it all into his go-bag. When the clothing is packed I look around for any last minute things before we make our way back. Checking the time, I cursed under my breath. The boys will be getting out of bloodwork and headed straight for the Psych Evaluation. Helena and her team will only take thirty minutes each, then she would send them off to the viewing field. I would have liked to have listened to their sessions with her but at this moment my priorities are drawn elsewhere. "Let's go."

The way back is smoother with Aurora walking with me. Out of the corners of my vision I watch her drag her hand along in simple patterns. I know she sees something different in her eyes, but she doesn't speak on it while she continues her "software updates". Her term, not mine. We go upstairs immediately, becoming an audience just in time for Kestien's parting words to his husband. "Fique atento às ordens. Você sabe todas as maneiras de entrar em contato comigo, então, certifique-se de me procurar assim que ACHAR que precisa de ajuda. Não depois. Stay on orders. You know every way to get a hold of me possible, so be sure to check in as soon as you THINK you need help. Not after."

"Amore mio, sai che non devi preoccuparti per me. Tornerò da te, non importa chi devo lasciare per arrivare qui. My love, you know you don't need to worry about me. I'll be coming back to you no matter who I have to drop to get here."

Milo's tone is softer than it ever is for anyone else as he speaks to reassure his husband. Their mismatched conversation is so cannon in their relationship that nobody in the room even bats an eye.

"Não é nunca se você vai voltar para mim. O que me preocupa é sempre como você vai voltar para mim. It's never if you'll come back to me. It's how you'll come back to me that I worry about." Kestien sighs, his reluctance to let Milo go has its good reasons even if he knows that I wouldn't send him away if I could trust anyone else to see it done. "Eu te amo. I love you."

"Ti amo, mio leone. I love you, my lion." They embrace. Then their lips meet. It's always uncomfortable for me to watch them be affectionate. The jealousy I feel inside makes me a little bitter, as I haven't felt my husband's touch in years. Though in my heart of hearts I know I may not get to ever again after he knows the truth. I hear Aurora clear her throat before she speaks.

"I know there is another reason why we are here, but I need to say something." We all turn her way. The boys instinctively tense, waiting for a backhanded comment that I just know isn't meant for them this time. "All the good men are either gay…"

She waves to Kestien and Milo, who have now relaxed slightly in each other's arms. "Or apparently…RELATED TO YOU! You bitch."

"Ohmygod I KNOW RIGHT!" Kiari calls out dramatically as she shoots back into the room at a speed only she can move at. A small smile touches my lips and I say nothing to feed into their banter, only causing them to do it louder amongst themselves while I speak to Milo one last time.

"Keep it simple." I'm serious suddenly, passing him the duffle bag. "Names. Faces. There's something going on here and he wants us to follow him down the rabbit hole to find it. Don't be obvious. Whoever is behind this is going to know I'm sending you."

"I haven't been caught yet." He said. I wince outwardly as he receives a loud thwack to the back of the head from Kestien. "I said 'yet'. I'm aware of the issues. I'll be back in time to get the boys to the rumble just like you planned, Captain."

He kisses my forehead. "Try not to worry about me, he's going to do enough of that already for the both of you."

Aurora goes to the hall again. The upstairs hallway closet at the end of the hallway was built specifically for jump point travel. Unlike the rooms they have on the mountain, we wised up after the preventable death of a fellow soldier. The room was basically the same in itself. A nook built into the wall where the shelves of a normal home would probably be, padded with pillows and memory foam cushions. The bench opens up to reveal an array of blankets and some heat pads for the winter. In the corner there is a fully stocked snack fridge Kiari insisted on painting with black chalk paint. Noting the boredom of someone who would need to stay and man the door, unlike Aurora who only needs to open it once if she so chose. The biggest difference between our rooms and the ones in Deadman's Land are the double doors. This particular design choice has Aurora's name all over it.

Most who are able to create jump points need to focus their juggernaut abilities on the physical door itself. So once the door is connected properly from here to wherever, the secondary door on the inside of the room is closed and locked. Allowing them an added layer of protection in case someone decided to go snooping. This also works as an alarm system of sorts, since most won't need to be making contact with the door to close the jump point in case of emergency.

"Jump point's ready." I call out to the others when I hear the second door's lock latch. I'm nervous. This is the first time in four years I've had everyone I care about so close to me, and yet everyone is just out of reach to me somehow. The three of them walked out of the Library and into the hall with me. "Are you all set?"

"Packed and ready to roll." he beams a confident smile at me before pecking Kestien on the cheek, and giving Kiari a sideways hug.

"One week." I stress once more before he places a hand on the doorknob turning back to us once more. "Don't make us come for you."

"Copy. Copy." Milo nods once and makes his way through the door.

Once we are alone, I make a quick beeline to the monitor Kestien has set up in the exam building for a quick check on my boys before heading back to my primary bedroom in the safe house and cleaning up after the last time I was here. Milo went through smoothly about fifteen minutes ago and Aurora will already be at the viewing by now. We will receive no communication until Milo is either in trouble or coming home. Kestien will be a wreck until the moment his husband sets foot back on safe soil. I know this feeling all too well, and will try my best to keep him occupied with a search of his own. While her brother finds himself engrossed in his task, Kiari comes to lean against the doorframe of my bedroom. "Shouldn't you be heading to the viewing gallery?"

"I've got time." I shrug, still trying to avoid the real questions.

"Do you have time? Or are you procrastinating?" she presses, raising an eyebrow when I pause but don't respond. "The legendary Special First Captain Kaila Jane is afraid of confrontation."

I bark a deep belly laugh.

I'm not afraid.

I'm fucking terrified.

"You can't bullshit a bullshitter, Kaila. Sufres porque quieres. You suffer because you want to." Her tone grows as harsh as her words. "You're afraid they won't accept you this way."

"That's not it." I said, too quick for my own good.

"Then what is it, Captain? Are you afraid they won't believe you? I know there's more to this than you're letting on but..." she softens, but only just. "Haven't you been through enough for these people? I know you're tired of being a war dog in someone else's power game. You have the power to bring it all to the ground, so why the charade? We've followed you through so much these last few years, and we will follow you through this. I just-"

She pauses to move closer, taking my hand in hers and forcing me to look her in the eyes. "We would follow you out of the fire if you chose to light it. Screw what the elders say. For every inch you sink into the void, we will be that much closer to remind you to come back from it."

I don't speak because I can't trust my voice right now. I can see the soft hesitation in her eyes, the more she wants to say, but she holds her tongue and I am grateful for it. "Enough of that. Let's get you to the gallery before someone finds a way to get their grimy hands on your boys."

I take a deep breath, nodding before grabbing my pistol from the end of the bed and holstering it to my right thigh. I allow my thumb to trace the name engraved on the hilt. "Petras" it reads, the same as its sister. The action calms me just a little before I reach for the dual sword hilts hanging from their hooks. The hilts with no blades that I keep secure in their homes at the small of my back. After making it through the jump point back to our room on the mountain, Kiari and I walk down the hall as unbothered as possible. The crowds of new blood now have been replaced by the much thinner crowd of more seasoned teams. Most captains head the same way, equally unbothered in the neutral ground we all occupy. In the hallways, none are above the other. We are just people. The formalities usually end the moment we are officially ranked, classified, and initiated as a member of the Dead Army so here in the hallway we are all indifferent to one another. The few friends we make are far between, but a few stand mingling in their own rightful groups. However the real trouble is when the challenges present themselves. The moment rank matters, and egos are forced to clash.

The Viewing is one of those times when we are pitted against one another. This is like our football league, where the Captains of each team are allowed to pre-screen the new candidates assigned to them. Captains are allowed to make trades, and employ the absolute veto. This being when a candidate is basically passed from captain to captain until someone either takes him, or the candidate is fed to the dogs. In a word, it's cruel.

When we walk up to the entrance elevator, I know Kiari is itching to come with me. There are no rules against it, but it's sort of an unspoken agreement. No kids in the parent's meeting. "Are you sure I can't go in with you this time?"

"I never said you can't go in. I said this is a Captain's thing." She huffs at me, crossing her arms under her breasts in a childish way. "Did you do what I asked?"

"You name it, it's done. You know that." she says matter of factly, dropping her hands to her hips. I chew my lip for a moment, waiting for a few to pass and get out of earshot. With the release of a breath I speak reluctantly through gritted teeth. I shouldn't ask, but I have to know.

"How is he?" With a hard jab to my arm that would've probably hurt someone else she looks around lowering her voice when a group of captains brush past us and onto the elevator. She manages to compose herself before whispering her response.

"I fixed the papers like you asked. Helena said they tried to lie, so he was in the room when I showed up. I think you're right about his juggernaut, his eyes are shifting like mine did."

"Did he give you a hard time?"

"Define *hard*?" She wiggles her eyebrows in a suggestion I never want her to make again.

"I will throw up on you." I cringe. I knew exactly what I was doing when I sent her after him. A necessary and unavoidable play to keep the boys together. I can't have any of them collared for the game. "You know what I mean."

"No captain, he was a gentleman but I'm sure Helena will have something for you later." She answers softly, but I see the way sunflower yellow worry bleeds from her pores, I know she is hiding something. I also know I can't ask. Plausible deniability is a bitch when you need it.

I take a steadying breath to compose myself, sending Kaila off before I enter the elevator. When I turn, it's just in time to see my least favorite person in the Dead Nation stepping onto the elevator behind me. I roll my eyes. I can't help it. Her entire being irritates me to my very core. Something about her, even from the moment we met, makes my skin crawl. Her attitude alone makes me want to gag. Just my height but rail thin even with all the training we go through here. Pale like parchment paper and the kind of pretty you see on the Victoria's Secret billboards. Fake as all hell.

"Kaila Jane." She says it like one would say "roadkill" only with more disdain.

"Narcissa Cox." I let my smile curl at one corner of my mouth. It's her name, but I never quite say it the way it's spelled. Her hatred for me is palpable even without my juggernaut ability, and it isn't hard to tell that I enjoy making myself an inconvenience in her life whenever the opportunity presents itself. I'm damn good at it too.

"I wonder what kind of scum they dragged up this year." She rolls her eyes, attempting to sway the conversation, checking her nails to show me she isn't the least bit bothered by what she's saying. "Lord knows you do get the bottom of the barrel when it comes to talent. What is that now, sixteen candidates in three years?"

"Seventeen." I correct sharply. Admittedly, the accusation in her voice pains me more than I would ever show her, but I kept a firm face. "If I recall correctly, and I do, your candidates don't even make it out alive. At least everyone called to my team is worth their salt enough to prove themselves a warrior. Rather than fighting to be one."

"Stepping stones." She scoffs. "This year's candidates are more than promising. I just have to make sure I get the best now that I've worked my way up to First Captain."

I scoff right back. "The only thing you've ever worked your way up from is the floor. The only reason you're a first captain is because your predecessor is dead."

"We're all dead. Aren't we, Kaila?" There's a mischief in the tone of her voice that makes me tense, slightly curling my fingers more around the hilt of my gun a bit more firmly. At that same moment the elevator doors opened up to the viewing gallery. With a prideful "hm", she skips away to find a seat. I brush the comment off for now, heading to the Masters Box. A personal viewing area overlooking the arena. This is where the big dogs will be watching.

Units are classified A to Z, with the hierarchy going from Z to A. There is no limit to how many can be in one unit, but with the work that we all do, real death has taken at least half. When a team is taken out completely, a new one is activated to take their place. I've seen too many fall, and even less rise who are worthy enough. Which is what makes these games we play so important. It's the same thing that makes them so tragically deadly. When I enter the room, the door guards salute quickly before returning to attention. I return the gesture, turning to the right and heading to a small ladder bolted to the wall.

"Finally!" Special Lieutenant Black's boisterous voice cuts through the murmurs of the others in the room. "Captain Kaila has taken refuge in her perch. Can we get this rat race started please?"

They always wait for me. They always seemed to take stock in my opinion, and I am always being closely watched. The Perch, as Black called it, is reserved for the strongest person in the room. Meant as a post rather than a privilege, this is the spot that gives the best and clearest vantage point over both the viewing and the arena. It's a way to keep the game fair. Since this was one of the few things the Lieutenants and Generals can't interfere with unless asked to by three confirming parties involved in an altercation.

I take a moment to look over all of the "top dogs", or "Top Problems" as Milo has named them. Everyone is getting restless, waiting for their new candidates to begin. Slowly I let my eyes fall to Special General Short Shit who sits smug with his second, who sits locked in a staring contest with me for not enough time to be as intimidating as he wants to be. His colors tell me everything to know. The man hates me, and he thinks he has something worth the bright red pride wafting off of him until finally the red bleeds away and is replaced with the shock yellow of panic. With a short chuckle I draw my eyes to the arena below.

The powers that be have chosen The Mirage as this group's first testing field. The first test is designed to get a baseline for each candidate by using their psyche and forcing them out of the plane we reside in currently. A fighter is fine and dandy but if they don't have the mentality strong enough to endure then they really are of no use to anyone here. We don't get to see what happens once the tester(in this case they've tasked Moira of unit L) infiltrates the minds of each and every one of them and basically runs them through a controlled simulation. This shows us how they are able to assess, strategize, and overall how fast and strong they are mentally without the use of their abilities if they have any. Until now, juggernaut abilities are a concept to those who don't already know about them, but this will give any doubters a real taste at what they are getting into. Tell a soldier they're outgunned and they might believe you for a bit. Show them, and they tend to work a whole lot harder to stay alive.

At that moment my eyes find them. They are standing together, Augustine with his back against the corner of the room. Marco stands across from him, slightly to the left so as to leave the view unobstructed. Max and Vince stand at either side of them, shoulders turned out slightly so they can see either side completely and clearly. I breathe a quiet laugh through my nose, they look so strong as they watch, ready for anything that gets close. Taking in the surroundings before them. So much trust in one another that I know they are each sharply focused on their side and their side alone.

Poor Marco, I think to myself as I watch him shift uncomfortably in his spot. When his eyes came into their potential last night, every ounce of my being wanted to be with him. A few well placed notes are good and well, but I am more than sure he is struggling with the adjustment alone. I feel like an asshole for not warning Vince to watch him too, but I can't pull all the strings. Even the ones I have pulled could have been the end of us all. My attention goes to the man who goes to speak as proctor of this part, Special General Short Staff himself. Pale skin, crooked teeth, unkept beard, and still the man doesn't scare me the way he seems to scare everyone else. He hates that, but I don't fear evil the way I should anymore.

"Welcome candidates. I know it has been a long day for some of you so I will get this going as quickly as possible. If you would all please find your assigned treadmill and listen to the safety briefing we can begin the assessment." I wonder if they've eaten lunch, but am given an answer in the form of a loud burp from Vince. My eyes draw back to my boys as they are escorted to their places. Some of the other candidates are watching them closely. Those from the altercation earlier being the most obvious. A growl ripples low in my chest, prompting a heavily forced cough from Black down below before my phone buzzed in my pocket.

Clm dwn

The message states dryly. I sniff and put the device away while clearing my own throat and shooting Black a look. I turn back to listen to the safety briefing with no enthusiasm, watching as nurses place the wiring system on my husband's now shirtless chest. At this moment I am grateful for the advantages of my own eyesight as I take the personal time to trace every ridge of his body with my eyes. Kiari would approve, but something about watching my husband when he doesn't know I am watching him tickles me inside. He can't put on a show this way. The natural state of him. Thinking back to the days when he was teaching me how to do tricks on my skateboard just so I could come with them to the skatepark. It's a full circle moment I will probably never get the chance to share with him fully.

"Alright! The way this works is, I will broadcast the simulation into your minds. The fancy dancy gear you are all being strapped into, is the latest fashion we call Isdyf. Long version? It's so you don't fall." Moira begins her speech. To them she probably looks like a low threat, but everyone up here knows way better.

"HA!" Marco bellows a laugh along with a few of the other candidates who get the acronym and I shake my head in amusement.

"My name is Moira Jeseph. As you are all becoming aware, these restraints are binding you at the abdomen, but the system is designed to move with you. These nodes our nurses have attached to you are to monitor your vital signs, which will be displayed on this monitor above me for the nursing staff to better be able to keep you alive. Should it so happen that your vital signs should become a worry, I will shut down your simulation promptly, and you will be asked to exit. Should you choose to remain against medical advice, you will be allowed to continue at your own expense." The last part is a contingency. It lights a fire under them, playing to their egos in a way that will make them strive to prove they are not in need of removal.

There is no such thing as removal.

There is only true death.

I trailed my eyes over the other faces. My abilities give me certain liberties into people's souls, as well as my former Psychology degree which gave me certain liberties into people's minds. I count seven souls who won't make it the first hour of this. This particular part of the candidate pool is made up of the unfortunate few who got curious enough to blackmail their way into a shot at feigned glory, only to have a heart attack because they aren't made for this place. There is one girl of those seven who I can already see going mad once the images begin to play in her mind. She will somehow make it out of this with pity ensuring her survival. Sent off to finish her days selling crazy stories for antipsychotics.

How quickly those who deem themselves mighty fall.

Chapter Eleven
Augustine

This contraption they have us all strapped into is unconventional to the eye, but still not quite like anything I have ever seen. The way the belt is both completely secure but still freely moving with me makes no sense in my brain, but it's only when Max speaks up that I figured it was best to just chalk it up to something I probably won't. "Woah! Can I play with it?"

"No." I bark, knowing he doesn't mean he wants to just press a few buttons to see how it works. One of the nurses helping him giggles and whispers something to him. She is a bit smaller than the other nurses. With blond hair and a smile showing in her eyes behind her mask. The teenage boy in me wants nothing more than to give Marco hell for the way his cheeks light up. However, I choose to promise to roast him for it later in the form of a look I exchanged with Vince. Though we can't hold back our snickers when he is left nodding and too stunned to speak. I make a mental note to ask him about it later, but for now I do my best to listen to the woman who had introduced herself as Moira.

"In a moment I will start bringing you all into the simulation. In order for me to broadcast it to you, I am going to walk your minds blank. It's a trick you'll probably recognize if you know anything about hypnotherapy. Whereas it is easier if you close your eyes, I do understand the issue with doing so, we are all soldiers here. As such, I would ask you to keep your eyes on the red duct tape 'x' on the wall behind me at all times." The woman isn't much for looks, but the strength in her voice is strangely soothing. In a way it reminds me of my mother in law and my heart sinks a little. Glancing passed the others, I notice the men from earlier shooting daggers at me. I won't say I feel threatened by them, but there is a rumble in my chest at the rank stench of bad intentions and I don't drop their eyes until Moira's voice cuts through to us. "Let's keep focused on me fellas."

Slowly I drag my focus back to her, taking note of Vince's watchful eye. I noticed it during breakfast, but it's starting to irritate me. He has bigger things to worry about. Though, I suppose I do, too. "As I was saying, my ability works in the mind. For this, I will be using it for a specific purpose. Once I've walked you under and you follow my instructions, your job is to find an object or person specifically important to you. This can be a person or object from the now, or from your past. The object can be anything from a coin to an elephant. All you need to know now is that it will be important and that once you find it, you have to get it back to where you started. We'll be getting to it in just a few minutes, so try to get as prepared as you can."

She walks off to the corner where some nurses have a tent set up with bottled water and first aid. This place is massive, and I wonder if we are still inside the mountain or if we took the jump point to an entirely new location. I turn to see Vince and Marco bickering about something in sign language yet again. I notice the way they try to do it discreetly, signing with one hand at their side so I can't see. We all know sign language, a skill my wife insisted we learn in case of an emergency. I never did admit that I learned simply because she was the one to teach me. I watch them for a short moment, knowing I will never see what they are signing from where I am. So I turn to Max instead, who has taken to doing the only thing he can not to take the whole mechanism apart which is, unfortunately, biting his nails.

I sigh at the thought of how long it's been since I'd last seen him do this. It's almost unnatural for me to tell him not to go nuts, but I don't trust anything about this place, and I don't want to find out what happens when we break their toys. I can't risk us getting separated when it's already looming over us as a strong possibility. I know the others will be starting to suspect the same, if not now then soon. They have allowed us to be together through everything so far. So it would only be natural for them to want to see what we can do alone.

"Calmate. Calm down." I whisper harshly.

Max jerks out of his anxious fit before turning to me with a slight embarrassment to his smile. Before he can say anything to me, Moira claps her hands loudly and all of us snap to attention once again. "Alright. Here we go. Remember, eyes front or closed."

I've decided to keep my eyes open. Locking the red x in my sights and taking deep, even breaths. Moira's voice comes again, only this time, I feel my whole being freeze. Her voice has changed, lacking its powerful tone from before and having been replaced with a calmer one. The lights begin to lower, until darkness falls on us, with only the x's on the wall ahead visible by dim spotlight. "I want you to imagine an empty waiting room."

The darkness falls into an eerie silence around me. A force that is both muting any outlying sound and keeping me stock still except for the steady rise and fall of my chest. I try my best not to panic, keeping myself focused on her voice while she speaks softly but audibly. "As you walk around this room I want you to think about the things you notice first. Maybe it's the smell of fresh paint or mildew carpets. How many chairs are there? What kinds of sounds do you hear? Do the lights flicker? Look at the colors on the walls. Picture them in your mind."

I do as instructed, but the more I picture the room, the stronger the force becomes around me.

"On the walls of the waiting room you should start to notice photographs. As you begin to notice the photographs you will start to see one become clearer than the rest. You will start to feel yourself being drawn closer. Closer. Closer. As you get closer to the photograph, notice yourself gravitating to touch the image. Allow yourself to give in to what your body wants."

Maribel Navarrete

I reach out to the black and white photo on the wall. A simple picture that has enough weight to mow me over. I can't understand what is happening, but nothing about what is happening right now is any form of normal. A very large, very old willow tree in the clearing of wildflowers. The very same one I proposed to my wife under. The last thing I hear before everything changes is Moira's voice once more. Only this time, her voice comes out split into three different sets of whispers all saying one word.

"Dive." The waiting room around me shifts sharply from left to right before the entire thing tips and I am thrown into the painting. Falling toward a black and white tree that just keeps getting farther and farther away the further I fall until unconsciousness takes me and the image fades altogether.

***

When I come too, the first thing I notice is that the landscape is completely different. Instead of looking at a photograph while standing in a waiting room, before me stands the willow tree in all its glory. Surrounding me are the wildflowers that accompany it. It's like I can feel the mechanism holding me in place, but the world around me in itself has changed. I can feel the breeze, and I can smell the flowers just as clear as I did the last time I was actually here. I take account of my body, noting that the apparatus is no longer visible to my eyes. The treadmill under my feet has been replaced with crisp dark green grass scattered with limbs and leaves that have fallen with time. I turned to look around, walking forward four paces and back five just to see if I can actually move around. Everything is so vivid, and it occurs to me to check the tree for authenticity. Striding toward it and instinctively going to the bottom of the trunk. There in the bark are two sets of initials, as fresh as the day I put them there.

I feel a pang in my chest and force a breath to fight back the threat of very real tears. When I have my composure back, I suddenly remember the reason I'm here. I'm alone in my immediate surroundings, but moments later I see the others come tearing through the tree line, waving me down like mad men. Once they catch up to me, a couple of things become very apparent.

One: These are not my boys.

Two: They are not friendly.

The fake Vince comes at me first, barreling into me with not nearly as much force as the real one would've hit me with. His tackle is weak enough that the elbow I slam down into his back is enough to loosen his grip on my waist. Throwing out my hips to break his hold completely I reach over to grab the seat of his pants to throw him off. Fake Marco and Fake Max are both on me quick enough but I've already managed to break for the trees. My feet pound on the earth beneath me but they're fast enough to snag my shirt. Two of us tumble in a clash of fists and limbs until I'm on my back with a slightly disfigured Marco above me.

He bares his teeth at me and just when I'm about to throw him off I see it. The gold chain hanging from his neck isn't what causes my pause. It's the diamond ring hanging from it, and just like that I'm not in a simulation. That ring didn't disappear with my wife. No. Right at this moment, everything is absolutely real when my fist connects with the fake Marco's jaw and I use the momentum to throw him to the side. I'm on my feet quickly and my eyes are narrowed at the ring. A devilish smile pulls across his lips as the other two come up on either side of him to face off with me.

"Give me that. Right. Now." I growl with my teeth clenched. I can feel the switch coming. The thing that happens when my control is outweighed by my drive. Right now my control is hanging on by a thread.

"This thing?" He asks, lifting the chain up with his thumb.

"If you hand it over this doesn't have to get ugly, but that doesn't belong to you." I hear my voice, but it doesn't exactly sound like mine. It has hollow undertones and a sharp echo that I'm not entirely sure is being heard out loud or in my own mind. The fakes make a show of deliberating and I already know they're not going to give me what I want. Which is fine. I gave them the opportunity the way I always do. It absolves me from ever having to feel bad for what's about to happen next. Because if I'm being honest, I really like what happens next.

"Nah." They all chuckle like something is really funny. "I don't think I will."

From the minute I got off my back I've been in a crouch ready for them to come at me, but at his admission the final switch flips inside me, and the little voice I've been running from for four years lets out a high pitched three-tone trill of excitement through my lips.

I am no longer in control.

I don't know what it is.

I don't know where it came from.

All I know is that when our objectives collide, nothing stupid enough to be in the way of it makes it very far.

The present becomes a scene I'm watching on a monitor. My body. My rage. Not my wrath. Not my ruthlessness. Not my savagery.

"Ugly it is." We speak, the hollow tone having completely taken over now. The amusement drops from the fake faces of my brothers just in time for the psychotic one to settle on mine. Quick as a blink I have fake Vince by the throat, windpipe practically disintegrating under my hand. Strange images flash in and out, images I can't read but they aren't there long.

Gasps that sound more female for a second too short for it to matter. My head turns languidly until my eyes lock onto Max's doppelganger, then again to lock onto Marco's when I drop the body and straighten up. They stand frozen for a single second before taking off like the prey they are now. I take a deep breath and the thing inside me lets it out on a contented sigh. "Now you've done it."

Chapter Twelve
Vince

When I get my hands on my sister, she won't need to tell anybody she's alive because I am going to kill her myself. The moment I got chucked into the painting of my old Commanding officer's office, I felt like I'd been tased. It's like I can feel this chick Moira rooting around in my brain and I don't fucking like her here. Like a splinter you can't see. You know it's fucking there, but you can't grab the little sucker.

When I come too, I'm sitting in a chair I helped to build years ago, that I haven't seen in almost as long. Pristine office carpeting, a six drawer file cabinet, mahogany desk, and right in the center of the desk that I really hoped I would never have to see again is a single, silver bell. One of those bells you see at hotels to get the attention of the staff, only the only thing encouraging you to push this little thing is temptation. I have always loathed this damn bell. Which is how I know it's my objective. How am I so sure? This bell doesn't actually exist anymore. I blew it up in his face the first chance I got, the second I outranked the man who owned it. Twice. The older brother in me wants to throw a fit at the sight of it because somewhere in the back of my mind, I just know the little shit I call my sister is watching somewhere laughing her ass off. With a grumbled curse, I take the bell off the desk. However, the instant I have it in my hand, everything around me does a strange flash in and out before it changes entirely and I'm suddenly staring at all three of my brothers. The four of us are surrounded by the huge boulders of the stream's edge and the dense trees of the Boise National Forest.

Nothing feels right. There's a dull pain behind my eyes for a moment before it's gone. Before I have a second to question it, the boys turn to me with eerily blank expressions. Like wax statues. I'm still holding the bell in my hand when the emotion finally breaks over their faces. When it does, the thing that looks like my baby brother surges forward, ramming his shoulder into my stomach and kneeing me in the balls. Not expecting it, I double over and almost throw up. The bell falls from my hand carelessly when I go to cradle my junk. The world around me blurs but it isn't my vision, it's the actual world around me. For a fraction of a second I'm back in my C.O's office then right back in Boise. The confusion is enough to help me ignore the ache between my legs. Standing up straight I clock that little sucker gunning it toward the thicket of trees, the bell clutched in his hand. A snarl rips from my throat when I reach for my gun, making sure I take the other two in my vision before lining up my sight. I am not about to run when my bullets are faster. My eyes narrow down the barrel to shoot him in the back. I would take the headshot but I'll be damned if I miss. All of a sudden the world around me flashes three times.

Once to the office then back to Boise.

Two to the treadmill then back to Boise.

Three and I'm still in Boise, but the cockroaches I'm aiming at are closer. Perfectly close.

I push past the pulsing in my brain and fire.

Three quick position changes, three bullets.

Three men down.

My head is screaming and the anger rises to create heat in my ears as I make my way to the bell. A few strides away from the object on the ground, the screaming starts to feel like needles stabbing in fast succession into my skull. With my eyes sealed shut and jaw locked together, I take a shaky breath through my nose. I take the step before I open my eyes again, but something stops me. Slowly, I open them, turning to see what is holding me back and praying for the first in years to a god I may or not believe in. The brick walls seem to build around me and the few short seconds it takes for me to turn around are like a millennia. When I see it, everything gets really far away, and I'm suddenly a teenager for a second.

A single shackle on each of my wrists, leading to its bolt on the brick wall behind me that has replaced the forest from before. At this moment I've forgotten about everything that is happening around me. Taking in the scene with wild eyes now I realize I am back in the middle of one of my worst nightmares. My worst personal nightmare. This is no longer a simulation. I had an objective, but fuck if I can remember it right now. This is very real. I'm chained up and in a solid room with no walls or windows.

The hyperventilating starts at the confirmation of confinement. All logic of this not being real went out the window. I start flailing. Yanking on the metal cuffs on my wrist as the images start flying across my field of vision. Superimposed over the room and the chains that just won't give. I know the sounds of foreign voices aren't real, but it doesn't stop them from forcing the banging in my brain to step up to a fever pitch. I'm forced to my knees by the pain, clutching at my head in hopes that the pressure will relieve some of the tension caused by the panic attack.

A single thought begins its crescendo until I realize I'm chanting the words, building from a whisper, to a growl, to a roar.

"Out. Out. OUT. OUT. **GET. ME. OUT!**"

I feel rough hands on my shoulders shaking me harshly until my eyes snap open and I'm looking into the bright ass blues of Special Lieutenant Black. He's talking to me but my hearing hasn't fully returned. When it finally does, I hear him whisper in a harsh and hurried tone.

"You need to calm the hell down! You're out." I look around, finally. Chest heaving when I realize I'm back on the treadmill with a team of nurses looking at me with strange expressions behind their masks. Immediately I check my wrist with a sigh of relief when they're free of shackles. I should feel foolish, but I still stand there panting while they extract me from this contraption. Once free, I step off looking around the room again as a way of being positive I won't end up in that damned room again. Everyone else is running with blank expressions on their faces and clouded eyes. Well, everyone except for Augustine.

While everyone's expressions are void of any emotion, Augustine wears a look that I will never openly admit is fucking terrifying. Captain is hunting something. Another phenomenon that has this place making a bit more sense. I feel really bad for whoever decided to run from him.

"You shouldn't have been able to do that." Special Lieutenant Black grumbles low to me, pulling me by the arm away from everyone who seems to be staring. "Listen to me very fucking carefully. Moira's team is pissed, and you need to stay as far away from that dumpster fire as inhumanely possible. I don't know how you did what you just did but when you figure it out, do not tell anyone but your team and ONLY after you make it to the choosing game. Do you understand?"

He's leaned in close to me so nobody will overhear. Something about it spikes my anger again. I snatch the front of his shirt and pull him closer. Locking him in place and bringing my voice as low as possible without losing the intensity. "I don't know what kind of shit my sister has us all in but the secrets better not pile up much higher. I know you know, so you can tell her I said that."

The chuckle he lets out is dark, and his next move is snap quick. In a flash the amusement drops from his face and he bats away my hold like it's nothing. His hands clasp on my shoulder and he begins applying pressure that amps up to vice-like almost immediately. Confusion causes my eyes to widen, and I look at him in shock as he lowers me down to the bench behind me. "If you think for a moment I would fear you, more than I fear and respect her? You are poorly mistaken."

With the amount of pressure he's putting on me, I have to wonder how my shoulders don't break in his hand. Instead he forces me to sit on the bench behind me. Pushing me further until my back is firmly pressed against the wall and my ass is planted.

"We all have a role to play here, sport. You have your orders. I have mine. She's doing more for you than you'll ever know. If you bring your living relationship out in the open, even breathe a word about your connection before it's time, and I will have you in the hospital faster than anyone will be able to ask questions. Are we fucking clear?" I nod. He releases my shoulders with a slightly questionable grin. "Now wait here until the others are done. Once your whole team is ready I can bring you back to your rooms and you will be considered dismissed for dinner. You will be allowed to debrief and strategize."

"How much longer does this usually last?" I grumble, feeling unusually defeated. While mentally cursing Judge Jackass, as Black will forever be known, I turn my attention back to my brothers.

"That depends on them. Hours at minimum, but due to one little shit in particular Moira has orders to pull them out herself at sunrise." he sighs, sitting beside me with a groan. "The test itself is like a pre-screen for mental stability. We lost three before you…passed."

"Lost?" My eyes look over the blank faces to notice three other treadmills empty along with my own. "Do I want to know what happened to them?"

"Going soft on the competition so early?" Black pushes his shoulder into me and I shoot him a dark look.

"Giving a fuck about what happens to innocent people isn't soft." I bite back.

"I'm inclined to agree. But not one of these treadmills is ever occupied by anyone *innocent*." His entire demeanor changes when he speaks now. The word itself puts him on edge, and I don't blame him. I can't wear the badge either.

"Whatever." I say finally. Wanting to be done with the conversation entirely. Glancing at the screens, I notice something strange and my eyes go wide suddenly. Black seems to have taken notice already because he stand's to shield my reaction from the rest of the room again.

"Don't draw attention to it. The nurses working on him have already begun to whisper but it needs to look as normal as possible for now."

"There is no way those are real." I whisper, trying to maintain my composure when I see the stats of everyone on the screen. I'm no doctor, but ONE of these things are not like the others.

"Look, try to take a nap. You boys have readable facial expressions and this is going to take a while. "

"If they are checked out. I'm not. Besides, if that shit is accurate then I need to pay attention." I say firmly, fixing my face with a stern look. "Like you said, I have my orders."

Black nods, clearly understanding the sentiment but he doesn't turn to acknowledge me again. After a moment he walks over to a small group of nurses. One of them being the nurse who was flirting with Max earlier. Something I am just itching to bug him about, and mercilessly. I watch the way the nurses seem eager to discuss with him, but he makes a single quick motion with his hand that they all seem to understand. The group all stop chattering quickly and disburse without another word. Except for Max's girl. I see her lock eyes with the Special Lieutenant, her face falling seriously before she gives a subtle nod.

She walks off cooly and unassuming. I track her across the testing hall all the way to a second tent. This tent looks like a tablet charging station, and I noticed the nurses using them to monitor us when we were being hooked onto the treadmills. The girl starts chatting with one of the nurses. Real slick even in a room full of soldiers. The touch she skates lightly over the back of the other nurse's tablet causes it to light up, and the nurse quickly puts it to sleep again. That's when Max's girl ends the conversation and walks over to lean against a wall by herself. Her light expression drops and her focus zeros in on her own tablet when her fingers begin to fly over the screen. I've seen Max's hands fly pretty damn fast when he's at his computer, but this girl's fingers on her right hand are almost invisible. It doesn't take long before she returns the device to sleep and relaxes entirely. Then she returns to the nurses station like nothing happened, and I suppose nothing did. Until I return my attention back to the wall of giant screens full of our vitals. The strange readings on Augustine's screen are still showing concerning levels, until slowly the numbers start to drop. I don't draw attention, instead I glance quickly back to Max's girl, who's eyes catch mine for a microsecond then back to the conversation she's having. Confirmation enough for me that this is her doing, and something I will have to keep in mind.

I have a wonderful vantage point from where I'm sitting, which makes me think Black did it on purpose. It's dark in the testing center. The dim light is just enough for me to clearly see what is happening with the other candidates. My eyes drift to Moira after having enough time to sort out my current priorities. She's standing with her eyes shut tight and her head down. However, before we all were sent under she was alone at the front of the class. She now has three soldiers marked with the same letter L as on her breast. I look them over, noting the only man on the team standing guard. Close enough to reach each of the women on his team with no more than four easy steps in either direction. It's a tactic I've used before and is effective when needing to guard more than one.

The tallest of the women, with long red hair and a deep concern in her Hazel eyes behind the hard concentration on her face. She is dabbing gauze under Moira's nose, and I realize that Moira is bleeding, and her breaths are heavy as her chest rises and falls in rapid succession. Something tells me it's my fault, and it isn't just because of the man on Moira's team shooting daggers at me with his eyes.

Before I can decide if I want to ignore Black's warning and see if Moira is going to be okay I hear Max gasp. His little nurse's attention snaps to him and immediately she snags a water bottle from the table and runs over. Max thanks her but doesn't take the water before his head whips around until his eyes locate the others beside him. I clear my throat, making his eyes snap to me. I can see his shoulders relax before he turns his attention to his girl once again and finally takes the bottle of water she's holding out to him. I continue watching as they remove him from their system, watching to make sure he doesn't start biting his nails again. They smile at one another in that dopey way I hate, but it doesn't take long before he's walking over to me.

"If I didn't know any better, I'd say you tapped out." Max whispers, tapping his knuckles to mine and plopping down beside me. I can feel him trembling from all the running and his breath hasn't quite evened out just yet. As of this point, they have all been under for about two hours more than myself.

"Good thing you know better." I grumble, displeased with the reminder of my own unclear results. I notice he hasn't even opened the water bottle yet. "Drink."

"Give me a minute, man." He breathes in deeply a few times, gulping down half the bottle before speaking again. "I feel like I just got hit by a bus. If they go on any longer we're going to have to carry them."

"They can't expect them to-" Before I'm able to finish my sentence, the sound of a heart monitor flatlining calls our attention. On instinct I check on my little brother first, then the Captain beside him. Both of them continue to run in a trance like state, faces unchanged. I turn my attention then to a treadmill surrounded by nurses. The commotion is brief before they all slowly disperse with heads hanging low, and a horrible scene is revealed before us.

A young soldier, a girl no older than eighteen is hanging in her contraption. Limbs dangling to the sides...lifeless legs skidding as the treadmill comes to a complete stop. I don't breathe while I watch as a few nurses slowly get her out, attempting not to jostle her more than they have to. My eyes drag back to our boys, and I can feel Max adjust his position to watch them now, too. I know that our attention will stay on them from now on. The rest of the room just became irrelevant to the both of us. My dad used to call it "feeling the real". That moment when rumor and truth mix to create the perfect cocktail of reality.

People. DIE. Here.

"What do you think is happening to August?" Max asks in a cautious tone. "His stats are way too normal for the way he's booking on there."

"You can thank your little girlfriend for that. A few hours ago they sure as shit didn't look like that." I lean forward as I answer, bracing my elbows on my knees and resting my chin on my knuckles. Kaila told me to pay attention, to watch, but she never told me what to watch out for. Now I get it a little more.

"Sophia." Max corrects, the smile on his face audible. Without looking, I lean back and jab my elbow into his side with a short chuckle. Then I lean forward again, back at it. Other candidates are beginning to wake up, gasps start to popcorn down the line, but we don't pay them any mind. Instead we stay fixed on our own, but our ears are open. I can hear sobs from those who are waking up to find out they've lost someone, but everyone does their best to remain as silent as possible to allow Moira to work. It isn't until hour five that Marco finally comes to, causing Max and I to let out a breath of relief.

"Three down." Max grunts, adjusting his position again to sit on the floor. Marco hobbles over to us after his nurse finishes up her questions, looking particularly green. His knees are knocking and I just know that after five fucking hours, he's gotta be dead on his feet.

"Not the three I would've put money on." I stand quickly, meeting Marco half way and hooking his arm over my shoulder. He doesn't give me all his weight, but as soon as I get him close enough, my brother collapses onto the bench, something close to a small sob leaving him. His breathing is completely ragged, and I can see his pulse trying to continue the race he just finished. I notice the way he is only breathing through his mouth, the same as he was this morning. Again I don't question it, deciding that it still isn't a priority. I will be getting to the bottom of it soon though.

"You doin' alright, track star?" Max chastises from his spot on the floor. Keeping his eyes on Augustine while I take care of Marco. Marco opens his mouth to respond, but thinks better of it, nodding instead.

"Yeah, he's gonna be just fine. Sit up, little brother. Gotta hydrate." Knowing that he's probably feeling about as boneless as a wet noodle right now I press my back to his after I push a water bottle into his hand. He's in no shape to do anything but breath at the moment. Another hour passes before Marco is able to drink a full bottle of water without feeling woozy. Another thirty minutes has the color in his face returning to normal, but the tremor in his legs remain. I make him drink two more bottles before I let him sleep. Two sets of eyes work just fine for now.

Finally after a grueling sixteen hours we hear Augustine gasp and it sets us all into motion. Marco shoots up, looking better but still not the best, his eyes falling to the commotion around our Captain. The nurses work fast to get him off the treadmill and by the time the last connection is loose Max and I make it to him. Augustine's eyes stay open long enough to see us, then he drops. Whatever he was chasing, I know he caught it. He wouldn't have let go if he didn't.

I begin to feel the stairs of the other candidates gathered in sporadic groups around the testing center as the lights begin growing brighter slowly. Without hesitating, I hoist August over my shoulders like the sack of potatoes he is right now. I don't bother checking to make sure if the boys get the message. I know they'll follow me. By the time we make it to the door we came into this place from, Lieutenant Black is already holding it open with a stone face in place of concern and leads us the hell out of there.

A nurse follows us from the testing center and through the jump point back to our rooms to check August out. She says he is suffering from some sort of dehydration, but it's the unsure tone that sits heavy in my gut. So after two bags of whatever liquid they pump into his body, the color returns to August's face, letting us know he's out of the woods. Once the nurse and Black leave us alone, I refuse to leave August's bedside. I make the boys take a shower and try to get some rest after the beating they just took, allowing me to lose myself in my thoughts for a while. I don't know how long I dissociate into the events of the day but I jump when I hear Marco speak. I frown at him, unsure of when he came back in after his shower or how long he's been standing there. "I can watch him for a while, if you want to go grab a shower."

"I'm fine. You need to get some sleep. You guys had a rough day." I whisper, trying to stay respectful. As expected, Marco just takes a chair to the foot of August's bed and gets comfortable, giving the captain a quick once over then turning his attention to me.

"Yeah, you know I was a bit surprised to hear you got out first. You want to tell me about that?" he asked, making no effort to beat around the bush. I wanted to tell him everything, but I have no information to give other than the speculation.

"You're breathing like a fucking moron. You want to tell me about that?" I parrot back to him. We stay there, eyes locked in a battle of brotherly wills, but we both plead the same thing. *Please don't push.*

"I think I'll keep that card in my pocket for another time, thanks." Marco says, readjusting to lay his head back before changing the subject. "Do you have any idea what's about to happen tomorrow?"

I contemplated for a few minutes, trying to figure out how I am going to get us as prepared as possible without the Captain's input. Not to mention without telling my brothers what little information I do have. I have watched August time and time again make solid plans under a hail of bullets, but I have never been the team strategist. My range extends as far as my fists or bullets fly.

"Fuck, I don't know man. Did Max manage to pass out?" As if my question summons him, Max strides into the room, hand buried in a bag of chips. I glare at the crumpling of the chip bag and he stops when he notices the noise difference from the other room to this one. Discarding the bag in the bin by the door as quietly as possible, Max wipes his hands on his jeans and makes his way over to one of the empty seats we brought in earlier and brings it over to the empty side of August's bed.

"Anything?" Max asks, scooting closer to the bed to check the tablet he has set up to monitor Augustine's vitals. Frowning at what he sees.

"Not a thing." We allow the conversation to die there as we all sit with our thoughts. 'The real' my father always spoke of settling between us like a lead weight. "Truth. People die here."

"Truth. We are all going through some kind of…change. And until we figure out what's happening, we can't talk about it." Marco offers, cautiously looking up to see if we agree. I glance at Max who nods, glancing at the captain.

"Truth…" Max pauses like he is trying to decide a way to say it without ruining a surprise, but gives in anyway. "I have something for you guys."

He stands up and walks out the door, peeking back in when we don't follow. Marco takes the hint, springing up and exiting quietly. I look at August over one more time before following, too. Once in Max's room, we notice the mess of wires and parts sprawled across the workbench in the corner. I smile a little knowing he has everything he needs and he didn't have to steal it. That is, until I realize I've seen this project before. "So, you guys remember when I stole your watches and made them walkie talkies?"

Marco and I grimace at the memory. When our father was still alive, he had given me and my brothers our first watches and told us to guard them with our lives. One day, Max gets the idea to make them into secret spy watches, along with a couple toy watches my brother and sister had at the time. Needless to say, I got the worst of the punishment for it because I found out only after the fact that the watch that had been given to me had been my Grandfather's. Marco got a pretty good talking to as a result. Max just chuckled, and I could practically hear him thinking "But they worked" without him even saying it out loud. Marco's delay in panic beside me startles me. "Bitch, did you jack me for my watch again?"

"No." He replies flatly. The last time he took our watches, Augustine almost killed him. He even made Max put every piece of each watch back in front of him. The justice was there after one watch, but the light died for Max after the second one. "I made us some."

Chapter Thirteen
Marco

I know that face. I hate that face. It's Max's 'look what I did' face. Over the years, that face has been the reason for so many nightmares. The lengths this guy is willing to go through for some tech is psychotic at best. A tendency I realize is one we all share in a different way. Though Augustine did his absolute damndest to keep us all in line after my sister's passing, the psycho part of each of us was kinda allowed to run rampant after my sister's passing. We were all rightfully worried about him in general, but a truth I was unwilling to share was that I was seeing a bit more than the others.

His chest was moving, and his heart was beating, but there is something about the way the other candidates and proctors were looking at us when we left the testing center. There were the obvious faces of disgust from those cocksuckers trying to start shit with us earlier, but there were more that displayed shock. I made it a point to sneak a peek at Moira before we left, noticing that she had also fallen into a coma at the same time as August. Moira looked a bit worse for wear than our Captain. Deductive reasoning would tell me that his simulation was way different from ours. Max walks over to a drawer by his bedside table, pulling out a long box. Taking a spot on his bed, he waves us over and pats beside him with a grin.

"Truthfully, I've been working on these since Captain got pinched and sent to Limbo. Before this whole thing started, we had orders not to break him out. Which we had planned to ignore. He would have undoubtedly sent us home and stayed anyway, so I took the liberty of creating a contingency plan. In case there was ever a chance he wanted to come home on his own and needed our assistance."

"What are they?" Vince asks, impatience bleeding into the anxious tone of his voice. He's been a live wire since the testing center, and I know that he's itching to get back to watching August.

"He's gonna be okay." I state, knowing both of them will understand. We take a moment of agreeing silence, but then Max clears his throat to answer the question we really want to know.

"These are," he pauses dramatically. Fumbling with the box until he has it open, pulling out a silver chain with a hollow circle pendant just larger in diameter than a penny. "M.W.T.D's."

Vince and I wait for him to explain further, confusion on both our faces. When we don't give him the reaction he wants, as it happened every single time, he frowns and dives in with a defeated sigh. "Micro Wire Tracking Devices. I haven't come up with a cool name for them yet, so I guess I'll explain. These chains are made from a braided Micro wire casing and tungsten pendant. A nano wire that's been specially crafted to withstand water, heat, and more importantly, if they could make armor light enough, it could essentially stop a tank round."

Max hands me my own chain. Gold instead of silver. "The pendant is a hollowed out penny filled with a tungsten marble. The copper acts as a signal boost for the Micro Wire, while the tungsten I wrapped with a preset signal, so that way the circuit is allowed to stop somewhere, with only two commands. Trace, which obviously keeps track of your location but only when activated. And the second reason. I designed the pendants to recognize a three finger pattern. I've already downloaded the programs and fingerprints accordingly. If we get separated at any time, all we will have to do is press the pendent between our fingers by hooking our first finger over the top of the chain, and pressing the pendent between your thumb and middle."

Max shows us the motion on his own, both of us frowning when nothing happens.

"Right hand, pendejos dumbasses, it's not an emergency."
Max says, rolling his eyes. "Anyway, there's a catch."
"There's always a catch." I groan. He snickers, shoving
into me.
"I just mean that once these things are on you and I've
activated them, they ain't coming off." He yanks on his chain
hard to show what he means, wincing at the chain biting into
his skin. "I designed them from the materials I did so that they
can be used as a form of last line defense in any scenario no
matter what. This kind of wire is only being used by the United
States military as a tripwire for counter strikes with special
sanctions because they can't be cut or set off accidentally.
The material is basically indestructible, but as the
technological community has come to understand, it is
extremely volatile when coupled with a charge because it's
like a small scale atomic bomb if deactivated incorrectly."
"You're trying to make us wear bomb jewelry." I say
incredulously. Vince and I suddenly hold our chains as far
from us as possible.
"Of all the ways I figured you'd find to kill us, little chains
are not what I would've guessed." Vince chastises.
"No." He barks, annoyed with the insinuation that an
invention of his might not work. "What I'm saying is that I
designed them so that they can't ever be taken off by force.
These *little chains* broke scissors, cutting shears, six bolt
cutters, three table saws, and two industrial hydraulic
presses."
"And a partridge in a pear tree." Vince and I whip our heads
to one another, our personal childishness showing just a bit
when we whisper loudly. "Jinx!"
We laugh, but it's short lived when I draw back to the chain
of wonders hanging from the tip of my first finger. I know
exactly why Max would make something of such
permanence. Something he kept hidden away from us as a
way of keeping it out of the wrong hands. We all feel a deep
sense of guilt over our sister. Compensating in our own ways

for what happened that day, and every day since. Vince made it mission to never get beat again by living at the gym during the day, and finding any underground fight he could at night as a way to keep fresh. I made it mine to learn as much as I could about any type of aircraft ever built. Flight projections, aeronautical maps, I even studied the weather in my spare time. Which I had a lot of when August was locked up. Max has it a little worse in a way. No matter how hard he looked, how many drones, tech or bots he sent out, he never found her or even her body. He was never able to forgive himself for it either. I nod at this understanding, pulling the chain around my neck only to realize there is no clip to fasten it.

"Hold it out and hold still." Max instructs. I look up to see him coming at me with his portable soldering iron. The smallest bit I've ever seen looks like a white hot needle at the end of the handheld machine. I gulp, lifting my chin as far as I can get it, but I can still feel the heat radiating against my Adams apple. I open my mouth to say something clever out of pure nervousness but he quickly shuts me up.

"Don't move." He demands, no joke in his tone. My jaw snaps shut, not wanting to get burned, and after a few seconds the heat pulls away and I am left sitting there. "Count to five and you should be able to put it down."

I do as directed, giving it an extra few seconds before turning to watch Vince go through the same process. I adjust the chain, treating the pendant like the bomb it is as I placed it in the center.

"It's not going to explode!" Max insists with a hiss. But I still watch Vince do the same thing which forces Max to roll his eyes even harder this time.

"What's not going to explode?" Augustine's gruff sleep addled voice snaps all our attention to the doorway, breathing a collective sigh of relief. Although he's leaning on the doorframe for support, he's awake and talking.

"Captain!" I call, moving quickly to help him to the desk chair.

"Back from the dead I see?" Vince grumbles our little inside joke, still irritated, but there is still no mistaking the relief in his tone.

"Maybe we should throw that whole joke away at this point. Don't you think so?" Max grimaces. We all agree silently.

"Yeah, the lingo around here is probably going to have us rewriting most of our banter material." August winces when I help him lower himself into the chair. "What did you steal?"

"500 miles of deactivated micro wire." Max admits outright. There's no point lying to this man anyway. "I took it when we did that Bolivia job. I have yours here."

Max takes a moment to re-explain the necklaces. Demonstrating the activation process a bit slower this time. Augustine shrugs, moving his face to give Max access to the invention around his neck. Once August's is in place, Max slides his desk chair with the Captain still in it out of the way, pulling another chair over. His fingers start ticking against the keyboard at a ridiculous speed. A program with a black screen and white letters that makes absolutely no sense to me begins to run on four of his nine screens simultaneously. Each screen has one of our names on the bottom right hand corner. Minutes pass when he abruptly ends his typing, turning to face us again.

"Now, because I wanted to make sure these things were never rendered useless, there is an emergency voice activation protocol that I have taken the liberty to implement. I just need your repeat word, and a five digit code starting with one letter and four numbers following."

"Chicago. X1594." Vince states without missing a beat. Max swivels around, typing it in manually while the system itself registers my brother's vocal patterns. It doesn't take but a few seconds before Max is waving his hand for another one of us to answer.

"Brazil. Z2233." I said, thinking of the firecracker who filled out my paperwork and some random numbers I'm sure I'll never forget.

"Kingston K1114." I knew the captain would figure out a way to make his password about my sister in some way. Kingston is the town he grew up in, the first letter of her name, her birthdate. Always the sentimental one, our Captain. Once Max is finished putting in the final codes and scanning the captain's voice, he presses enter. This prompts a simultaneous and faint ding from each of the necklaces.

"Now you need to remember that these are not the inventions. These necklaces are like a homing beacon for the invention with the added bonus of making it easy to find you if anything happens. I have a few minor touches I would like to add after today's events but if we get separated the way we think we will, they will be ready when needed as always."

"I look forward to seeing what you've managed to create for us this time, Max. I know you've been working on these for a long time." Captain gives his praise, earning a proud smile from Max in return. "Let's get some food going so we can debrief about those simulations."

We all freeze. None of us were quite comfortable talking about it. Though it was clear we all had a different experience. He must pick up on our discomfort, and apparently had some of his own judging by the way his shoulders relax a bit. "Maybe we just eat and get to this welcoming thing. Anybody need to sleep?"

"All of us, but we can sleep after dinner. I took the liberty of making sandwiches since the housewife doesn't want us in her kitchen." I smile at my brother's face. Vince loves to cook, and he's damn good at it. Which is the only reason he's allowed kitchen rights. The rest of us are limited to easy makes and special occasions. Like if Vince ever slips into a coma for example.

We all file out of Max's room to the living area to eat, attempting to maintain at least an hour of normalcy.

After a while Vince decides to pull out a deck of cards for us to play. The time passes quickly but still gives us enough time to sift through our personal issues on our own. It's something we learned to do a long time ago as boys. Before my dad died, he taught us that it was never okay to ignore what was bothering us, because it would fester and grow to control us. He used to tell us that as men we are taught by society to ignore our feelings, so in his house we were to be taught how to address them silently. That way when we are able to speak about it, even if it was just amongst ourselves, a proper argument could be formed in place of the one we would have had in the heat of the moment. After our father died, playing cards to think is something we developed from his guidance.

With the second game's ending the tension in the room successfully lifts, and we all disperse to clean up quickly. We are all about to enter our rooms when a knock is heard from the main hall door in Augustine's room. Instinct takes over, causing us all to stop in our tracks and turn to one another. When the knock comes again, August moves to the door, the rest of us following at a reasonable pace. August opens the door to reveal a rather exhausted looking Special Lieutenant Andrew Black and we all relax into our annoyance. Not bothering to wait for an invitation, the special lieutenant shoves past us and into the room.

"By all means come in." I grumble sarcastically, feeling the exhaustion slip into pissy behavior. He waves off the comment, sliding his hands down his face with a big sigh.

"I'm here to take you all to the opening ceremony. Leave any personal effects here if you don't want them confiscated." he plops down on an empty chair, waving us off.

"Looking kinda rough there, Special Lieutenant." Vince says it with all the venom he can muster, hissing the man's title. Black chuckles, amused by my brother's disdain.

"I notice you aren't looking as rough as the others, Vincent." The goading is lost on me, but the Lieutenant's words seem to set my brother off entirely. In a flash Vince has Black by the shirt and up against the wall.

Can't say I didn't call it.

Chapter Fourteen
Augustine

Vince's hold on the Special Lieutenant leaves no room for confusion. Vince doesn't do well with the kind of game I can tell Black likes to play.

The Special Lieutenant sighs, unphased by his shirt wrapped in Vince's hands. A small smile pulls at the corners of Black's lips. The second I see it, alarm bells go off in my head and the cotton candy scent of excitement fills my nose.

"Vi-" The warning dies on my lips. The Special Lieutenant is a blur of motion for a fraction of a second before he has Vince's face pressed against my desk with his arm gripped firmly, outstretched dangerously behind him. I hear the groan of the desk under the force Black is using to hold him with.

"You really need to learn some self control, or we're just going to keep ending up in this position." The boredom in Black's voice is not subtle, snapping us out of our stupor. I draw my gun knowing it's already way too late. Before Max and Marco have the chance to follow, Black whips his head to the side, eyes locking with mine and not showing an ounce of the playfulness I've come to recognize. "Think about it."

I already know without a doubt I will never get the shot off before he does any damage. I don't holster my gun, but I make a show of pulling my finger off the trigger. "Smart. Now, I am exhausted and my patience is pulling from its reserves. I'm going to let you up. Do not swing. This is your final warning. Am I understood?"

Vince reluctantly nods his head as best he can, accepting the defeat. I can tell just by the look on his face when the Special Lieutenant lets him go, taking two steps away. I holster my weapon, but I see Marco and Max moving in to attempt a take down. I shoot them a warning glance, forcing them to stop. Vince storms off to his room, locking the door behind him. I try to listen for shit to start breaking, but no sound comes. When he doesn't return right away, I narrow

139

my eyes on the Special Lieutenant. "You ever put your hands on one of mine in our home again, I'll have your teeth on a necklace faster than whatever the hell it was you just did."

He smiles pulling an amused snort from his nose but says nothing further on the matter, glancing at the door Vince retreated through. "Is he off to throw a fit?"

"You know? You really do have a big fucking mouth, payaso. Clown." Max argues, trying to take a step forward.

"Enough!" I bark, stopping him again. "Let him cool off, he'll be back in a second. This is your last warning to quit being such a prick, Special Lieutenant. That big ass mouth of yours will get you jumped. We don't care about your rank in this room, and I couldn't care any less about what you can do. I will find a fucking way."

"Alright, alright. I'm done." He holds up both hands in surrender before moving to the living room and onto the couch as if he had been invited to do so.

"Who the fuck is this guy?" Marco breaths, just loud enough for us to hear. I know exactly what he's talking about, too. Special Lieutenant Black has been a conundrum from the very beginning, but if there is one person out of the three of us who thinks Vince is unstoppable more than Vince, it's Marco. "I'm gonna go-"

"No." Max and I say, cutting Marco off roughly. We all fight. We all lose. Vince's fights always get particularly gruesome, and he wins just fine. However, his losses have always been something else. So we always make it a point to keep Marco out of it whenever we can. He's still seen his fair share and participated when necessary, but unlike the two of us, Marco only has the slightest idea of how dangerous his brother really is when he is angry. I can only imagine how he would be now.

"He should be out in a minute. The best thing we can do for him is stay out of his way 'till he calms down." Max explains. A yawn ripples through all of us as we empty our holsters on my bed before we decidedly make our way to the living room where we see the Special Lieutenant has made himself at home. Having propped both boots on the coffee table in front of the couch.

"Baja los pies de la mesa, carajo! Get your feet off the table, damn it!" I shout immediately. No longer able to contain my irritation for him in this instance. He grumbles something unintelligible but brings his feet down without any more protest. I stop in my tracks to close my eyes and take in calming breaths. Just a second before the next thing starts fucking with us. I scented it from the second Black stepped through our door. Deception. It's wafted from him a few times already, but he reeks of it now, along with softer tones of reluctance.

"Anybody ever told you that you have boundary issues?" Marco asks, echoing something I know he learned from my wife.

"Ha!" Black bellows harshly. "Only every damn day kid. Is he going to be done with his hissy fit anytime in the near future or are we in it for the long haul? I hate to be late, even if they won't start without me and I don't really want to go."

As if on cue, Vince emerges from his bedroom, a hard but seemingly calmer expression on his face now as he makes his way to stand beside me. I nod to him once in question, and he nods back in reply before turning to point a warning finger at Black. "If you give me a chance, I'll take it."

"When I give you the chance, I'll expect you to do just that." Black's sneer is a challenging one, and it isn't lost on me that he said 'when' and not 'if' like Vince had suggested. Tension passes between us, somehow thicker now than it was even moments ago. Palpable as he speaks again. The coolness of his tone does not match the tightness of his shoulders. "If you are all ready to go, I won't stir the pot without a little truce planned."

He pulls a pint of whisky from his inside jacket pocket, shaking the contents while wiggling his eyebrows at us. Seemingly back to his younger personality.

"OOH." Max loves whiskey. So the girlish excitement doesn't surprise me.

"A shot or two before we leave won't hurt." Vince says, retrieving six shot glasses from the stocked dish cupboard and setting them down on the coffee table in front of us. I haven't taken my eyes off the Special Lieutenant in probably too long. Something isn't right about what he's doing, and everything is telling me not to take the drink.

"I know I didn't hit you that hard, kid. There's only five of us here." None of us entertain his question while Vince arranges the glasses so one sits face down in the center. The Special Lieutenant clears his throat uncomfortably, the heavy spike of guilt too sudden for me not to know he won't ask again. Removing the topper from the bottle he pours the last of the contents in our glasses, coming up short when it gets to his glass. Ever the kindest of us, Marco saunters to the cabinet above the stove where he found the selection of liquor last night and returns to fill Black's shot the rest of the way with a different brand of whisky. Max visibly winces, but says nothing to deter the gesture. "To those we've lost, and the knowledge that we may find each other again. Cheers."

"Salud." We raise our shots in toast before downing them in an easy gulp. Max's face twists slightly and I can see him looking at his shot glass curiously from the corner of my vision. He shakes his head, probably deciding it isn't important before he collects our now empty glasses, washes them quickly, then meets us all by the door Black came in from.

When we enter the hallway, I'm a bit shocked. I expect the halls to be filled with other teams as they had been earlier in the day, but instead we are met with an empty hall and some breathing room. Our hallway is unassuming, identical to all the others we've been in, but something about the door directly across the hall from my own draws my attention. Most have names on them, initials at least, but instead only a Z adorns this one. Another thing to keep in the back of my mind, though that bag of shit is getting really fucking full.

"Where is everybody?" Vince grumbles, more than likely relieved with the elbow room.

"You all were my last stop. The door here at the end of the hall was temporarily cordoned off as a jump point for today. Everyone else has been sent through and is waiting for us." Special Lieutenant Black says through a yawn as we walk the way to a waiting Aurora sitting with her eyes closed, leaning back in her chair lazily. I know she knows we are here, and I know the moment they begin talking in code, too. Both moments bring more scents that just bring me closer to losing my shit on everyone to find out what the hell is being kept from us. I need some real fucking sleep. "Draw the short straw, Donovan?"

"Volunteered." she calls as she stands, meeting his eyes for a quick moment the same way she did back at the boarded up convenience store. "I'm coming through with you, so let's get going."

"Nice to see you again, Aurora." Vince's wink at her is audible to me and I groan inwardly. Noting the subtle hints of lust coming from her now as she watches him walk toward her. The light air of amber under the different shifting scents coming off of her and Black is a decent enough reprieve. Not enough to ignore what is happening in front of me as the warm, spicy scent becomes stronger, and is now coming from Vince too as we get closer.

"Oh, choke on it." She bites back in reply. I almost fall on my face, and Marco and Max make no attempt to conceal their laughter. Vince's smile widens at the mistake she just made. We all know it, but she hasn't realized she walked into the lion's den with meat in her bra.

"I suppose that depends on how determined you are." Vince drawls. She freezes, the way her shoulders tense should indicate anger, and she does a good enough job emulating just that when she turns to get in his face. However the same can't be said for the slight pull to the corner of her mouth and the fact that the same anger doesn't reach her eyes. She stands about a foot and a half shorter than him, but the fire in her eyes makes my heart ache.

"Determination doesn't matter when you're sucking on a tic tac." The boys erupt in "ooh's" at her quip. This girl has no idea that he will never let her go now. I have never seen anyone come back at him and still get that close. I myself am thoroughly impressed.

"Guess that'll be for you to confirm for yourself." He chuckles. Aurora rips open the door in front of her before shooting daggers from her eyes at Vince once again.

"Wouldn't you like that?" she hisses before walking through. Vince's hand goes to his chest when he suddenly stumbles back dramatically.

"Dear GOD, yes! Mmh!" he shouts before following her like a puppy. I smile to myself, breathing out a laugh before following with the other in a line behind me.

We make it through the jump point to find a grumpy Vince waiting for us. It doesn't take a genius to understand that his new purpose in life left him high and dry. I shake my head with a smirk before looking around the nearly empty lobby of a run down auditorium. The building is different from where we were this morning. Instead of an Olympic size gymnasium, we now find ourselves in a movie theater-esque place. The closer we are led to the first door inside, we can hear the crowd, the commotion of tense conversations in my ears. The barrage of varying emotions and intentions filling my nose.

When we join the sea of candidates, Black waves us into the back row of seats. We shuffle down the row, each of us taking in different aspects of the area. I watch the Special Lieutenant until he disappears from my field of vision when Vince grumbles, stifling a yawn as he sits down. "Three major exits, and I'm assuming there's a fire escape behind the stage."

I nod as a hush falls over the crowd, so silent every scrape of our pants against the beat up seats feels like it's echoing off the walls around us. Before I can drop my eyes to roam across the faces surrounding us, the lights lower and Special Lieutenant Black makes his way to the podium.

"I'll spare you all with the assumption everyone knows who I am." He begins sternly. In this instance I can see Judge Jackass making an appearance in his tone.

"As you are all aware, before bringing you here each of you shared a shot of whisky with me. Now while I do think it is a crime to taint a good hooch, I also think it's unfair to drug you and not at least tell you about it." The murmurs begin, a look shared between Vince and I quickly when the Special Lieutenant continues, unbothered by the information he's giving. "Mixed with the alcohol was a mixture of herbs. A concoction designed to induce heavy sleep, which should begin its effects within the next ten minutes if it hasn't already begun."

Murmurs erupt into panicked whispers around the room. I turn my head to find Max's face twisted with a knowing expression. "I knew it. That disrespectful fuck."

"Do not be alarmed. The amount administered to each of you will only keep you under for the time necessary to place you around the game board." Black's bid for reassurance is cut short with the rising hostility.

"ENOUGH WITH THE BULLSHIT!" Someone shouts from the crowd.

"HAVEN'T WE DONE ENOUGH!" Calls out another. The room grows more and more restless as the Special Lieutenant speaks a bit louder.

"From the moment the liquid touched your lips, you all entered The Choosing Game. Our final proving ground and rite of passage for anyone with even a small hope to become a true Dead Soldier. This game is designed to make sure there are no flukes in our system. We make it a point to keep you as uninformed as possible. As Dead Soldiers, we walk this world with what we have, and what we can create ourselves. This is where you prove to us, as well as yourselves, whether or not you have what it takes. I would like to take a moment to explain the few rules that we do have in place. First and foremost: Under no circumstances should you attempt to exit the test of your own accord. Any attempt to leave the testing ground after the testing has begun will result in the direct forfeiture of your life by the hands of a Ranked Dead Soldier. Second, unlike the aptitude tests where you were all strapped in snug and safe to keep from hurting yourselves, the island you will all find yourselves in will very much be a hostile environment. Therefore, the rule of survival stands. Any means necessary." The room grew even more restless.

"Now as a precaution, there is a third rule. If the Choosing game is ordered to cease for any reason over the next four days, orders will be broadcast to each candidate via a telepathic Juggernaut. A unit of Ranked Dead Soldiers will be tasked with rectifying any situation, and the situation assessed from there." Black clears his throat, stifling another yawn. "You will have four days to reach an extraction point. As easy as it sounds now, I can guarantee most of you are going to lose purely on the fact that you will underestimate the challenges of the days ahead. You are to hunt, trap, and kill your own food, and track your own water sources. Survive."

I can no longer hold back the yawn that has been trying to rip its way out of me for five minutes, covering my mouth with the back of my hand. I begin to realize just how uncomfortable I am in this seat, and begin to stir with heavy limbs. Quickly realizing the others are doing the same, I glance around the room to see the collective discomfort spreading throughout. Whole sections in the front of the theater have already begun to slip into unconsciousness and I watch a few heads bobbing forward trying to fight it off. A few heads already hang loosely, snores breaking through the bickering that seems to be moving father and farther away from my ears. Without another word, Black exits the stage, locking eyes with me from across the room and sending me a wink that I can't be completely certain wasn't reassurance of some kind.

"August?" I can hear the lazy panic, but I can't tell who said it,

"Mwaht?" I giggle incoherently at the sound of my own voice. Whichever of them called to me doesn't say anything further as unconsciousness takes me by the balls.

"Damn, that's some good shit." I don't know exactly, but I'm guessing Vince said it.

And, fuck if he ain't right.

Chapter Fifteen
Kaila

"Let's make this clean." Aurora barks, shooing the gaggle of female soldiers scattered about the stage now that the candidates have all fallen unconscious. The only reason I move my attention to her is because I have been staring at my husband and brother's sleeping faces for entirely too long. It doesn't take long for everyone to leave the stage, giving Aurora a wide berth to do what only she can do. Eyes closed she faces the curtain backdrop, filling her lungs with a slow suck. The chatter in the room cuts off, everyone turning to watch Aurora with no small amount of fascination. On her exhale, the energy in the room becomes mute and I know she has begun. With hands folded in the prayer position, she drags their position from chest to right in front of her face. From where I stand I have the perfect view of the stage curtain splitting in the center like someone is pulling at the ropes. I know that isn't the reason. Aurora separates each of her fingers like the pins in a lock, each deliberate movement guiding the red velvet curtains apart.

When she interlocks her thumbs, bringing flat palms out she holds for a second before her right palm snaps to face down. With a hard yank of her right hand the curtain flies open the rest of the way. The energy Aurora was holding as she worked breaks free and everyone takes a collective breath. Spinning on the heels of her boots, she starts barking orders, setting everyone in motion again. "Start from the bottom of the roster with Unit A. You will each have exactly one hour from the first step on the island to place your candidates and their support item with no less than thirty feet of space between candidates. All support items and weapons need to be secured before you walk through my portal. You bastards like to lose shit along the way and I'm not cleaning up after you! If you lose it, consider it gone. After your hour is up, and the last candidates have been placed, this door will close. Find your own way home after that."

The room erupts into movement. It won't take long, but we will have to wait for the end before we can move. Aurora jumps off the front of the stage, everyone being respectful enough to move for her. Black finishes his conference with a few of the other young soldiers before joining Aurora as she walks, their never ending bickering match already begun. Just before they reach us, the colors of worry and fear grow brighter to my eyes. My eyes narrow on them both, and my own aura must alert them to my attention because both of them whip their head around to lock eyes with me. Aurora can't hide her facial expressions from me the way black can, so I lock in on her first. "I assume I'm not gonna like this?"

She gulps, but recovers quickly. "Special Lieutenant Black's been poking the bear again."

"Is that what we're doing now?" Black's face breaks into an incredulous expression directed at the side of Aurora's face before he turns back to me. "I didn't hurt him. This guy just has a short temper and might actually have the fight in him to back it up."

"You're fucking right about that." I risk the knowing glance at my oldest brother's sleeping face. Noting the fact that I have never not once seen him look so peaceful. I itch to ruin it, it almost feels wrong. Bringing myself back to The Special Fucker in front of me I take a step to close the gap between us just enough to drop my voice to an audible whisper. "Don't pretend you aren't deliberately baiting him, Black. I know you. You put up a good front, but I know you. You're like a child that gets one more piece of candy than the rest of the kids."

"I have a job to do." He offers a subtle reminder. I feel the curiosity from my unit as well as Aurora. The parts of the plan even they aren't privy to showing their ugly heads. I'm so fucking tired of this game. The emotions of every single person in this auditorium seeps into my pores at a snail's pace, weighing me down all the more.

"Don't I know it." I chuckle, bitterly. "Now I want you to listen to me, *very* closely. These boys have enough on their plate right now to be worried about you poking at them for reasons that for now, they do not understand. You are playing with toys that do not belong to you, Black. Am I clear?"

The intensity of my aura has caused sweat to form on his forehead as he tries his best to maintain his devil may care mask. The others have taken deliberate steps away from us now, trying to make themselves look busy, but ultimately they've been listening intently to this entire conversation without interrupting. This is the way the twins always are. Milo may be the master at gathering intelligence, but the twins are the King and Queen of gossip. He listens for the sole purpose of reporting back to his husband upon his return. She listens for personal entertainment. Which, if I'm being completely honest, makes her the more dangerous one.

"Crystal." He smiles wide, making a move to close the gap but is quickly stopped by Kiari.

"We should get them up there, Captain."

I move to the side, giving the twins room to grab Marco and my husband. Lieutenant Black shuffles passed me for Vince. Once they're over a shoulder, I hoist Max over mine. Turning to face the others and losing the battle not to laugh at the sight. The four men I have looked up to like gods, slung over the shoulders of their little sister and her friends. "Aurora."

"Captain?"

"You do what I need?." I ask quietly.

"Duh." Aurora chimes from behind me. There's a tense silence as Narcissa's unit moves through the jump portal, their eyes locking with ours for a second before they walk through. The smug smile she throws my way is in no way subtle.

The same moment they walk through, Kiari scoffs.

"Deixe que ela olhe para você assim de novo, capitão. Eu vou consertar isso para ela. Let her look at you like that again,

Captain. I'll fix that for her." Nobody needs to know Portuguese to understand the hate in her voice. Narcissa Cox and her team of fodder has been a point of anger for all of us in different ways. Not a big dog I know that likes a snake in their bed. However, Narcissa's reputation is one that doesn't seem to hold water to evidence. In other words, people fall for her bullshit. "Our turn."

We all walked through one after the other, leaving Aurora behind.

The first thing I notice is the sky. The gray and pale blue clouds rolling in over the horizon. The warning of the coming storm, causing my own worry to spike. The storms out here are no less brutal than the island itself. Torrential rain, massive lightning strikes, and winds strong enough to rip the trees out from the roots and send them somewhere else to rest. I adjust Max on my shoulder, turning to face my team. Special Lieutenant Black doesn't wait for me to speak, knowing his role better than anyone aside from me.

"You have the capsules?" I ask. They nod once, pulling the capsule disks out of their pockets. I nod my approval. Kiari's nerves heighten, causing Kestien's to do the same.

"What is it?" I bite.

"We decided it's best if we don't show each other the secondary item." She braces for my response.

"Como que 'we'? What do you mean 'we'? Not me." I declare, pointing to myself. Without looking at one another, a bet is settled before me when Kestien hands his twin sister a rolled up bill. My face falls, annoyed knowing the argument that is about to begin. Deciding it's best to just agree, I turn on my heels and head to Max's location, leaving them to their sibling banter.

I smile to myself as their argument plays from memory anyway. The gist is that whenever they make a bet between themselves, the money is never "folded correctly". Kiari is usually the one who complains, and in turn does the majority of the arguing, being the one who has a wallet full of neatly stacked and folded currency from various countries. While Kestien, ever the instigator, only rolls his money into a tight little coke straw just for the sake of seeing his sister get ticked off about it.

I make it to the cave we planned for Max to start from, taking him to the very back of the cave and propping him upright against the wall. I take the moment to look at him, pride blossoming in my chest for the boy who just showed up one day, now a man. I remember him having short hair, short on the sides but longer on top, just enough to ruffle. He started off hating when I did it, but I never did care, and eventually neither did he. From the moment we picked Vince up from the jail, Max was with him waiting outside the gate. I remember how skinny he was, and all the bruises that adorned his face and hands. I recall the sick feeling we all shared when they both climbed into the car without a word. Not that we needed one, Max was part of the family from that moment on.

Max stirs just a little, breaking me from my memories enough to get back to the task at hand. I pull the capsule disc out of my back pocket. The information about who invented these things has been lost to time, but the use is timeless in itself. Pressing down on the center, a button depresses soundlessly before the whole thing springs open on an airy thunk. A big pill with a flat bottom now rests in my hand, one of the handiest transportation containers in the Deadlands. Turning it flat side up, I press down lightly on the edge, opening the first compartment. Once Max wakes up and finds it, his pre-programmed biological signature will pop the compartment open to reveal the pistol and full magazine I'm securing inside. Once the gun is removed, however, a smaller secondary compartment will open at the top of the canister. Though all teams are allowed to leave their candidates a weapon, the secondary compartment is not a privilege held by any other than those of my own team. A precaution I've had prepared for months, finally being used in the way it was intended. Still there is a part of me that is nervous that the design will prove faulty, even though I know it won't. We tested them enough.

I take the flash drive from my cleavage and slide it into the secondary slot, close the compartments quickly and place the container at Max's feet. When I stand, I finally look closer at the chain around his neck, pride growing to a fever pitch at the one part of their survival that I've been banking on from the beginning. "Atta boy, Max."

***

After the twins and I return to our quarters, I decide to retreat to my bedroom. It's depressing as ever, no real personality. Nobody is allowed in here, and nobody will ever be allowed in here. I don't even sleep here. Fuck, I don't really sleep, just another downfall of my ability. Even with the collar I can't turn it off long enough to find some fucking peace.

The energy radiating from my pores by the time I make it behind my closed bedroom door is enough to overload my collar, but I don't care. The fact that I know the twins won't bother me, at least until they think I'm unconscious, settles my worry a little. They think I don't know they're the ones cleaning up my mess, but Milo doesn't clean anything but wounds. I allow myself to unleash. Thick waves of color blasting out of me at a pulse. Though there is no body to the colorful smoke-like waves at the moment. Unlike my tails, which require epic amounts of focus to contain, the sheer force created by the cacophony of colors is enough to slam the bed to stand upright on the headboard. A strained sob escapes me while I try to reign it all in. My body is beginning to tremble under the weight, and I try to force slow, deep breaths. Spots start to create holes in my vision. I've been holding on well enough, but today's talks and events have me all over the place. Too much, too fast, too long. Until recently I've maintained a strict routine. The other's called it my "personal time" while I called it a "smoking session" for my own entertainment. For no other reason than the gaseous menagerie of colors that now occupy all the breathable space in my bedroom. I gasp involuntarily when the force grows exponentially, feeling the blood pooling in my mouth from biting my tongue in an attempt to dampen the scream that threatens to rip its way out.

Another wave and I drop to my knees, the pain just too damn much. I double over and clutch at my stomach and chest, hugging my body as tight as I can. This is it, the moment I dread every single time. The release. The moment the energy fully absorbs into my body, the ringing in my ears grows to a deafening volume, not even my ragged breathing audible over it. My vision begins to blur as the threat of unconsciousness looms over me and the door starts to open. Kiari's worry is bleeding into the room now, the smoke-like manifestation of her emotion flying toward me with purpose, allowing me to feel her without lifting my head. I can't risk the scream to warn her, my grip fading fast. With the last of my consciousness I whip out my hand, sending a surge of shock yellow to slam the door shut again. The guttural groan that comes from my lips when the feelings begin to swell again. By the time it's over, I am nothing but a pile of sweat and a heaving chest on the ground. My body aches worse than it did the last time, and I struggle to even roll over onto my back.

As my breathing slowly returns to normal, I manage my way onto two wobbly legs that barely carry me to the overturned bed. It's completely upside down now, and when I try to flip it, my breathing hitches and I cry out. Fuck. I broke some ribs this time for sure. I'm too weak to try again, knowing I won't get anywhere. A small sob leaves my lips, nimbly grabbing the pillow that's been thrown nearby. It hurts like hell, but I finally get down on my back to try to sleep, knowing I won't get any, but the slip into the void is slow. After what feels like a long while, I hear the door opening again and Kestien's worry tickles my nose. I can't protest when he comes to flip the bed, doing his best not to make any noise.

At some point I lose all feeling in my body, the pain giving way to shock. All I can do is listen.

"Oh, Captain." I hear Kiari breath, no doubt gawking at the destruction I've caused. I want to call out. Send them away for trespassing in the one place they know they shouldn't be like always. However, the relief that I'm not entirely alone right now is enough. I listen to the shuffle of papers in the background, Kiari's attempt to straighten up. I know the desk is broken, it wasn't even strong enough to survive the initial blast. I managed to shatter the vase I keep by my bedside table. I know from the sound of glass scraping together while someone sweeps. "She's been skipping personal time."

"I hadn't noticed." The undertone of anger in his voice overshadows the sarcasm. The attitude that comes with being Kestien gone completely from his words.

"Não fique chateado com ela. Ela tem o suficiente para lidar. Temos que apoiá-la. Don't be upset with her. She has enough to deal with. We have to support her." Kiari hisses, someone dumping the contents of the dustpan into the garbage can they brought in from the kitchen. I stopped keeping one in my room after one too many times cleaning trash up when it gets caught in the shitstorm.

"Eu a apoio, mas você não pode continuar nos pedindo para ficar para trás e vê-la sofrer assim. I support her, but you can't keep asking us to stand back and watch her suffer like this." Kestien snaps back. I feel myself being lifted off the ground, I know it's Kestien holding me, but I can't feel above light pressure. It's like my nerve endings are dead.

"O que você gostaria que fizéssemos? Aumentar o poder em seu colar de novo? Entorpecê-la ao ponto da mecânica? What would you like us to do? Increase the power in your collar again? Numb it to the point of mechanics?" Her whispers grow harsher, and I feel guilt playing at the atmosphere around me. Kestien doesn't respond right away, and I wish I could see his face at this moment so I would know what he's thinking. I'm given my answer anyway when he speaks again.

"E se apenas disséssemos a eles? What if we just told them?" He sighs, resignation and reluctance heavy in his words.

"Kestien!" She gasps, and reason becomes foggy with the panic I can't voice. "Você não faria!? You wouldn't!?"

"Olhe para ela, Kiari! Olhe para esta sala! Look at her, Kiari! Look at this room!" His words came in almost bellows, apparently having come to the conclusion that I won't be waking up any time soon.

"O que você quer que façamos?! What do you want us to do!?" The sob is desperate. Like she's just begging for an answer.

"WE HAVE TO DO FUCKING SOMETHING!" His shout rings out into the room, hanging in the air. The room falls to silence. Only their ragged breathing fills the quiet until Kestien speaks again, softer now, with tears in his own voice. "We have to do something. Because I can't keep watching her like this. Her Juggernaut is killing her, and plan be damned I will tell them. She would've found a way months ago if it was happening to any one of us, and you know it. If we can't help her, if this keeps getting worse, then I will make them help her."

Kiari breaks into sobs that slowly become muffled when I can only assume Kestien embraces her. "I don't know how to help her anymore, Kestien."

"Nós vamos descobrir isso, irmãzinha. We'll figure it out, little sister." he whispers, a new determination bleeding into his words. They sit for a moment in silence, most likely making sure I don't start seizing before I hear the door open and close again, leaving me to the darkness. It doesn't take much longer before the void swallows me whole.

Chapter Sixteen
Marco

I shoot to my feet as soon as reality comes crashing back into me. Stumbling, I brace against the wall as all my senses return in waves. My hands land on a rough surface, rocks falling from beneath them. The earthy smell in my nostrils is extremely telling, and I am suddenly very aware of the silence. I force my eyelids open, my vision focusing like a camera lens and I see that I am, in fact, completely alone.

"Shit." A string of curses leaves my lips while I do my best to gather myself. I take in my surroundings, simultaneously running a personal check for any wounds. Finding none, my eyes land on a weird pill looking container on the ground next to where I woke up. Curiosity tells me to see what it is. Training tells me to treat it like a trap until I learn otherwise. My default setting is and will always be a kid brother first. It's my way of keeping everyone out of the dark, but it's moments like this when I am what I need to be. When the child I'm very comfortable being is put away. Only the soldier remains. The one my captain trained me to be, and my brother raised.

I walk from the back of the cave, muscles coiled and ready to jump if necessary. When I see light, I hiss at the sting of the sun. How long have I been out? It was night time when Black came to drug us. Something I will not be forgetting any time soon. Coming to the mouth of the cave, I am relieved to have my natural eyesight for the moment as green overtakes my vision. The landscape over what I now confirm is a mountainside is breathtaking and I have to wonder if I am even on the same continent as I was when I passed out. Instinctively I wonder what this place would look like from the windows of a jet. The sea of treetops that bleeds into the shore of ragged grass, rocks, and boulders. I risk the few steps away from the safety of the opening, craning my neck quickly and focusing hard. My pupils dilate and all of a sudden the world sharpens again. At quick glance, I count eight more caves just like this one above me scattered along the mountainside. I make the educated guess that the same can be said for below me. I won't go far enough from the cave to confirm that theory just yet. Instead, I let go of my focus, which reverts my eyesight back to normal, and I return to the safety of the shadows at the back of the cave. I return my careful attention to the container still on the ground where I left it and inspect it closer. I listen for the tell tale tick of an explosive, picking it up when I don't hear it. I don't realize there is even an opening until a soft click and release of air draws my eyes. I turn the container over to see the pistol embedded in what looks like soft foam. Once I have it out and in my hand the first thing I notice feels like a joke. Not only are there no bullets, the magazine is missing altogether, a folded note resting in a slot that looks like it's supposed to hold the clip. I listen to my surroundings as I remove the note and unfold it carefully. The words themselves are enough to launch me into confusion, but the real kicker is the second click and release of air.

A second, smaller compartment opens on the dome side of the device and when I look inside, I see two black rings protruding from the foam. My heart speeds up in my chest, and if I'm being completely honest, my pants are a little tighter. Like a kid on Christmas morning I use the middle finger on my right hand to pull both rings out as carefully as possible. I know exactly what these are before they're even visible, but the beauty that's revealed is enough to short circuit my brain entirely. Damascus steel, rigid like stone, fixed karambit knives. With talon-like blades that I have no doubt in my mind will slice flesh better than scissors cut wrapping paper that almost looks like they just flow from the hilts. I know these knives. My heart crashes against my ribs now as I try to understand.

When we were younger, Max and I went into my fathers office. It isn't like we weren't allowed in, we just weren't supposed to be there without supervision. The reason for that was my fathers extensive knife collection. Something I was always obsessed with. When our father died, my mother gave me these knives with the notion that my father would have wanted me to have them. My brother put them away and was supposed to give them back the day I turned eighteen, but the house was robbed and the knives were never seen again. The fact that they're in my hands now means more than I am willing to admit, and I am the optimist of the family. I can only imagine what the others will say. I glance at the note in my left hand after dropping the canister on the ground.

Accuracy matters.

What the fuck is that supposed to even mean? Cryptic motherfuckers are getting on my nerves, but I don't have time to dwell on it. I sheath the knives in my boots, hearing the fabric tear easily due to the curvature of the blades themselves. Jumping up and down to make sure they won't fall for any reason, or slice my Achilles tendons, I take a deep breath to steady myself. I recall the briefing we had over breakfast, then what Max showed us right before the shit started. After a few more calming breaths, I reluctantly push the button on my necklace, bracing myself for an explosion that doesn't happen. Instead I hear three faint but distinct tones, then nothing happens. I know it isn't faulty. If Max made it, it'll work exactly the way he wants it to. Knowing that for a fact is enough to push me forward.

I exit the cave at a creep, focusing hard to steady my vision. I need to figure out which of the X's I ended up being on the secret map August found. The map in my head isn't near as clear as it probably is in Augustine's head, but I did take the time to memorize the scans Max took. There were four black x's on the mountain, and I remember Black saying we would be placed no less than thirty feet apart. The moment I peek out of the cave's entrance, I realize I'm the furthest from the bottom. The air should be thin up here, but it feels amazing in my lungs and I inhale deeply. The only thing to do now is find my way down this damn mountain. Sliding as close as I can to the ledge in front of me, I lose control of my eyes again, as if they've adjusted to the altitude and space. It would be shocking, but now I can see even more gorgeous details of the island itself. Fruits peeking out of the leaves, the colors of birds and the songs they're singing. If I could die anywhere, it would be here.

Maybe, not the best thought to have right now.

While I'm entranced by the scenery, a bullet zips past my ear. I don't think, I just break into a run, somehow feeling noticeably lighter on my feet. It's like that first shot was the signal to let loose, because the gunshots start ringing out from all directions, echoing off the mountain walls. One thing becomes really clear in my mind, I need to find some rounds for this gun and fast. So I slide to a stop, almost falling over from the sudden decision. Before I can even turn my head to find a place to hide and pinpoint a shooter to take out, the shooters fire into the rocks above and below me. I duck and cover my head with my arms, feeling the PTSD creeping up my spine when I press my belly to the ground. The shooting stops, lighting a fire under my ass with no hesitation. I push off the ground, hauling ass and not waiting for these bastards to shoot at me anymore. The rocks are loosening around me and I know this ledge is about to give. My brother's words slam into my brain, pushing me forward. *"If the gunfire stops, go fucking faster!"*

Just as the shooting starts up again, more sporadically this time, I hear a noise so sweet to my ears I could cry. My eyes locate the origin of sound and relief washes over me so strong I would probably collapse if I was standing still. The rumble of the ledge above me starting to slide forces me to make a choice and I twist on the balls of my feet faster than should be possible without obliterating my ankles. I don't think, because I don't have the time. I just run straight for the edge as one of Max's drones comes straight for me. A small metal box hanging from a heavy link chain. I launch myself at the drone, gripping the chain with both hands for dear life. I know it isn't going to hold my weight, but I'm hoping it will slow the fall somehow. I'm almost right, too. Until I see the first ledge fly by my face. I have too much momentum and am now hurtling down the side of the mountain.

The second ledge is coming up fast, but I'm going to miss it if I don't do something. I start swinging my legs, trying to force myself and the drone forward. If not for the hand that whips out just in time to grip the front of my shirt, I don't know what would've happened. My fight instinct is in full swing, and my adrenaline is rushing too hard not to assume it's a threat and ask questions later. So when my feet are firmly on solid ground, I'm surprised to see Max's wild eyes.

"Did you just ride my fucking drone?" He calls out, eyes wild with adrenaline and clearly not impressed. I breathe a quick sigh of relief that's cut short by the sounds of pistols firing. We duck into a run, dodging as much of the debris as we can manage, careful not to lose sight of one another. Max bellows from behind me. "Grab the damn box!"

I do as I'm told, struggling a moment to undo the clip from the drone that seems to be following me. I finally tear it from the chain, opening it to reveal a very, very unique looking watch and I'm immediately extremely pissed. I've been looking for this particular watch for over a year. "What the fuck is this?"

"Your new watch." He pants as we run. We start to hear yelling behind us as the ground assailants gain on us. From what I can hear there are at least three people shooting at us but I'm not stupid enough to look over my shoulder. "Duck!"

I throw myself into a barrel roll, smashing my shoulder into the ground a few times on the way. I skit across the gravel to a stop just in time to look up and watch Max grab the chain on the drone, spin, and launch it at the space behind us. We watch it fly, and it swings hard into the first man to come up over the ridge. Before I can praise the hit, the drone explodes completely.

161

I stand to my feet with Max's help and dust off my pants. I take a second to try and see if I can spot the shooters that were firing long range artillery. Content to find it clear as far as I can see. Completely out of the original shot line, we take a moment to breathe, but don't stop moving. Heavy breaths overtake us before I slip the watch onto my wrist and let out my sarcastic surprise as I mock him. *"I made you a watch. Fuckin' tech junky thief."*

"I improved your watch. The company that made that piece of shit should be indicted." Max spits before taking my wrist and turning it over. He presses the only button on the watch then lets go. Two quick beeps and the watch face burst open. The best way I can describe the material that crawls out of the watch and up my arm is millions of tiny ants. The substance begins to settle, the weight of it not heavy, but more noticeable on my skin until it settles and solidifies fully on my inside forearm. I can't even voice my praise, but he beams with pride at the look I give him.

"Your micro-tech?" I ask, taking a shot. Confirmed by his nod I ask "You got it to work?"

"I didn't just get it to work. I got it to fucking sing." He blows a chef's kiss before both the screens on our forearms start flashing. "That's the signal for incoming that isn't one of us. I programmed it to read heat signatures within a 300 mile radius"

"Vince said orders were to meet under the mountain bridge, if they haven't run into an ambush like we did that's where they'll be headed." I tap the screen on my skin and the screen starts flashing with two red dots, and a lot of blue ones.

"What do you want to do?" Max asks. I glance again at the red dots. One stays unmoving while the other is moving quickly away from us. "Something's wrong with Augustine. He's been stagnant for too long."

"Let's handle the ones coming at us, give us less to worry about later. I need to find a clip for this gun before my brother pitches a fit and kicks my ass." I say, looking around for places to hide. An ambush will be our best bet for now.

"I should be able to kick your ass as a proxy." he chuckles, nudging me with his elbow. I slide both knives out of my boots.

"Well, I'm not totally unprepared." I shrug, brandishing the weapons for him to see. He sucks in a breath of shock, face contorting into that of surprise.

"Are those the real ones?" he breathes. Stepping closer to examine the weapons in my hands.

"Or a fucked up joke." No time to question it now. We both fall to seriousness, nodding before we each take off sprinting in opposite directions. A row of bushes that hides a piece of ledge and now hides Max's body just enough to not be noticed right away. I take to higher ground, free climbing until I find a sturdy enough branch with a big enough bush of leaves attached. I swing myself up onto it and my heart races a bit faster when the branch gives just a bit, but not as much as it should. Now that I'm up here, I am well aware that the damn thing is not strong enough to hold my weight, but I'm really glad it is. I settle myself and position my body just in time to see a group coming up the path and into view.

"Where the fuck did they go?" the shrill voice of a woman fills the air, and only after do I see her face. Unlike the men we blew up, I recognized her along with two others from the simulation room. A stocky Asian woman, followed by a smaller blond, and a larger, bald male. How had the whole team found one another so fast? I make note of my curiosity for later.

"They went down this way. They're probably heading down the mountain like we're supposed to. Why are we hunting them again?" The man whines, shaking his light brown hair out of his face when they stop.

"Damien has a map of all the rendezvous points to make it out of the choosing game. As long as we can take this group of normies out and bring Damien their heads, then we'll pass together with no casualties to our team. Breezy." The Asian woman's words intrigue me. Max's eyes lock onto mine, but I shake my head, deciding it will be better to listen a little longer.

"What's the big deal about a bunch of powerless punks? They're probably not going to last through tonight without the whole candidate pool gunning for them." The man gripes some more. He's clearly upset about the ordeal, and probably thinks he's the toughest guy out here. "I could take them both out without breaking the pace of my breathing."

Sure, buddy. I think to myself.

"You heard about what happened during the simulation. There's no way they're all that powerless." The quiet one murmurs, earning a scoff from the big guy.

I raise an eyebrow at Max, which he mirrors immediately. Turning back to look closer at Mr. Confidence, I'm even less impressed by the sight of him. He's big in the shoulders and arms, but he doesn't look like the threat he so clearly thinks he is. My brother was twice his size by the time we hit high school. I've learned enough up to now to know that some people here already have these "Juggernauts" the Lieutenant keeps going on about, but as a soldier who is trained to know the threat just by looking at it, this guy isn't setting off as many warning bells as the shrill one.

"I already told you everything I know! Powerless pukes who for some reason are set to pass the choosing game as the secondary team to the strongest unit ever known to the dead army. If we take them out before anyone else and make a name for ourselves on this island then we can take that spot. Our lives among the dead should be smooth sailing after that." She turns on him, lashing out with a handful of claws and tearing three long gashes into his face. "I *fucking hate* having to repeat myself."

I know this will be our chance. I signal to Max with a nod and I don't have to check it's him when I hear three shots. I pounced out of my own hiding spot. I almost feel bad for taking the quiet one out first. She never even got a chance to talk. My brothers taught me how to fight men both bigger and smaller than me, but my sister made sure I would never lose focus on account of my kind heart when it comes to a woman in combat. I catch her off guard when I land with both feet on her back, and waste no time sinking a blade deep in her neck. Looking up, I see that Max has emerged from his hiding spot with his gun trained on the shrill one, having taken out the big guy with three shots to the chest and one to the head for good measure. We turn to the shrill ringleader, Max slinking closer from his side.

Max wants to catch her off guard while she's distracted by me. He most likely sees the fact that she can't be more than 5'0" and looks like she weighs a cool 125lbs which should make her an easy kill. What he doesn't see is the way her skin is beginning to stretch as her muscles contract. Slowly at first, the woman goes from stocky to fucking huge. Muscles increasing in size, limbs lengthening as the transformation quickens like my heart rate. Her voice grows deeper when she sneers down at us while we gawk and stand frozen in shock. "I would have taken them out eventually. My team was decent, but they were too stupid to see the big picture."

She snarls gutturally, her voice taking on a monstrous tone. "At least I won't have to lie about taking you two down myself. I'll be sure to make it quick when I scatter your bones across the island."

The she-beast lunges, but somehow I'm too fast for her as I'm jolted into action. I hear Max letting off more shots but I don't focus on if they hit or missed. Instead my focus is lasered on closing the gap. She wants to come for me first because I'm smaller, they always do. Sprinting straight at her my eyes are so sharp it seems to affect time as I see it. Slowing down my target to the point I can see her muscles tensing, and the way her jugular bounces under the skin of her neck; But it's the click of her shoulders in the wild swings of her arms that catches my immediate attention. Her left shoulder is a weak spot.

I'm aggressively smaller than her now that it seems the transformation has stopped. It's for that reason, I don't have much of a problem faking right and pushing off the earth hard. Before she knows what's happening, I've stabbed both knives in her massive bicep, causing her to cry out and flail. I use the thrashing to swing out and over until I manage to crouch on her massive shoulder. As fast as I remove my blades from her arm I slam both knives downward into the injured shoulder, and her screech is so high pitched next to my ears that I almost let go to cover my ears. Thrashing and wailing like a bull in a balloon shop, she's trying her damndest to throw me sky high. Instead I manage to yell out through the sounds of her madness. "MAX!"

My voice seems to shake him of his stupor. Max takes a step, lining up the shot before he shoots five rounds from her belly to her throat. The fourth bullet stutters the screaming, the fifth cuts them off completely. The body stiffens, rocking once before falling backwards and taking me with her when I am unable to get my blades out of her shoulder fast enough. The impact is enough to pull the blades out and force a groan out of me. "Ayúdame, cabrón! Help me, dude!"

"If I wasn't here to see it…" He trails off, yanking me up with a grunt. "What the hell even was that?"

"If I knew what the hell was actually going on with any of us then this would be so much easier. Wouldn't it?" Dusting myself off and returning my weapons to my boots I let out a sigh of pure exasperation. "We need to find the others. I don't think it's going to be safe enough to meet at the pass like we had planned. The guy said the whole candidate pool is after us and we know fuck all about any of them and what they can do."

"I think you're right. The fact that their whole team was together already has to mean something that can't be good for us." Max says as he checks his device and our surroundings. I check mine too. "It looks like Vince is still heading that way, but I can send him our location when we find a better spot to rendezvous."

Max does something with his fingertips on the device, probably looking for a good spot to lay low and figure shit out. A few seconds pass before he asks, hesitantly. "Are you alright? You did great, but you took out two women."

"I'm fine, no point in feeling sorry for someone shooting at us. I'll admit I feel a little bad for the little one, but as far as I'm concerned this one is a dude in disguise. Did you see how fucking big she got?" I breathe, noting the way the beast's body has started to return to its normal shape and size.

"I shot her ten times! Did I see how big she got?!" he scoffs incredulously. Shaking his head like he is still having trouble believing what just happened, Max walks over to each of them. Picking up the guns they will no longer be needing and removing their clips along with the bullets in the chamber. "We'll take the clips we find. If we're wasting full clips on one person, we're going to need to strategize before we run out of bullets."

He tosses me a fully loaded magazine that I shove into my own gun before cocking it. Instantly I feel just a little better. "What's the next move? We have more incoming."

He pokes at the device on his arm again before my own device pings. I find the coordinates to what looks like a cave just before the bottom of the mountain that has no heat signatures within it. It's our best bet for now, so I nod my agreement before he sends the same to Vince and Augustine. "Eyes peeled. Let's take a good pace. Hug the mountain when you run, not the cliff. I was getting shot at from the trees earlier."

Without another word, we start off again. Listening to the eerie silence of our surroundings, dodging sliding rocks and sharp drops. It would almost be easy to forget we aren't just kids having fun. If there wasn't, you know, a bunch of people trying to kill us.

Chapter Seventeen
Vince

Getting the location ping from Max after hearing that feral scream rip through the air so loud I was almost forced to cover my ears is enough to calm my heart even just a bit. I glance down at it again, trying to get a good idea of just how many of the other candidates are going to try getting in the way of me getting eyes on my family. There's an anxiety in my chest that's making me feel queasy. Something I doubt my younger siblings even realize I'm capable of, but this feeling is as recognizable to me as the love I have for them. When we were younger and it was just Marco and I, it wasn't as bad. More than likely because we were just kids and we were both boys. Then came my sister.

I have a lot of memories of sitting beside her crib with worries bigger than myself for the first time in my life. She was so tiny at first. I would sneak out of my bedroom with a blanket and a pillow as soon as my parents were asleep and curl up as close as I could. I remember getting in trouble for breaking her first crib because I would climb in there with her at first. After that I pulled a chair up to the bars and slept there. The day my mother finally realized what I was doing, I spilled my fears and anxieties with tears in my eyes. I'll never know if my mother understood, but from that night on there was always a chair beside the crib waiting for me. As we all got older Marco joined me, and eventually when our sister was old enough for her own big girl bed the only way we could all sleep was with a baby monitor set up to connect our rooms. The addition of Max into the family just gave me another person to protect, and I never wanted or needed my own room for fear that something would happen that I couldn't prevent or protect them from. I watched them grow up under my protective eye, and now we are in a place where not only are they somewhere I can't reach, but somewhere that I am fully aware there are people trying to do all of us harm.

I shake my head to clear it of my thought spiral, resuming my steady pacing within the cave as I start taking stock of myself. No head trauma, nothing broken, no bleeding, all set. After the forty-five minutes it's taken me to understand this damn watch Max created, I know it's time to get my ass in gear.

I feel the pistol that was left for me tucked into my waistband at the small of my back. They might as well have sent us in here naked with all the good our clothes on our backs would do for us. I can do damage with a belt, any soldier worth a damn can. It's for how long that's the problem. I take a glance at the surprise that was waiting for me in the secondary compartment of the weird gun case that was sitting at my feet when I woke up. They look like any regular pair of brass knuckles, but imagine my surprise when I close my fists and an alloy covers the parts of my fingers that would connect to anything if I threw a punch. Open hands? Open hands make the damn things basically melt into full on gloves. I can't call the strange alloy metal, and brass isn't even close to being pliable enough to move with my hand and do the melty thing.

A noise from the tunnel leading to the outside stops my examination, the switch from curious civilian with a new toy to a soldier. I listen hard and stand as still as I can, the scuff of boots and shifting rocks telling me that whoever it is isn't trained enough to make sure they don't make a sound. Right over left I hide behind a big boulder to the left of the only way in. My fists close, allowing the alloy to cover my knuckles as I ready myself for the inevitable fight. I count my breaths as three men of varying sizes try but fail to sneak up on me.

"They said the big one would be in here." One growls.

"If we don't find him then we're fucked." Another spits through clenched teeth. "I can't stay on this fucking island."

"The boss said whoever kills them gets to leave. We find them, then rip them apart." The first guy turns and a feral smile spreads across my face as he locks eyes with me. His surprise is what costs him giving me the opening I need to use the stone wall behind me to launch myself at him. My fist connects with his jaw and the thump of the connection and the loud snap of it breaking fills the cave and breaks the other two of their trances. I drop my stance just in time to watch the bright blue sparks dance over the shorter man's fingers on his left hand. Changing my tactic to avoid his hand, I block the impending blow by gripping his left wrist and bicep before spinning hard. Wrenching his shoulder out of its socket and forcing a roar of pain from his mouth, the sparks die just before I use his body and throw him into the last man standing. The guy with the broken jaw stirs from unconsciousness and I take the opportunity while the other two are distracted trying to untangle themselves from one another to drive by boot down on his face hard enough to cave it in.

"You son of a bitch!" The short one snarls, hugging his busted left arm to his body while the sparks start to dance on his right hand. The taller one inches away, his brow furrowing over his slate gray eyes like he's trying to set me on fire with his mind so hard that sweat starts to break out on his forehead. I stand ready, calculating all the ways they can come at me when sparky rears back his arm like a pitcher. I weave out of the way just in time for an electric ball blasts at me, blowing the stone behind me apart on impact. My eyes widen in disbelief as he rears back again, but it's clear to me that he's throwing with his non-dominant hand because he's giving away the trajectory. I dodge two more times while subtly inching forward for a takedown and keeping grey eyes in my sights. The next time Shorty rears back, I'm closer than he realizes and park my boot right in his chest. His head cracks off the stone hard and he crumples to the ground in a heap.

Gray Eyes doesn't give me the chance to celebrate before he jumps on my back to try to bring me down, but once you've grown up with my siblings you know how to keep your footing.

Gripping his forearms to keep him right where he is, I jump up and throw all my weight back to land right on top of him. We grunt on impact, but I hear the air leave his lungs in a huff. I roll off of him, whipping out my gun and pressing it to his forehead with my knee in his chest to hold him down. "Who sent you after me?"

He wheezes and snarls angrily but doesn't fight anymore. "Fuck. You."

"You ain't my type." I smash the butt of my pistol down on his nose, effectively breaking it before resting the barrel between his eyes again. "Who. Sent. You?"

"You might as well kill me." he groans. Deciding I don't have time to get the information out of him, I pull the trigger and end him like he asked. Adrenaline coursing hard in my veins, I check the short one for a pulse and find none, but I still put one in his brain to be thorough before swiping their clips and hauling ass out of the cave.

***

The sun is high over the mountain, shining over the valley full of so many shades of green that I wouldn't be able to name ten and be close to all of them.

No debate on beauty.

No doubts about danger.

The note my sister left was vague, but something tells me that there is a right time and place to understand it.

Shields and tanks are the same if used creatively.

Coming up to a ridge, I hear the slide of rocks behind me and immediately hit the breaks. I skid just a bit, twisting around to get eyes on the threat. My fists are up, ready for the fight I know is coming when my eyes land on a guy about my size, with a really punchable mouth turned up in a wicked grin. He sizes me up, trying to hide the surprise at being caught, but I saw it already. Target Mouth rolls his shoulders, holstering his weapon as he starts to advance. I almost laugh, but the excitement for the impending brawl has me so focused I almost miss the vibration under my skin, if not for the way my spine suddenly feels noticeably stronger. I've been training for long enough that not even that distracts me. What does it is the way the earth lets out a sickening crack. The rumble under my skin is gone as both of us look down to the ground under our boots with just enough time for the whole thing to crumble under my feet. Time feels like it doesn't exist the same as I find myself falling with a shower of rock and rubble. How did this happen? I can't just die like this. It can't end here, not like this. I have to find them. I have to protect them. I can't leave them alone. I. Refuse. To. Die. Here.

I hold my breath for the impact, hoping that I can brace the fall somehow. The last thing I expect is to land with both feet on the ground. Throwing my arms over my head, I'm prepared for pain as the rest of the rubble continues to fall on top of me, but the pain never comes. When the crashing and rumbling finally stops, I peel my eyes open slowly, taking in the rubble first while lowering my arms. I'm standing in a small crater, the stone ground around me coming up to mid shin, but otherwise, I'm alive. I'm fucking alive.

The breath I let out is both relief and disbelief. "Holy shit."

A long whistle catches my attention, prompting me to spin and crouch low. Ready for a fight again. Instead of the man with the mouth, in front of me stands two teenage girls. They both look completely different. The paler one is smaller in stature, with dark brown eyes and short, curly light brown hair to match. The other one looks to be just a bit older, with jet black hair pulled up into a small tight bun. They can't be much older than late teens, pushing into their early twenties. I soften but don't dare lower my guard an inch.

"A few more seconds, Dariah, and he would have been dead." The brown haired one says, a twinkle of fascination in her eye when she turns to me. "But if you don't move the bullet *will* kill you."

I dive forward out of the hole and roll just before a round too big for a pistol blasts its way into the rock right behind where my head just was. I whip my head up to see the one named Dariah grab the small one's hand before growling my way. "Come on!"

I hesitate to follow. Uncertain of why they even want to help me in the first place. Another shot slams into the wall no more than a few inches from me, telling me that whoever is shooting at me is shooting blindly, but is trained on the exit waiting for me to come out. The girls stop short of being swallowed by the darkness further into the cave, whipping their heads back and pinning me with narrow eyes.

"We should be more concerned about whether or not we can trust *you*. Now move it!" Dariah barks before taking off deeper into the tunnel. The shots are coming in heavier as the commotion from outside tells me that they've realized I'm not coming out. I let a snarl echo out before taking off after the girls, but as I go I realize that the tunnel immediately starts to narrow. It doesn't take very long before I can't completely stand up all the way, the tunnel itself forcing me to walk in an uncomfortable crouch. Just when I think it can't get any worse, the shrinking forces me to my stomach where the girls are only dropped to a crawl. My claustrophobia is screaming right now, but I'm doing my damndest not to freak the fuck out because I'm too fucking big for small spaces. I slide on my belly through a much smaller opening after the little brown haired one and I release a heavy sigh as I bring myself up to my full height. "We have the chance to take him out, Sue. Are you sure this is the best option?"

I stiffen, palming the gun at my back.

"You know I am." Sue shrugs. "They're our only chance to survive."

"Or our best chance to die." Dariah grumbles before moving farther into the darkness. I don't know how I can even see. It's not completely clear, but for some strange reason, I am nowhere near as blind as I should be in here with how dark it is. I track her for a little while with a scowl, now thoroughly annoyed that they're talking about me like I'm not standing right fucking here.

"Don't mind Dariah. She's just cranky because there's no coffee out here in the wild." She smiles softly, waving for me to follow. Sue waits until I'm right next to her before she starts off after Dariah at a leisurely pace that doesn't match the situation we're in. The silence makes the cave seem smaller to me, so I open my mouth to speak, but am quickly cut off by Sue once more. "We know who you are. Vincent Ronaldo Arrio. You go by Vince. You're 6'7" and pushing three hundred pounds."

"Hey!" I interrupt. It's true, but jeez.

"You are the second in command for your team. When you were younger, you sat beside your sister's crib and told her stories of wild places. When you were in middle school, you went to juvie for beating the shit out of a kid that cut your sister's hair."

"How the hell do you know this stuff? Why are you telling me this?" I back up a step, shocked by her knowledge and the fact that I know she has more of it just by the way she's spouting it off.

"Because I need you to understand quickly that we are your allies."

A snarl that isn't entirely human rips from the dark when Dariah stops to turn on me, getting in my face suddenly as if to try and catch me off guard. I'm not phased by the sudden action, and I realize that I am growing more accustomed to the difference in speed everyone seemed to have. "If you get her hurt-"

"I wouldn't dream of it." I cut her off because I know what she's trying to say. I would say the same, and I have more than once. It's obvious they aren't siblings but they mean more to one another than friends. I can see it in their eyes the way I used to see it in my sister and Augustine. "Look, I have absolutely no idea what is going on here other than the fact that it seems like everybody I come across is targeting me and mine. I just need to get to my team so I can keep them safe and we can find our captain. Did..."

I want to ask if Kaila spoke to them, but I don't want to risk betraying her by accident. The point is irrelevant when Sue speaks up next. "I don't know your sister personally, Vince, but your secret is just as much ours. There are twelve minutes of tunnel left. Your brothers will be coming this way and we can meet them. From there is the tricky part, well, for you anyway." Sue shrugs again. She has an odd way of speaking, and her gaze never settles. Darting back and forth from time to time in an unfocused way. It's more like she's looking *through* everything. Sue surprises me yet again by pulling me from thoughts I haven't spoken yet.

"The probability of you finding answers to your unasked questions is lower when you don't voice them." She sighs, stopping to turn to me. "You're wondering about my eyes."

"I don't mean to be rude-" I stutter, seriously wondering how she's doing that.

"She doesn't like it when people stare." Dariah interjects, casting a sullen look to Sue before answering for her. "She's seeing paths. Her Juggernaut makes her see the possible future, constantly. It's superimposed over her natural vision, which is why her eyes move so much."

I nod, looking at Sue a bit differently. How curious it must be to see things all the time, I wonder. She smiles wider this time, like she is having an epiphany and something brilliant struck her. "The younger two of your group should meet us at the mouth of this tunnel as I predicted so long as we keep this pace without stopping more than once."

"On your lead then." I smile back, bowing rather dramatically. She laughs and Dariah is less than impressed with my antics. We walk and fall into a more comfortable silence than when we started. I watch the way the two of them interact and come to a few simple conclusions. One, that Sue isn't a fighter. Two, Dariah is. Three, these girls are together. And four, I can trust them both.

After a few more minutes Dariah stops, turning to hand me the flashlight and giving me a look I've given my siblings more than a few times. It tells me to play along, so I nod slowly once, taking the flashlight and keeping it pointed at the ceiling while she addresses Sue with a tone so light I almost don't believe it's coming from her. "Okay, baby, it's time for our game."

"Awe I hate this game! It's not any fun!" She whines, stomping similar to a child when Dariah pulls a neatly folded scarf from one of her cargo pockets.

"Come on, Suezoo. Just for a bit." Dahria begs. I chuckle at the nickname, but Sue doesn't seem to hate it.

"What kind of game? Would it be easier if I play, too?" I ask. Sue looks at me for a moment to gauge if I'm serious before bursting into a haughty laugh when she finds that I am.

"You can't play this game, silly. It's the special game we play when Dari'dear doesn't want me to see the ugly stuff twice." Dariah winces at her words and I have to clench my teeth hard not to laugh at her pet name. "If I can make it to the end without opening my eyes, she usually promises ice cream I never get. No. I won't put it on and we have to go."

"Can I make you a deal?" I interjected. "If you can make it with your eyes, and ears covered completely, I'll teach you how to take me down. How's that sound?"

Though she mumbles to herself, Sue still closes her eyes and turns her back to us. Dariah shoots me a grateful look as I tear a long strip of cloth from my shirt and split it in half with another pull. "Okay Suezoo, Vince is going to put something in your ears so you can't hear. Gotta make sure you don't cheat."

"I do not cheat!" she whines, indignantly. After a few moments, we're checking to be sure she really can't see or hear anything before pressing forward. When I finally bring the flashlight down on the path ahead of us, I begin to see the reason for the sharp stench that has been causing my nose to wrinkle and my stomach to turn.

Bones scattered along the ground only mildly warn of what is to come. The smell of old blood and rotting bodies begins to fill my nose the closer we get to the light on the other side. Bodies in varying forms of decay litter the base of the walls. Some look as if they had stopped to rest and simply stopped breathing while others lay with missing limbs and terror frozen faces. I try to count the number of uniforms covering the carnage but there's just too many with and without them. I let my eyes roam up the walls to see crimson and death paint them almost completely. I draw in a sharp breath, almost choking on the thick smell of human feces and destruction when I see what looks like human remains literally smeared on the walls. My stomach hasn't stopped flipping in what feels like too long, and I'm very liable to puke.

"What the hell is this?" I whisper in shock.

"There are tunnels like this all over the island. Bodies piled up from the ghosts of our predecessors." Dariah replies, a somber tone bleeding into her words. "Some people think it's a good idea to wait until the game is over. Finding hiding spots in tunnels, caves, and tree trunks to try to survive the game the cowards way. If you notice how little room there is in here, you realize this tunnel, like a lot of the others, is man made. They were carved out as a way to keep away from the carnage. But this game doesn't work like that."

"All of these were candidates?"

"Most. Some are the prisoners kept here." She replies with a slow nod. "The hurry up and wait plan only works for a few days before someone realizes they can either seal the tunnels, or start shooting around in the dark. Some of the more close combat Juggernauts take the time to hunt at the entrance and stash the bodies in here. Then there are the predators that call the island home, or the prisoners who will likely never leave that hunt candidates like us for sport."

I find myself angry all over again as I come to realize that this was what Kaila had been trying to warn me about. This is a glimpse at what she went through. On her fucking own. "What happens to the ones that survive the choosing game?"

"Kills are racked up like points. Captures even more because it's so hard to keep anyone in line long enough over the days here. So nobody really chooses that option in the end." Dariah continues to explain as she leads with Sue's hand in her's. "Most of the people hired as obstacles, basically just Dead Soldier Convicts who are working on a promise. True death or false freedom if they survive."

"That's…" I'm appalled, but the sadist in me is also highly impressed. "Wrong on every level but that one I suppose."

"You're kinda twisted." It isn't a question, but I let my grin respond for me anyway. She breaths a chuckle, glancing at Sue's hand with fondness in her eyes. This is the first time I truly see her guard lower in front of me. "The exit is right up there. I'm gonna make sure it's clear."

"Wait here. If my guys see you they'll shoot first. If they've been running from someone at all they aren't worried about questions." I unholster my gun and follow the wall without touching it. It doesn't take many steps before I'm able to see out of the entrance that lays hidden behind thick bushes. My eyes are taking a moment to adjust to the onslaught of the sun when I hear heavy breathing and see the backs of two familiar heads. I whistle short and quick, prompting them to whip around until their eyes both land on me. They survey their surroundings before ducking inside with me. Marco looks like he's going to wretch immediately but I cut him off when I pull him chest to chest with me. Our faces are close enough so he has no choice but to look me in the eyes. I point to Sue and Dariah with my eyes and my 'watch your mouth' look. My brothers shoot me a questioning gaze, but I don't get to warn them anymore than that.

"Did you fight Alida and her team or Dannon by himself?" Sue asks rather loudly, the makeshift earplugs still in place. I release Marco and wait for Dariah to remove Sue's blindfold and the cloth from her ears, making sure to keep Sue's back to the visible carnage. Sue's eyes land on Marco with a focus I have yet to see from her. "Good. So you killed her?"

"The big bitch?" Max raises an eyebrow, slapping me on the back like he's making sure I'm really alive. Sue nods eagerly. His reply is simple. "Yes."

"Perfect." Dariah sighs in relief before turning to give me a sympathetic look I don't understand. "You should probably stretch, big guy."

"Guys, this is Sue and Dariah." I introduce them, shooting Dahria a questioning stare.

"It's nice to finally meet you both! But no, seriously, you should stretch." Sue giggles.

"Likewise!" Marco smiles wide before turning back to me for business. "You get ambushed when you woke up?"

"They tried but were too slow to catch me off guard. You?" I ask, ignoring the girls' strange warning. Marco and Max both nod in response. I check my clip out of habit even though I haven't used any rounds since earlier. Max makes it a point to check his before reaching into his cargo pants and handing me a full magazine.

"Took them off the big bitch and her team. Figured it'll help us, these bastards don't go down easy at all." I shake my head and show the three I stole from the men who tried to ambush me in the cave. Max nods in understanding at the same time I catch Marco reaching for his boots. I watch his hands curiously until I see them. Our father's karambit knives.

"Where did you get those?" The question is only partially for appearances, since they can't know Kaila is actually alive and I'm positive she found a way to leave them. A smaller part of me wonders how she would have gotten ahold of them to begin with considering that she was alive when the house got robbed and they were taken. I don't have time to dwell on it now.

"Secret compartment." Marco reaches into one of his cargo pockets and hands over his secret message and I notice right away that the handwriting is not my sister's. "What'd you get?"

"Accuracy matters?" I raise an eyebrow. More cryptic shit. Fucking great. I shake my head and hand it back so he can pocket the note before I raise my hands and show off my brass knuckles and what they can do. "You get anything, Max?"

"I didn't get anything fancy, but I did get coordinates and a note that said 'part one'. I'm betting whoever is watching over us intends for us to head there." Max swipes at his forearm before the coordinate marker pops up on my own device.

"You should have stretched." Sue mutters, drawing our attention. The annoyance on her face is clear. She seems more timid than in the cave. Her eyes dart back and forth over her personal visions, but I notice the crease in her brow like she's worried about what she sees.

"Why should I stretch?" I ask with a raised eyebrow.

Sue points to the air at the same moment a beast like bellow shakes the earth from a distance, too close for my liking. I start hearing the heavy, booming footsteps coming in fast. I look to the boys to make sure they're with me before clicking off the safety on my weapon. Marco spins one knife gracefully, reminding me of our father, before palming it and taking a ready stance. Max has his weapon ready, giving me a nod. I turn back to the girls. "Stay behind us, Sue. Dariah, I'm sure you're capable, but I'm going to ask you to stay behind us anyway so you can keep an eye on your girl. Respectfully."

An expression passes over Dariah's eyes that could be mistaken for grateful, but she masks it too fast for confirmation and simply nods. As we carefully exit the cave's safety, the monstrous roar comes again, this time dangerously close. Sue's hand on my elbow stops me before I get the chance to search the trees.

"This one is just for you, Vince. You can take him." She smiles sympathetically before backing up to stand beside Dariah. I nod, confused and unsure of what she means, but I lead them all out of the tunnel anyway.

The onslaught of light causes us all to hiss, but there isn't time to adjust before the noise reaches our ears again, coming from right the fuck in front of us.

"Lead them out of here, Max!" I bark the moment my eyes take in the beast before us. I risk a glance at Max who hesitates but thinks better than to argue before his fingers fly over the device on his wrist. My eyes lock with Marco, the worried look on his face one I hope I'm not mirroring. I would be real damn stupid if I wasn't afraid. "Sue is your responsibility, Marco. Listen to her until I catch up with you. Find some cover, Max. Marco, get your ass in the trees with her and somebody find our fucking captain!"

"We can't just-" Marco tries to argue, but as my full attention returns to the problem, I see no time to argue because the threat is about to come to me.

"NOW!" I bellow, shoving him in the direction of the trees to get him moving. With a snarl of defeat they all break into a sprint across the large open grass area we find ourselves in and head straight for the tree line. Marco reaches out as they run to pull Sue onto his back and she wraps herself around him to keep herself secure.

Like the cross between a rhinoceros and a man, it scuffs at the earth twice before charging at me with an earth shaking roar. The space between us isn't much, and the speed it's gaining is horrifying. It's clearly trying not to give me a chance to think. Sue said I could take him? Take him where? My funeral? I'm a cool 6'5" but this guy is pushing nearly 8ft tall. Gray skin encompassing his arms and torso like armor and a wild look in his eyes like he has every intention of stomping me the fuck out.

I dive left, but he's so big I almost don't make it out of the way in time. The way he makes a big loop around to redirect himself at me tells me that he can't turn on a dime, but the speed he has is the big problem I'm having as he comes at me again. Can I take a hit from him head on? I ask myself. Suddenly, something stupid comes to mind as my sister's note floats through my memory. I huff out a few breaths to gather whatever courage I've got while bouncing on the balls of my feet and shaking out my arms. Instead of running away like I damn well should, I start sprinting straight for him. I hit a hard right hard when he's close enough and put some distance between us so he can round on me again. I do it again, banking left at the last second. Admittedly, I'm scared shitless to follow through with what I've got planned but I can't keep playing with it. I just need to find my balls.

The beast skids to a stop and turns to me again. His heavy breaths chuffing out of his nostrils so hard I can hear it from where I stand. Looking into his eyes I see the moment he decides he's coming with the intent to end it. Eyes black from corner to corner, like the animal is fully in command over man. I watch the humanesque parts of his body fade into the gray armor of the beast. The horns on his face grow in both size and sharpness and a shudder rocks my body at the sight. I try to think but I'm overwhelmed with what I see in front of me. His body pitches forward until he's on all fours and I'm staring at a mutant sized mammoth of a mother fucking rhinoceros.

That's when a bullet ricochets off one of its horns, snagging its attention from me. The animal's attention and mine both snap to the direction of the bullet's origin. To my horror, Max is shuffling right foot over left foot quickly with his gun trained and his face screwed up in fury. Whatever he's yelling at me is lost in the adrenaline that rushes through me, making my blood start to rush so hard that my hearing becomes pure white noise. I feel the rumble of the earth under my boots before I can fully process the nightmare about to unfold before me. The beast tears at the earth on a direct path at him and everything starts going in slow motion. Instinct takes me over, my body hurdling forward without thought. I can't feel my heartbeat all of a sudden, but I can't think about that now. The words in my head keep repeating over and over as I fight to close the agonizing distance in time. *Hit it hard enough. I just have to hit it hard enough.* I can't hear the scream I let out just before I make contact. I don't know what I expect to happen when my shoulder slams into the rhino man's midsection, but when we both go smashing across the grass the "how" is the furthest thing from my mind.

I don't know how many times we roll hard and heavy before I'm able to dig my fingers into the ground like a cat to stop myself. On my feet quickly, I turn in time to see the thing skidding a few more feet before it thrashes around to get back on all fours. A short but guttural grunt reverberates from him, and his front hooves buck at the ground angrily. His attention is back on me like I want it, with no opportunity to check where Max is because I know this fucker is coming to finish this.

"Not my brother you big bitch. Come at me." I spit.

He charges with single minded purpose, hooves thundering against the ground so hard the earth tears up beneath them. I'm on the move too, but I am done fucking around. The balls of my feet dig down for me to launch into a sprint but apparently, my body has other plans when my first step launches me forward, bypassing about five full strides completely. I'm...bounding. Yes, bounding hard and fast, closing the gap to him way faster than he is closing the gap to me. The moment we clash I lock my right hand over top of the longer of his two horns using his momentum to whip myself around and smash my hip into the side of his jaw. I don't have a second to breathe, bringing my left hand palm down on top of his giant head, forcing it down and causing him to tear open the ground more as we slide to a stop. I'm not done yet, though. With all my newfound strength I yank his whole head toward me while he's still stunned, and I hear the loudest and sickeningly satisfying snap when it's neck breaks. When the body goes limp, I finally release him.

Stumbling away from it, the fight replays in my mind. I search the grass until I come to what I'm looking for. Max stands with shock and awe in his expression, the others standing around him with matching looks as they watch me pant and try to get my bearings. I take a quick last look at the body, noticing that it seems to be reverting back to its human form. After a few short seconds, a young man lays on the ground with his head facing the wrong direction in the dirt. Definitely dead.

When I reach the group I expect questions that never come before I have Max's shirt in my fists to pull him to me. "En qué carajo estabas pensando?! What the actual fuck were you thinking?"

"Estaba pensando que estabas a punto de ser pisoteado por un rinoceronte mutante! ¡Ella me dijo que le disparara! I was thinking that you were about to get trampled by a mutant rhinoceros! She told me to shoot at it!"

My head whips to the side to glare at Sue who just shrugs and says "You needed the opening."

I let him go with a huff and a shake of my head before checking on Marco who just looks at me with a sense of pride in his eyes before asking the only question he is ever allowed to ask me after a fight. "Aces?"

I think for a moment, shooting him a bewildered glance as I start jogging. His chuckle was short but understanding. The truth is I have no idea.

"Max. August?" I asked, hoping to change the subject as we set off at a jog as a group.

"Moving finally. Pretty fast too from what I can tell. Headed our way." he pants. I can see the tree line now only a few more feet in front of us.

"Down!" Marco shouts suddenly. Instinctively, I dive to cover him and Sue, but Marco seems to have other plans. I smash into Sue with the force it would have taken to tackle my younger brother, twisting as best I can at the last second to soften the impact of the fall so I don't crush her. Once we hit the ground, I roll onto my stomach and whip my head around, ready to call out to him. What I see makes my breathing stop, and all I can do is watch and listen in terror.

Chapter Eighteen
Marco

Call it instinct. Call it the ancestors. Call it blind stupidity. I don't care. I haven't been able to reset my eyes since the encounter with who I've been calling Big Bertha. While it is annoying, I'm growing more aware of how much of an asset my new eyesight really is. So when I see the sniper aiming at us from the trees, I just keep going. I have to take him out before he can hurt anyone in this group, and the only way I can seem to think to do that is by the element of surprise.

When my siblings and I were younger, I would always get into trouble for climbing trees. It was easier for me than all the other boys in the neighborhood and nobody could ever climb higher than me. I used to be able to climb until the branches themselves couldn't hold me up, and I made good money taking bets for a few summers. It was easy…but it was never this easy. I started with a single minded mission and now it's like my body has taken over to accomplish it. I jump-well more like launch- myself at the first tree in my path. I planned to get high enough on the first tree trunk to monkey my way up and shoot the sniper. What really happens is that when I jump, I soar straight over the nearest branch and straight to the next tree. My boots touch the large branch but I've got too much momentum for them to stay there. So I crouch into the landing and push off, right onto the tree the sniper is using as a perch. This time I'm ready for it and go right in for the tackle. We fall to the ground in a hail of fists, him trying to fight me in mid-air is a futile attempt when I spin him. He cushions my fall and I hear all the air exit his body in a loud and pain filled 'oof'. I flip him onto his stomach and press my knee into his back. One hand in the hair to expose the neck, and the sharp tip of my blade pressed flat against the carotid artery.

"Move it and lose it." I snarl. I can hear the others closing in but don't look away from the man in my hands right away.

After I'm sure he isn't going to move, I look up to my group waiting a safe distance away. "CLEAR!"

I see Vince's worried expression when he sort of bounds toward me. I noticed the motion when he was fighting the rhino guy. Almost as if he's using the strength of one stride to blow past a few others. It's efficient, but he looks ridiculous. Even more so when I realize that he doesn't know how to stop. As ungracefully as possible, he skids to a stop on both knees hard, bringing one up and drawing his gun to the guy still not trying to struggle underneath me. The others come up after him, but only Max seems to be doing it with any haste. Breathing a sigh when they see I'm fine. I turn back to the guy. "I'm going to let you up now, but you aren't going to fight. Blink twice so my brother can see that you understand."

Vince nods at me once to confirm and I release his head a bit harder than is probably considered respectful. I get up but don't bother sheathing my weapons. The guy stands slowly, showing his hands. His skin is darker than the rest of ours, but his eyes have a strange glassiness for only a few seconds before it's gone. I wonder for a moment if my eyes look as strange as they feel, but the thought is cut short when Dariah speaks in a strong but hurried way. "Name."

"I don't have to tell-" He starts, but is shut up by a large fist to the gut. Vince hates it when people try to play like they have the upper hand. I don't particularly like it myself, but his tolerance for it is nonexistent compared to my own.

"She asked you a fucking question." Vince growls.

"Silas Raynes." The guy answers through a cough.

"Who told you to park it here?" Dariah asks without skipping a beat.

He shrugs smugly. Vince sucks his teeth, rearing back for another punch. "You must really want to get your ass beat."

"Speak!" She calls, stopping Vince short and earning a grumble that I'm positive is anything but respectful. Vince looks to Sue as if waiting for her to chime in, but she doesn't meet his eyes and remains silent as a mouse. She knows something she isn't willing to say, but Vince isn't pushing.

"My captain. Alida Hee. My orders are to take the small fish on the mountain." His nonchalance is forced, but he's good at the mask. The name of his captain rings a bell. Sue said Big Bertha's name was Alida. I meet Max's eyes with a knowing smirk that Silas catches. "What happened to Alida?" The worry is evident in the words but it doesn't quite reach his eyes the way it should.

"I killed her." I shrug, hoping to get a rise out of the guy. He's too passive.

"Good job!" he says. His demeanor melts into a relaxed attitude, confusing us all. Except Sue, who just casts a bright smile and a quick wink my way. We all look at Silas completely baffled, but he doesn't wait for any more questions as the mask he was just wearing falls away.

"You don't seem too heartbroken about your captain." I spit.

"You're right about that. Those of us that aren't activated as a pre-standing unit are thrown together. She was only my captain by name. No love lost." He scoffs. "Listen to me very carefully. Alida was working for a guy named Damien Mikhailov. Supposedly they are, well I guess were, together and had been for a long time. Damien and his brother Ascher are dead army royalty with a contact on the inside who has been feeding them information about rendezvous points and the other candidates. The word around is that the brothers are working for an unnamed dead soldier who's been said to be making promises under the condition that you and yours never make it out of this game. They've got everyone gunning for you, including the criminals trapped here."

"All of a sudden you wanna talk a lot?" Vince sniffs the air, unamused and unimpressed. "How about you tell us something we don't already know?"

"How about the fact that the reason you all have a target on your back is because of the rumors that you're set to be the second most powerful unit in the dead army roster? Most of the time, teams are ranked after the choosing game based on the points we rack up for kills and captures, but whoever is feeding Damian and Ascher their information seems to think that you four are basically just here to prove you belong in the spot you seem to have already."

"Has that ever happened before?" Max inquires.

"Not even once." he shrugs.

"So who the hell is the most powerful unit? We heard Alida mention them earlier. What's the deal with them and why would we be ranked behind them with no idea what our juggernaut abilities are or if we even have them?" My confusion seeps into my tone as I scan our surroundings.

"As the story goes, they conquered the island. There was a huge uproar years ago when they were ranked, because nobody has ever held the Z on their breast before them. They say each member has more power than has ever been recorded. That's all most people know, which is why there's such a fuss over a bunch of nobodies coming out of nowhere, set to take the spot behind them." Silas offers plainly.

"So how do we know you aren't just going to kill us in our sleep and collect on these promises being handed out." Dariah speaks finally, asking a question I think everyone but Sue wants to know the answer to.

"Look, we're all just trying to survive out here. Most of us who grew up in the deadlands know each other, and Alida was always a power hungry bitch. Until now, she was my best chance at getting out of here. I'm not a ground fighter, I'm a sniper. My eyes are like long and short-range sights. I can take out a threat with my rifle like brushing my teeth, but I'm shit at close combat. I've never agreed with what they're planning to do before they leave this island."

"So why tell us any of this? Why let us catch you?" Max inquires.

"My cousin. I can't tell you his name or why he sent me. I was given very specific instructions not to say anything unless it was necessary to get you to believe me. I'm on your side, and you can use all the help you can get."

"Say we don't believe you." I ask with a raised eyebrow.

"You don't have to believe me." He scoffs. "But you can believe her."

Silas points to Sue, who still hasn't said a word. Her attention is split between this reality and another, a phenomenon I have questions about, but choose to ignore for now. Dariah must not like all the questioning gazes on Sue because she makes quick work of using her body as a shield to block Sue from our view.

"Nobody here is going to hurt me, Dari'dear." Sue finally speaks, resignation and exhaustion in her tone. She takes a second, sidestepping Dariah and pausing to choosing her words carefully before answering. "Silas is meant to help us. As far as snipers go, he's one of the best. Plus, his loyalties are sound as they come. I trust him."

"Do you even know him?" Max snorts. She doesn't reply at first, returning to her silence for a few heartbeats before turning slowly to him.

"I don't know you either, if you want to get technical about it." Her snarky tone causes both Dariah and I to snort. Vince doesn't even try to fight her on it, which is the real shock of the evening. Instead, he turns his safety back on and shoves his gun back into his waistband at his back. I don't holster my knives yet, but I do relax a little. No matter how confused I am, I'll always take my cues from him and Augustine. "We have to get out of here. It's starting to get dark and we are about to lose our daylight advantage."

"Advantage?" Vince grunts before starting to move further into the trees, following the map on his wrist. Silas follows, and his shoulders visibly relax a bit when he does. The action itself makes me feel just a little better, but I'll be keeping an eye on him just in case.

"The wildlife." It isn't just Silas who answers. The girls do too, making a shiver roll over my skin. Only Dariah continues.

"The wildlife here is different. It's like a cesspool of government experiments gone wrong. Only the government didn't have anything to do with them."

"They aren't just island animals either. Bears, tigers, jaguars, fuck. Even the birds swarm at night. The criminals on the island tend to stop their hunts when the sun goes down because of them. My dad used to tell me stories about this shit hole." Silas says the last part more to himself.

"What about August?" I ask in a whisper to my brothers.

Max doesn't get a chance to answer when Sue gasps and comes to a stop, Dariah beside her. We all stop short, turning to her with heavy breaths filling the silence around us. Sue gulps, eyes focusing. She's afraid, and every hair on my body stands on end. She turns to me but she isn't looking at me, she's looking through me. Every instinct starts to scream, and I turn as slowly as I can. I hear the rustle of the bush mid turn but I don't stop. Then I see it. A massive bear. A grizzly with dead eyes and blood-drenched fur. The way it stalks out of the foliage on all fours, hot breath coming out in loud grunts is one thing, but its size has me fighting not to pee a little.

"Oh fuck." Silas groans. "You should've let me go back for my rifle."

"Don't. Move." Sue's voice is so cold it could stop a war. All of us freeze as the bear rises onto its hind legs. We have to crane our necks to see the underside of its jaw, but shots ring out right when it opens its maw to let out a roar. However, instead of the bullets causing blood to erupt from the leviathan's fur, purple smoke blasts from the wounds and wraps around its body until it's fully encompassed. I hear Sue's sigh of relief as she whispers "Thank the gods."

I turn just in time to see the only thing I truly believe to be the most terrifying on this floating rock of bullshit. Augustine on the fucking hunt.

Chapter Nineteen
Augustine

I've been on a single-minded mission from the moment my eyes opened in that cave. The pistol at my waist is one that knows my hand better than my own dick. The surprises don't feel like surprises anymore, more like deliberate signs of something beyond our knowledge. I know for a fact the others are getting them too. What surprised me was the chip in the secondary compartment of the weird case I found beside me, along with a note that read 'part two'. Now, with the chip in my pocket and a little more blood on my hands than when I woke up, I'm tearing through the trees at a speed I only recognize from my nightmares. Most of my time since waking has been a blur, like I've taken up the passenger seat to my mind. I know I've killed two candidates after finding them waiting for me outside of my cave. I also know, the next three people I killed after that were not candidates. I didn't give them a chance to speak before I shot them, so I don't know where the hell they came from but I do know that all of them were desperate to take me out for some reason. Once they lay dead at my feet, one of them taking an unfortunate plunge over the side of the mountain edge after I planted my boot in his stomach, I was better able to control the need for blood I felt.

The sun has started to retreat over the horizon, painting the earth in a warm glow of oranges and purples. A beauty I wish I could appreciate even as I beat feet to make it down the mountain. I haven't encountered another living person since the sun began to set, but I've jumped and dodged plenty of dead ones. When I finally make it to the bottom of the mountain I allow myself a moment to breathe and check the map on my wrist. I have to hand it to Max, the device he's made is unlike anything I've ever seen in or out of the military. I see them clustered together, their tracking points blinking steadily with the two others they've had following them for a while. At some point a third heat point was added to their group, and it makes me wonder if they've picked up strays or locked down prisoners. I decide on a path to them, stretching my legs so I can continue when a gurgling sound in the distance catches my attention. It's the sound of someone dying but trying their best to hold on. I see the body lying in a heap on the ground about 10 feet away and am about to walk over to finish the job, but shrill screeching and the sound of wings beating quickly gets closer. I don't have to search long before I see a black cloud of birds diving directly at the body. Wet screams fill the space between us as I watch in rapt fascination while a misfit flock of different species of birds strip the meat from the bones of the unfortunate victim right before my eyes. If my stomach wasn't so strong, the contents would probably be on the grass. When the flock disburses back into the sky, only bones remain, and I take that as my que to run faster.

The sounds of other animals start to pepper the air in the distance, and I feel like I now know why my path was clear coming this far. The grass fades beneath my feet as I close in on my family, ready to find a way out of this godforsaken hell hole. As I run I finally hear them, and a whisper starts at the back of my mind as I get closer. *The bear. The bear. The bear.* It's ominous and not my voice, but it's one I've heard before. The same sensation I had while taking the battery settles over me. I can see sharper, and breathe easier, and I just know I could run for miles at this pace without much effort. Dark thoughts begin to flash through my mind. I don't know why I'm thinking like this. There is so much violence and the deepest parts of me crave it. The scent of bad intentions rides the wind, but the source is unknown for now. I just keep moving until I see exactly what I'm looking for.

I unholster my gun and take in the situation before revealing myself. My boys and three new faces stand frozen stupid staring at the gargantuan grizzly bear before them. The beast's chuffs turn white as the air blows from its nostrils.

"Awe fuck." the dark skinned new guy groans. "You should've let me go back for my rifle."

"Don't. Move." The smallest one warns obviously in a cold tone. I crouch, both hands on my gun as I inch closer. The monster grizzly pushes off of its front legs, rising to its full height on its hinds, letting everyone know it's about to charge. I shuffle faster until I'm close enough and raise my gun to line up my shot. The moment it opens its maw to roar, I let three shots fly. Two go wide when the big bitch thrashes his head, but the one that lands right in his chest bursts into some kind of purple smoke. I slam to a stop a few feet from my team. We all watch in complete shock as the smoke seems to solidify somehow, spreading along the animal's fur-like paint. I watch the animal's eyes widen, panic taking over its facial features in an almost sad way. It tries to thrash, but as the body becomes fully encased, still visible through the unexplainable color, the beast is still trying to fight against it. Until it just stops moving. The substance seeps into the fur until the only remnant of the color still visible is in the eyes of the bear.

"Thank the gods." I hear the little one's relief as the grizzly drops back onto all fours.

I move slowly until I'm planted between the bear and my people, locked in a staring match with the creature. Into eyes that could very well hold the depth of galaxies. I don't know how long we stand there before the feeling of understanding passes over me, and I somehow know the creature isn't going to hurt us. Instead, it sniffs softly and just turns and trudges back the way it came. I continue to stare in the direction it goes, but I hear the group walking over to me carefully. When everyone is a few steps away I finally turn. Blood is the first thing I notice, the second is that none of it is theirs. The third, fourth, and fifth are huddled together just behind Vince. I let my eyes drift over the three of them, dragging in a subtle breath through my nose. Jasmine tells me that their intentions are good. Enough for me to ignore the burnt sugar mixed in for now.

"Augustine?" Something about the way Vince says my name snaps my senses to some kind of normal, but not the normal I started with a day ago.

"Everybody else get jumped?" I shake my head to try and clear the last of the fog, unwilling to waste any more time standing still. My brothers exchange a glance I won't bother with just yet before nodding, but the sad look the smaller girl gives me makes the hairs rise on the back of my neck. There's a knowing in her shifting eyes and subtle hints of the sweet apricot smell of sympathy "I've dropped five. Not all of them were candidates I recognized."

"Two." Max checks his clip.

"Three." Marco eyes me.

"Four. Only one of which was a candidate. From what we've learned, the Island houses criminal juggernauts like some kind of fucked up exile jail." Vince gives me a look I can't decipher but the scent of his concern tells me enough as he moves to introduce the newcomers. "Captain, this is Sue, Dariah, and Silas. So far it seems these three are the only ones on the island not trying to kill us."

"Well, I can only assume that since you aren't sucking dirt with a bullet between the eyes we can trust you three. Whatever trust means here. Can you all hold your own?" Silas rolls his eyes, which grates on my nerves. The disrespect on this kid is palpable, but even though there is all this burnt sugar in the air, there's no melted rubber scent. I'll take the wins where I can get them and get answers when they matter later.

"I'd be able to do a better job of it if I had my rifle. Which is hopefully still in the tree the little primate over here knocked me out of." I pause, glancing up the tree to my left. Even the first branch has to be ten feet in the air. I make a note for later. Marco is the monkey of us all, but he would've had to get up to the first branch. I've seen him free climb some nauseating places and if anyone scaled a fifty foot tree, it would be him.

"Dariah can, but Sue isn't a fighter." Vince answers for them. I brace for impact.

"I can speak for myself. Thank you very much." Dariah snaps.

"Sorry." His apology is quick, but the terror filled shouting off in the distance is enough to get us all moving again.

"Well, if the rifle is something you can afford to leave, then leave it, and let's go. If not, one of us will have to go with you and I'm not exactly okay with that." I check the clip on my weapon, freezing slightly when I notice no bullets are missing.

"I'm not leaving my rifle and I don't need a babysitter." Silas growls indignantly.

"I wasn't giving you the option." I say matter-of-factly.

"I'll go get it." Marco surprises all of us when he speaks up.

"Absolutely not." Vince shakes his head, but Marco isn't hearing any of it.

"I'll be faster without worrying if goggles here can keep up." Marco sheaths his all too familiar knives before stretching a bit. I raise an eyebrow in question of the 'goggles' comment. "Kids got scopes for eyes."

"We're like the same age!" Silas argues, clearly peeved at being called a kid.

"Alright already!" Sue shouts. "You two will have all the time in the world to argue about whose dick is bigger but we don't have time for that right now. The night is on us and we've already wasted enough time listening to you all bitch."

"You all keep talking about the night, but I'm more concerned with the flock of feces looking to put us on the chopping block right in the daytime." Vince grumbles, incredulity bleeding into each word.

"You still don't understand." Dariah sighs. I turn to give Marco the order to stay put, but when I look to where he was just standing, the little shit is nowhere to be seen.

"Oh, he's been gone." Silas chuckles at the look of confusion that passes between the three of us.

"What the fuck?" Max gasps. Vince is already vibrating, cracking his neck before stomping in what I can only assume is the direction Marco just went.

"Did I not just say I wanted us to stay together. Where the fuck are you going?" I say, stopping Vince when he tries to stomp past me. He brushes me off, earning a bewildered look.

"I'm not leaving him alone on this goddamn island." He growls. His path is set until Sue surprises us all yet again by planting herself right in front of him, arms akimbo, and the force of a woman on her face.

"No." She barks. Vince visibly solidifies in place. I, for one, am shocked. "Marco is doing exactly what he needs to be doing right now. If you keep coddling him like a baby brother instead of treating him like the soldier he is then he is going to die. We have other things to worry about."

"Unfortunately, she's right." I sigh in frustration. "I watched a flock of birds strip a body to bones before I found you guys. The animals aren't something we can ignore if they're all the size of that bear we just saw. We need to find shelter for the night and get some sleep under our asses before we make any moves."

Max might shit himself holding in his laughter at Vince getting scolded by someone a quarter of his size. Sue waits until Vince gives her a tense nod of understanding, staying in place to calm himself and more likely trying to convince himself not to go anyway. Satisfied, Sue steps around him to face me again. "You have the chip?"

What she's talking about almost escapes me completely until it clicks that I still have the memory chip in my pocket. I slide it out of my zipper pocket along with the note. "Anybody have an idea of what 'part two means'?"

Max is already bouncing on the balls of his feet with a hand out for the chip. I drop the small device in his palm and watch him, for lack of a better description, feed it to the device on his wrist. I eye Sue. "So what is it that you can do exactly?"

"I'm what one would call a seer. And before you ask, Captain. There are some things best left unspoken and only so much I can say without changing what I see." she replies with a small sheepish smile. I roll my shoulders in an attempt to conceal the shiver that rolls through my spine. I watch her eyes dart for a couple of seconds before I hear Max snicker.

"What is it?" I ask, my gaze flipping over to my tech gremlin.

"Right now? It's putting a location marker on our maps, but it's different from the one left on the note I got stating 'part one'." He sounds amazed. I've heard the tone on a few occasions, almost all of them were times of his own works.

"What does 'right now' mean?" Silas scoffs. I see his left pupil dilate so quickly that it stuns me from speaking. At the same time I remember what Marco said before he disappeared, Silas stiffens. His reaction sets the rest of us off, Dariah moves Sue behind her while Max and I block them.

"Right now, means we should go. Like, right now. You can't fight Damien and his brother. Not tonight. We have to move." Sue doesn't wait for us, instead, she takes off to the right at a dead sprint, Dariah right on her heels. Max looks to me for a decision, but I see the hesitation on his brow to go after them. What surprises me more is to find Silas also waiting for my go-ahead. I don't question it, instead, I grab a still-seething Vince by the collar of his shirt with what should have been a thud. At least a smacking sound. Instead, I have the shoulder of his shirt wrapped in the palm of my almost dramatically sore hand. Instinct buries the questions for now and I take off after the girls, the boys right on my ass.

As we run, Sue calls out in breathless haste. "We have to get to the location on the chip. If we can get there we'll be safe enough to figure shit out for a little while!"

"Max, take the lead." I bark. Effortlessly, Max pulls in front of both the women, taking point.

"What about-" I know the ending to the sentence Vince doesn't get to finish because I'm wondering the same thing. "He'll meet us there!" Sue calls out, panting at an even pace. We run strong and hard long enough for the sun to give its last light of dusk. The sounds of collective ragged breathing around me bring to my attention my own breathing. Which is still steady, as if I haven't been running for what feels like forever. After a few more feet, Max stops so hard his feet almost go out from underneath him, our devices buzzing hard. Sue's voice comes in calm, but the panic behind her panting is obvious to me when the strong scent of licorice permeates the air around her. "Oh shit."

Before I can ask her what's wrong, my device vibrates more consistently as dark red heat markers start to pop up around us. At the same time, I start to hear the cackling of hyena popcorn through the air. Max, Vince, and I share a grimace and plant palms to weapons. The cackles come again, but then so too do the sounds of victims fill the air as we watch blue dots that I can only assume were other candidates start to disappear. All of a sudden the scent of gasoline and cinnamon slams into me, the force of Sue's panic and horror heavy enough to send me straight into a coughing fit as it burns my nose and throat.

Not. The. Time.

"Shut up, Augustine." Vince shakes me like I'm doing this on purpose. I manage to stop coughing as I adjust to the scent of her terror thickening, but the voice in my head begins to grow louder and more restless.

They're coming. Let me out. Let go. Give in. Stop fighting.

"Augustine." Max's breathy whisper is a plea as I double over and clutch my skull, gritting my teeth in an attempt to keep this growing feeling at bay.

Stop fighting. Stop fighting. Give in. It's time.

I hear the sound of weapons being drawn as the crescendo of static takes over my ears. Then I hear the rustling from all sides of us as the voice within me roars

'ENOUGH' and It's like it all just snaps. Something is different about this time. It isn't like blacking out, instead, it's like I settle into my own body. The heartbeats I hear make my mouth water, and that alone is new and unsettling. I know that there are six hyenas surrounding us, but I don't feel an ounce of worry about them. I do feel some for the rapidly approaching Marco. In my conscious mind I know he shouldn't, nor has he ever been able to run at the speed he's gunning. Even still, when Marco stops beside me like he just appeared there, I catch the way his pupils are almost nonexistent. Marco tosses the strangely modified sniper rifle at Silas who hugs it like a child with a teddy bear.

"We have to go, right fucking now." Marco doesn't wait for us to ask questions. Instead, he maneuvers Sue onto his back without her permission, but she goes willingly and without protest. Dariah, however, looks like she is about to rage, but is stopped when Marco cuts to her. "Stay on my ass!"

The rest of them don't bother waiting for more of a signal before they're all taking off in his dust. Nobody notices right away that I don't follow. The snapping of twigs and cracking of fallen tree branches being crushed turns me around just in time to watch the first snout emerge from the shadows of the forest behind me. Then comes another. Then another. When they're all visible, I notice right away that the left eye on what looks to be the leader of the pack is missing. In its place is the ugliest scar, like the eye was gouged out by someone or something even more fearsome than even this beast. My wife always had a fascination with animals. Predators are her secret expertise. Right now? Every single hyena fact that ever left her mouth is rattling around in my brain.

Did you know that hyenas hunt in packs?

Did you know that a hyena's bite force is eleven hundred psi?

Did you know that hyenas hunt mostly at night?

Now, my wife will be the only woman I will ever love, but right now I wish I didn't know any of that shit. The scarred one snaps its jaws, a warning of an impending attack or a taunt before one I'm not sure. The two on its flank let those damn cackles loose, and they're so loud they echo in the air. Or at least, that's my first thought until my wife's voice infiltrates my psyche once again.

Did you know that a hyena pack can have anywhere from six to a hundred?

My heart drops all the way out of my ass when that realization is further confirmed by more heartbeats, too many heartbeats. The fear in my mind and the fear in my chest don't match, and that same instinct that keeps finding ways to take over is comfortable right behind my ribs. My head turns slowly to the left, but I am painfully aware of the movement to my right. I'm surrounded, and that knowledge doesn't scare me as much as it should. The scarred leader snaps and snarls again and I surprise myself when an equally savage roar rips its way out from my chest. The sound blasts from my chest, the force alone rocks the trees I can see. Unlike the bear, where I somehow knew that the animal wouldn't hurt me after I shot it with the questionable bullets in my gun, I know deep in my soul that not one of these psycho dog cats can touch me unless I allow it.

I want to destroy them. Rip them apart for daring to come after what's mine. Show them what a true beast can do. Who the real predator is.

The sound of Silas getting into position with his rifle doesn't escape me, and neither does his cocky whisper. "A little to the left please."

Chapter Twenty
Vince

By the time we realize that Augustine isn't following us, it's already too late to go back for him. My heart stops when I turn to see his spot beside me empty and curse myself for not having noticed in the first place. Sue slows to a stop, realizing August stayed behind before slamming her hands into Silas' chest and pushing him toward a tree. "Get up there and help him!"

Silas doesn't question her, slinging his modified rifle onto his back and producing two knives. I know he's about to use them to climb, but I also know it's going to take more time than we have. Shoving him out of the way, I clasp my hands to give him a foothold. "You better be able to shoot straighter than you can see."

Silas gets his foot secured in my hands before scoffing. "Just get me high enough you giant."

"How's this for high enough?" I grunt before launching him upward and getting a sick sense of satisfaction from the surprised squeak that leaves him. He catches a branch and hoists himself up. Silas makes quick work of settling into position and lining up his sight. I hear him breathe out a warning I'm almost positive won't be heard for August to move a little to the left. My doubt quickly dries up when in the next breath Augustine puts right over left in a calculated single step to the left. Silas doesn't waste any time before I hear three whirring clicks. The way he maneuvers the rifle is pretty fucking cool, but it's what happens when the bullets reach their targets that drops my jaw to the floor. Each bullet not only tears straight through a hyena, but when the trajectory stops, all three animals fucking explode. I don't mean like a head one way and a big chunk missing out of a shoulder or two. I mean these beasts splatter over every tree trunk and grass blade visible to the eye. I gawk, the forest stunned to a pause. Except for Marco. Marco glides down from the high branch he'd perched on to keep Sue safe, something I guess he can do now along with the running at breakneck speeds.

"You were shooting at us with that!?" Marco snarls, incredulously. Marco makes moves like he's planning to jump up there and beat Silas' ass until Dariah grabs his arm to stop him.

"I missed, didn't I?" Silas calls down to us as he realigns his sights. My little brother tries to take a step at the tree again but I grip Marco's shirt, hailing him back beside me before they can get into it.

"Not the time." The hyenas that survive begin to cackle in a crescendo. The sound itself is unsettling, but it's the sound that doesn't match that sparks something inside me. It isn't fear, more like the desire and need to slaughter being awakened within me. The roar starts as a snarl and builds until it rumbles over the earth. The sound rolls over my skin, seeping in to rattle my bones. Marco clutches his chest beside me, but when Silas lowers his rifle I realize the sound is coming from Augustine.

"Mother of Gods." Silas gasps in disbelief as I settle my gaze back on August in the distance. When his growl breaks into a roar, it's like the very pits of hell have opened their maw to send their cries to the sky. The power behind it, the pain. Every single drop of anger. I have no doubts in my mind who the sound is coming from, but even in the sound, there is something deeper. A voice that isn't heard, but I can feel it in every crevice of my body. My soul knows it somehow, a calm stretching over me similar to coming face to face with an old friend I haven't seen in years.

It says "I have woken"

It says "I am vengeful"

It says "I am king"

The overwhelming urge to cry out in return almost has my knees buckling. My jaw clenches and I lock eyes with Marco, the same tightness in his cheeks as mine. And just like that, we're running toward him. Marco takes off ahead of me, but

I'm not far behind him this time as we watch the horde of hyenas descend on our captain. It only takes a few hard strides before we run straight into a swarm of absolute dismemberment. Literally, Augustine is tearing the animals apart with his bare hands, using his gun as a supplementary device on those he can't reach. The strange phenomenon that happened with the bear starts happening with each hyena that gets hit, only this time, the color is deep red. While the purple tendrils brought calm to the bear, this red has each one hit turning on their own in a fit of absolute rage. Marco and I watch in rapt amazement while they all seem honed in on our captain. If I had to hazard a guess, I would say there are about fifty four-legged bodies all desperately trying to return the ass-whooping August is giving them, but the man isn't letting up.

"Well, should we try to help him?" Marco asks, shouting over the concert of obliteration.

"Help him? What the fuck are we supposed to do? I don't even know how he's doing this!" I shout back. We share a look, both of us knowing that we will absolutely be going in. I groan reluctantly. "Keep close. We'll take out the stragglers together."

The sounds of limbs breaking and jaws snapping around me is deafening. I glance over for confirmation, only to spot the fast-approaching hyena that seems to have finally noticed us over my little brother's shoulder. There should be panic in me but there isn't, even as I push him out of the way to face the creature head-on. My focus zeroes in and instead of reaching for my gun, instinct drives me to pull back my metal covered fist and aim right for the fucking nose. About halfway through the punch, I say my goodbyes to the bones in my arm, but when my fist connects with its snout, I feel absolutely nothing. The hyena, however, feels a lot. Like the crunch of its face caving in, and the three of its friends he barrels straight through.

"What the fuck!?" I actually squeak in bewilderment, a sound I can honestly say I've never uttered in my life.

I hear another coming, but when I turn to face the hyena coming at me, it's too close to pull back my fist again. I barely feel the boots stomp up my back as I brace myself for incoming death before Marco is sailing through the air with his knives held ready to stab. Landing right on the animal's face, Marco slams both knives down into its skill. The hyena's eyes roll up as it dies and my eyes widen even more when Marco removes his blades quickly and runs over the dead animal's body. I watch him power slide toward the next beast coming, slice through the front right leg of another hyena, then whip his arm around to stab the bastard straight through the underside of its jaw. He whips around to face me as if surprised by what he just did.

A mutual agreement passes between us with a nod, and then Marco goes right and I go left. Of the about fifty that started, twelve are left with the way August is mowing through them. I wish I could watch so damn bad, but right now I have my own shit to worry about. My punches are landing like battering rams, sending anything I hit with a closed fist shooting at least fifteen feet. Silas seems to have snapped out of whatever stupor he was in, because hyena start to explode left and right. Two manage to get on me, but it takes minimal effort to snap one's neck and split the other's jaw wide open. I don't know how long it takes, but anything is better than death at any speed. The outcome of this chaos is nothing I would have even dreamed possible, but I am nothing more than grateful. I roll a hyena off of me to see Marco covered in blood and insides with a hand outstretched to help me up. I take it, panting while we search for Augustine the minute I'm standing. I don't have to search long, because he's headed right toward us with not a single spot on his body untouched by destruction.

"Captain?" Marco asks, cautiously trying to figure out if August even realizes what happened just now. Our answer is just as baffling when he turns to us with clear eyes, calmer than I've seen him in years.

"I can't explain it. So don't ask." He say's before we can even think to ask what the fuck just happened.

"Are you okay?" I question instead, dragging my eyes over the aftermath around us.

"I'm fine, Vince. I saw you both just now, too. It seems our reasons for being here are a little more warranted than we thought originally." His nonchalance earns a side-eyed look from Marco and I both. "I need to get cleaned up. How far are we from the location?"

"Not far," Marco's answer is slow at first as he eyes the captain a little more. For the first time in a few hours, I can see that Marco's eyes have returned to normal, and I didn't realize that I could miss the warmth of my brother's eyes. He continues, less skepticism in his tone. "The others are right over there."

Before we can head toward where we left the rest of the group a long drawn-out whistle reaches our ears. Silas comes closer tentatively, rifle slung over his back with a confidence I kind of understand now. "That was fucking disgusting."

"No kidding." I grumble, looking down at my blood soaked clothing and picking a piece of what I'm pretty sure is brain matter off my pants.

"What kind of sniper are you?" August eyes the man like he's the strangest person in the group right now.

"A damn good one." Silas smiles wickedly. "I made my rifle myself, it's one of a kind."

"I should give you a one of a kind beating for aiming that shit at us." Marco snarls.

"Like I said before, I missed. Use that bird brain of yours and think about why that is. Because what I aim at, I hit. And here you are, still breathing." Silas is about to get punched in the mouth, and I might let it happen because of the simple fact that he's getting under my little brother's skin. "Anyway, Max took the girls ahead to the point the chip was leading."

"Let's get to it, then. We all need some sleep, and a damn plan." August seems to be right back in captain mode, which I am happy about. Well, as happy as I am allowed to be covered in sinew. I look down at one of the dead hyenas, reverting to my comfort for cooking in my mind.

"Has anyone ever tasted hyena before?" I ask offhandedly. Marco grimaces but swallows back his bile before handing me one of his knives. I get to work cutting a meaty leg from the body, making quick work of it.

"There's a stream on the way to camp, we can get cleaned up before Sue sees us covered in shit." Marco suggests as I start dragging the severed leg behind me.

Night has fallen completely, and even though we shouldn't be able to see, we can. The night air cools the blood on my skin, making the itch start in parts of my body I hope never itch again. We stay silent as we trudge through the forest, and it doesn't take much time for us to see the stream Marco spoke of. Silas veers off to join the others as we stop on the edge of the freshwater, exchanging looks before Marco slowly begins to laugh. The sound doesn't match the circumstance in any way, but the louder he gets the harder it is not to join him.

"What the fuck are you laughing at, chuckles?" Augustine asks, trying to hold back his laughter but failing. It takes a moment for the little fucker to calm down enough to brace one hand on his knee and point to us.

"We look like used tampons!" He wheezes. August and I groan into a well-earned laughing fit, looking at each other and breaking out into it harder. After a while we get to work, peeling off our shirts and pretty much falling into the water. We take the time to scrub off as best we can, wash and ring out our shirts, and even scrub off our boots a little. Once we're clean, we jog the rest of the way to where the other's have set up a makeshift camp. We hang our shirts to dry over the trunk of a fallen tree close by then join the others huddled up around a small fire.

I catch Max's expression while he meets us halfway and I know somehow he got a front-row seat to the massacre. Silas has posted himself in a tree above us, low enough to watch and still participate in the pending conversation. Dariah sleeps with her back against another fallen tree with Sue nestled against her, snoring lightly. Max stands and leads us away from the girls and closer to Silas' perch, plopping down on the ground with an expectant look as we all drop down to join him.

"So," Max begins. "Super speed, super strength, and whatever the *fuck* that was that you did, captain. Can we stop sweeping shit to the back burner now?"

There is a hesitation that passes through the three of us that ultimately breaks into resignation. With a sigh, August opens his mouth to start, but Marco beats him to the punch. "I don't think it's super speed. I mean, I'm fast as fuck, sure. But it's more than that. If I focus, or if I'm in a serious situation, I can see fucking everything. Like far, and clear."

"What makes you think it isn't all about speed?" I ponder.

"When I'm running hard enough I don't feel like my feet are touching the ground. If I jump, it's almost like I'm weightless." He braces for a reaction, but what could we give him? If he decided to tell me he could shit rainbows, I would have no choice but to take him at his word. I trust my brother, and we can only work with the information we have.

"Is that everything?" I push.

"The breathing. I'm sure you've all noticed, but I'm finally getting past how weird it feels. I have to breathe through my mouth. Only my mouth. If I try taking a breath in through my nose it fucking hurts. I mean it really hurts. It happened the first night in the deadlands. I was panicking and no matter what I did I just couldn't take a deep breath. I was scared shitless until….until I heard a voice tell me to breathe through my mouth. I found a note on my desk that night along with some ear plugs. I don't know how it got there, but that night I plugged my nose and its like it reset the way I breathe."

"That had to have sucked ass. The notes seem to be a recurring thing for us." Max adds. He doesn't mean anything other than what he says, and I know his curiosity is exactly where it needs to be. However, I can't help it when my heart rate spikes a little, guilt seeping into my chest. I try to ignore it, bringing my attention back to the boys only to be met with Augustine's knowing expression. I have to fight the gulp because all of a sudden this forest is too damn small. What makes it worse is that he only eyes me long enough to let me know he's coming for me next.

"Whoever the hell keeps leaving bread crumbs for us is a fucking asshole that really needs a kick in the dick." Marco grumbles. *Or a punch to the tit.* I think to myself, holding back the snicker. Max shifts uncomfortably, his hand coming up like he's about to start biting his nails. A nervous habit he has when he's overthinking something.

"Out with it Max." I urge. He drops his hand, realizing what he was about to do and sitting on them instead.

"So...I've always been good with technology. If there's a computer to hack, I can hack it. I've been able to read binary since I was four and I started coding a year later. When the group home got me tested, the doctor said I was a genius. Only...I'm realizing now that it might not be that simple."

Nobody speaks, allowing him to get this off his chest. "Technology...talks to me. I don't mean like with an actual voice, I can't translate what it says or anything but I just kinda know what it's saying."

He hesitates for a moment, sighing as he removes the memory chip from his device and holding it between two fingers. "I can tell that this chip has a location activated switch embedded in its programming. I can tell that in its code is a kill switch that is meant to activate if anyone other than me gets ahold of it. I also know that whoever coded this chip knew my coding signature well enough to make sure I was the only one who could get into it. All without having to insert it into my device."

"That's insane." Silas interjects from his perch. "Fucking awesome, but super creepy."

"Who invited you into the conversation?" Marco sneers.

"Proximity." Silas shrugs, continuing his watch. We ignore him, unwilling to feed into their animosity anymore tonight.

"What about you, Vince?" The question is loaded, but I know damn well it's directed at me. And coming straight from my Captain.

"Well, I hit like a nightmare." I make the attempt at humor to gauge August's reaction, but he doesn't twitch but the corner of his mouth and I have to fight not to fidget and give myself away. He's looking at me like he can see straight through me, and there's never been a time I wanted to spill my guts more than right now. "I don't know. I feel like I could both stop a tank and be one if I needed to. My heartbeat gets really slow, and I might not be faster but I am pretty indestructible. A hyena got me with its teeth earlier, but it didn't even break my skin."

"And?" August asks, cooley.

"I can't really describe it, I haven't had the chance to explore it any more than what you've already seen." I dodge his digging, swinging the conversation away as slickly as I can manage. "Doesn't seem like mine is much different than yours though. From what I can tell at least."

His demeanor is so different from when this all started. Sitting in front of me is the man I secretly idolize, not the shell my sister left behind. His cocky demeanor is calm, collected, and there is nothing in his eyes to tell me he isn't rearing up for a trump card. "I don't know about that. I'm coming to understand that my Juggernaut isn't like anybody's. Unless you guys have a voice in your head. Do you roar?"

His pause holds so much weight before he says the one thing that makes me want to walk off a bridge. "Can you smell emotions? Good or bad intentions? Can you smell a lie, Vince?"

I freeze at the implication. Marco and Max exchange wary looks, scooting away as subtly as they can. August and I don't fight often, because when we do, we break things. Sometimes it's glass, sometimes it's bones. Right now, it's my will to live. I'm coming to the painful realization that my sister really doesn't know what his Juggernaut is, because she wouldn't have fed me to the lion himself if she did. By some gracious miracle, a crunch of dead leaves and sticks breaks the stare down I'm losing and calls all of our attention to the source. Sue's tired eyes meet us in the dark, the smallest hints of moonlight shining through the canopy of trees that cover us all. There's something deep in the way she looks at each of us, saving August for last and settling on him for a beat longer. I watch his reaction to her, knowing the information that has come to light. He softens, respectfully, but not much until she speaks.

"You all need to rest. Silas can handle the perimeter for now, Dariah and I will take second watch because you all need more rest than we do. We will be safe for the night as far as I can see. The game isn't over yet." Augustine visibly stiffens, and he takes a methodically slow breath through his nose. Sue closes the distance between them, coming to a stop right in front of him. Sue's eyes don't remain still, a phenomenon that I can see we are all getting used to. She speaks softly, directly at Augustine. "All pieces and players are coming into place. The unknown will be revealed sooner than anyone is ready for. For now, all we can do is rest. While we have the chance. Your answers will come to you. The patience and loyalty you have will be well rewarded."

Max and Marco stand up, dusting their pants off before walking over to where Dariah is now visibly awake and watching Sue. Sue follows them with a last look between us, leaving me with Augustine. We stand at the same time and I turn to face him, knowing better than to just walk away. Our conversation isn't over, and I won't get anywhere by trying to just get out of it. His next words stun me a little, but the relief they bring is amazing because it's his way of telling me he's dropping it for now. "You know what's gonna happen when I find out what you've been hiding the whole time, right?"

"Will it save my ass knowing it'll be worth it? Or that I didn't have much choice in the matter?" I ask, my last futile attempt to save my own ass.

"Not even a little bit." He snorts humorlessly, shooting me a sly grin I've seen a million times. The one that always sucks when it's pointed at you and not someone else. August's face drops back to a serious expression. "Something's coming that Sue isn't willing or able to tell us about. We need to be ready. I'll drop this for now, but you better hope you get the chance to tell me before I have to figure it out myself."

We end on that note, finding a spot with the others and getting comfortable in the grass. Marco and Max are fast asleep already, and it doesn't take long before my lights go out with one final thought on my mind.

He might actually kill me for this.

Chapter Twenty-One
Augustine

My body is still except for the steady rise and fall of my chest. I know it lays in the grass, surrounded by my brothers and the few friends we've managed to make, but my consciousness is somewhere else. Back in that space of ominous smoke and dark color, only there is no purple and my wife is not the one staring back at me. We stand locked in a battle of wills. I've never seen his face before, but I know it like I know my own. The deep galaxy eyes, the sunken face. Such anguish written in his features that reflects my own true feelings. This is who shares my body.

Without speaking, the man begins to circle me. Assessing as he does, his smile growing wider. His teeth could cut by accident, all sharp edges and points behind his split lips. As he assesses, so do I. This man is the culmination of fury. The power behind him is familiar, and volatile. Slowly he takes on my form, but his major features stay the same. Razor teeth and galaxial eyes. His voice is unnatural when he asks "Do you know who I am?"

I don't respond, so he comes to face me once more. "Do you know *what* I am?"

I grit my teeth and he chuckles to himself, both amused and impressed with my ability to become mute. "You can continue to ignore my presence, but I am here. I cannot leave anymore than you can cease to breathe."

"Why don't you cut the shit and answer the questions you know damn well I don't have the answers to?" I snarl. The savagery of the smile that spread across his lips is akin to cold vodka. Smooth, with a wicked bite that would send a shiver down a weak man's spine. I am no weak man, but I straighten my spine anyway in preparation for an attack that never comes. The next time he speaks, it's my voice I hear.

"The name I once had is not important, for in this lifetime it is yours I share. I have been with you from the moment you first opened your eyes in the world and in every moment after. I have waited. I have watched and listened. I have learned."

"What have you learned?" I ask out of pure curiosity. He chuckles, but even if it's my voice, the sound is broken and sounds uncomfortable.

"Where to begin?" He says hollowly. "You see, I have lived more lifetimes than would be possible to your naturally skeptical mind, but it is this lifetime that fascinates me the most. Not for the technology. Not for the cultures that have risen since time began, but because of you and those with which you surround yourself. It enraptured me from the very beginning."

"You don't make any fucking sense." I snap.

"And you don't fucking listen." He drolls. I snarl. He snarls savagely. "Pay attention, because I will not repeat myself and we do not have the time to slink around things anymore. Every choice you have ever made. Every path you have taken in your life has led you to me. Here. To this moment. At three years old, you were walking with your mother through an airport with a teddy bear in your hands when you came across a baby crying in a buggy…pardon…a stroller. The mother was flustered, her frayed attention shifting between the unruly desk agent and the child who wouldn't stop fussing. At three years old, any other child would have gone about their mundane existence, but you? You waddled over whilst your mother wasn't looking, handed the baby your bear and held her hand until the mother finished with the desk agent and realized there was a little boy soothing her child to sleep."

The confusion must show on my face, because he scoffs and then continues to spill moments of my life I never thought twice about until now. "At seven, when your father abandoned your mother for a secret family, you held no anger the way another child of the same age would have. You packed his things, left them on the front lawn, and proceeded to take over as the man of the house. You taught yourself how to mow the lawn, you kept the house in pristine condition, and you dutifully took care of your mother without being asked. You made sure she ate, slept, and had time for herself. You gave her the opportunity to mourn a relationship without mourning your own. You maintained the highest grades of all your peers, kept out of trouble, and made it your mission to excel in places others your age would have rebelled."

"At thirteen, you decided you wanted to go into the military. You asked your mother to send you to a military school because you wanted to grow up and be a Marine. Unbeknownst to you, your mother had just gotten the diagnosis that would kill her years later." He says this solemnly, and I clench my jaw in memory of my mother. "When she passed away, you were forced to live with your uncle and you took the move in stride. You were moved to a regular school where you got yourself into trouble for the first time for throwing yourself into a fight where the victim was unprepared to defend themselves. That summer, you were forced to attend classes in order to catch up on the things you needed, where you then met a woman who within the first meeting showed you she was able to match you in mentality and drive."

"Don't talk about my wife." I spit. The amount of information he's given until now hasn't shaken me. But her memory is the one thing I will not tolerate being picked apart.

"Do not defend her from me like I have not loved every version of her across the millennia." His words startle me, his fury mounting quickly and coming out dripping in pain. "You know nothing of the agony it took to get us here. No clue as to what lies ahead, for the both of you. It is time you accept your place, and my help. Stop being childish and let me out before you get us all killed."

"The both of us? My wife is fucking dead!" I push back into his space, but he doesn't budge until moments later. When he does, he backs off with a sigh and a shake of his head.

"You have never been stupid. Don't act like it now." He murmurs so quietly I almost don't hear what he's said. He doesn't give me time to speak after my sharp intake of breath. "The events are unfolding at a faster pace than ever before. Your awakening has triggered the decisions, and they will come now as they always do. Hold your ground. It will all make sense very soon."

My eyes snap open, the paralysis from sleep fading quickly as my surroundings come into my awareness. The soft swish of soldiers on the creep catches my attention and finger's brush mine on either side. It's a subtle signal that Max and Vince are awake and ready, keeping the backs of their fingers close enough to my own so that I can brush my knuckle down against Vince's to signal him to go for those ahead of us, and up on Max's to signal behind. We take three breaths, allowing the ambush to get closer before we spring into action.

Vince sits up in a flash, firing his weapon twice.

Max's arms go over his thrown back head to shoot from a lying position.

I drop my gun from my right hand to my left, throwing my arm straight out over Max's body to shoot the assailants coming from that side. I don't need to look over my shoulder because I can hear the thunk of blades landing in chests to the right of me. Marco's up too.

We burst up from the ground as a secondary wave comes through the trees. Before I can take out the guy who appears behind me, Dariah jumps down from the tree above, snapping his neck and riding his back down to the ground. Every time I shoot, a color takes over the victims they hit. Purple holds them still while the red turns them on each other. By the time they stop coming, ten are dead on the ground around us. I glance up to see Sue watching from the tree above. "A warning would've been nice."

"I wouldn't let her on account of the ambush." Dariah shrugs. "She knew you'd notice anyway."

"Where the fuck is that goggle eyed punk?" Marco gripes, removing his blades from two bodies.

"He went to relieve himself right before they showed up."
Dariah spits. Silas comes out of the line of bushes a minute
later, dragging three bodies unceremoniously behind him and
dropping them beside the others.

"Nothing like getting jumped with your dick in your hand."
Silas grumbles angrily.

"Just one hand? Tough breaks." Marco sneers. Vince and
I share a look and an eye roll.

"It's too early for a pissing contest." I warn. "Since we're
up, let's check them for any useful supplies. Vince, see if you
can get the rest of that leg cooked before we break down this
spot. Silas, get your ass back in that tree and scan the
perimeter. Marco, you too. Separate yourselves. I don't have
the energy to listen to you two bitch."

"Copy." They all chime in unison. I walk over to Max,
watching from the corner of my eye to make sure Sue gets
down from her spot with Marco's help.

"Talk techy to me." Max barks out a laugh at my humor,
not looking up from his device as he maps out the best route
for us.

"Looks like this was a scout group. If I had to wager a
guess, it would be that they were meant to take us out while
we slept. These people keep underestimating us and it's
specifically insulting." He begins, taking another moment
before sending through the next location pin to the rest of us.
"This is the next place that the chip wants us to go, but I think
we should keep an eye on the fact that the rest of the human
heat signatures seem to be moving like they're convening."

"Are we worrying about another ambush?"

"Not from what I can tell. The location we're headed to is
in the opposite direction they're all headed. I wouldn't worry
about the candidates but on the way to where we are going it
looks like a cluster of people waiting to road block us." He
explains. I nod, leaving him to his tech.

"Sue, how's the day looking in your eyes? Anything you'd
like to add?" I ask calmly as I sidle up to her and Dariah who

are watching Vince make something out of nothing. Before I can get to them, Sue gives Dariah a quick peck on the cheek and stands to pull me away from the group. When we're far enough for her liking, I watch her face fall to seriousness and her eyes settle completely on mine.

"You saw him?" She whispers. I startle slightly, eyes widening just a bit as I stare at her for a moment before I nod. Sue releases a breath it seems like she's been holding. Her shoulders relaxing under relief. "Good. Everything is going the way it should."

"What's that supposed to mean?" I growl, my exasperation mounting quickly. "If you know something, I need you to tell me because I am out of my fucking depth here, Sue. I can't protect everyone if I don't know what's coming."

"I don't think you understand how much this power I have sucks. I want nothing more than to tell you everything I know and see, but I can't. Ever. Not even Dariah knows what I do. She trusts me. I need you to trust me." Sue's plea has a desperate air to it that kinda breaks my heart. To see the future, every possibility, and be forced to rely on the actions and choices of other people for something horrible to be prevented.

"I'll trust you, kid." I relent. "Let's get some food in us so we can move out."

I start to walk away but she catches my hand before I can get too far. "When the time comes, don't let your anger ruin the chance to have everything you've so devotedly waited for."

"I don't know what that means, but I'll keep it in mind. Thank you." The smile I offer her is good enough to have her skipping back to Dariah even if I know it doesn't reach my eyes. Vince juts his chin toward the meat on his forest-made spit when I come back to the group. Everyone eats quickly before we break down the makeshift camp and snuff the fire out. As soon as we're satisfied, we head out. The group falls silent as we go, the only sounds besides that of the forest around us are our mingling breaths and the soundtrack of footfalls on grass, dirt, and branches. The trek is almost calming. Soothing in a way that lulls me into comfort.

Time passes and the forest passing just feels endless before I catch Sue falling behind us once again. I signal for everyone to stop, our panting breaths fill the space between us as I allow everyone to rest. "Max, how far are we?"

"Not far. But we should stop to set up camp before we get there."

"Shouldn't we all be a little more concerned with the fact that we haven't seen a single candidate or island prisoner since the ambush this morning?" Silas asks aloud with his hands on his knees to catch his breath. "Just doesn't seem right."

"I hate to agree with him," Marco says, breathing just as even as me. Neither of us looks as though we'd been jogging for hours like the others. "But he's got a point. We haven't seen any sign of anyone for hours."

"Isn't that a good thing?" Vince groans. I give him a dry look that he waves off with a wince.

"We should keep going. At least for a little bit longer." Sue's implication has us all sharing a nod, Vince and Max groaning like dying mules.

"Let's go boys. No time for sissy sounds now." Dariah finally enters the conversation and I finally notice how at peace she looks. The constant running should have her panting like the boys by now, but she looks like she hasn't broken the slightest sweat. The boys suck their teeth at her but straighten up and nod their readiness to me.

By the time Sue calls us to stop the sun is beginning to set once more. The colors begin to bleed out over the sky and the savage sounds of the island filter through the trees. Vince and Max drop to their backs on the ground with equally pained groans. Sue's knees buckle, forcing her to lean into Dariah's waiting embrace. Silas drops down beside a tree trunk, pressing his back to it to the trunk of it trying to calm his ragged breaths. Marco chuckles quietly, jumping up into a tree and surveying around us for any dangers that may be close enough to be concerning.

Taking pity on the group, I get to work building a small fire. In an ideal situation, we would have tools to build an underground fire to divert the smoke to keep people from spotting us, but nothing about these last two days have been ideal. Once I'm finished, Dariah volunteers to hunt us some food, I don't argue on account of the excitement I scent from her. Sue takes a seat beside me, bringing her knees to her chest while her eyes dart over the possibilities in her vision. The silence between us stretches on, the rest of the group slowly gaining their bearings and making their way over to the fire. Night falls quickly and completely before Dariah returns with a handful of rabbits. Vince gets to work stripping and cooking them, soft conversation passing through the group like this is any old camping trip. I feel the niggling of the being within me start to scratch the back of my mind. Not like a warning, but more of a reminder that he's still here.

"You're a good man, Augustine." Sue says suddenly, forcing the group to still.

"What makes you say that?" I ask, clearing my throat of the emotion welling up. Sue doesn't speak for a while, as if gathering the right words.

"When I was a little girl my mother would tell me a story passed down to her by her mother and so on for as long as you can imagine. The story of Ryn and Kyn." Her voice softens, like her mind has gone far away as she continues. "They were lovers, their fates woven like the thickest and most unbreakable branches ever known. Those who knew them, would speak about their love for one another as if it was something so unattainable, yet written by the gods themselves. Ryn was known as the mother of many. So caring and kind that the people followed her unquestionably. She fed the hungry, tended to the sick, gave home to the wild, and gave shelter to those without. Kyn was a savage man.

Hard of heart and mind until the day they met. She taught him to fight far better battles than the ones he sought, to love more than his sword."

"They spent years together. The life they built talked about throughout the lands until they were named King and Queen of the exiled. Those cast out of their homes by their rulers who refused to see them as people were taken in by Ryn and Kyn without question. Kyn built homes and schools, Ryn raised gardens and held sickbeds. The kingdom thrived under their love and care until the years passed and people from all over began defecting from their tyrannical leaders to pledge their loyalties to Ryn and Kyn."

"Unfortunately, the lovers attracted the attention and ire of a tyrannical King who was known for employing dark sorcerers in his court. The tyrannical king paid a great sum to have a sorcerer cast a curse on both the lovers. His curse was never known, but her curse drove her mad. Kyn was forced to watch Ryn die slowly as she descended into the insanity cast upon her." Sue stops for a deep intake of breath, all of us riveted by her story. "On one of Ryn's final days, during the last bout of sanity she could muster, the two of them took a final walk of their kingdom. Kyn led her to a flower garden he built for her where she could spend her dying moments in some semblance of peace. In the garden there was a woman, battered and bloodied on the ground. Ryn and Kyn helped the woman to a sickbed where Ryn nursed her back to health and patched her wounds. Unbeknownst to them, the woman was no ordinary being, but a goddess sent to test them. The way my mother told me the story, she said that the Goddess bestowed gifts on each of them individually, but her lover who was a god of great power bestowed a separate gift over the both of them. Nobody knows what the goddess gave them but the god wrote their love in the stars stating that for so long as the stars burn, so too will Ryn and Kyn's love for one another. So long as the sun rises in the morning, and the moon in the evening, they shall be blessed to meet again and again and again."

"Woah." Marco and Max breathe.

"Why are you telling us this?" Vince asks, feigning boredom even though he's just as enraptured with the tale as I am.

"Because," Sue shrugs before looking me dead in the eyes, "I want you to remember it when the time comes."

***

An eerie feeling in the air jolts me upright and out of sleep. Marco, Vince, and Max all burst with me, more alert than awake at first until they realize there is no danger around us that they can see. I search for Sue and Dariah but only see empty grass where they should be. "Where are the girls?"

Vince jolts, his head whipping around in search of them as if we missed them in the small campsite somehow. Max starts looking for them on his device, but the grimace and mounting scent of potting soil worry makes the pit of my stomach drop out of my ass. Marco's voice leaks through my panic and we all turn to see exactly what he's looking at.

"Guys." Silas' modified sniper rifle hangs from his perch by the strap, swaying in the wind. "I got money that says Silas doesn't take a piss without that thing."

"No no no no no. Fucking damnit!" Max snarls.

"What?" Marco, Vince, and I produce our weapons, checking chambers, and reloading bullets while Marco spins his blades like a pro. I am once again taken aback by the fact that my gun has no bullets missing. "Somebody's trying to hack my shit from the outside!"

"Can you stop it?" I ask.

"Stop it?! They fucking activated the kill switch in the chip and fried my goddamn system!" Max is infuriated as he reloads his weapon, the scent of it radiating from him only just overpowered by the worry and concern permeating from us all. I turn to snuff out what's left of the fire but am stopped when the wind changes direction. Mildew, rusted metal, burnt sugar, and melted rubber all at once force me to inhale sharply through my nose. My back stiffens, Marco's head snapping to the tree line around us for just a moment before we all share a look. Within a split second we've all turned so our backs are pressed together. "How many?"

"Too many." Marco and I whisper as bodies start walking out of the dark. I count at least twenty in front of me, which doesn't bode well for the count I can't see. My senses sharpen, the being within me offering some kind of twisted support as all the hearts beating become clear in my ears. The crowd parts, soldiers and what I can only assume are criminals who call the island home move out of the way for none other than the Russian prick with the snakelike eyes.

"Captain?" Vince grinds out through clenched teeth.

"Wait."

"Put the guns away, boys. Let's have a little chat." Damien drawls cockily. None of us move to put our guns down. Damien snickers and the sound is backed by a hiss. "Razoruzhites', ili ya prikazhu im vsem strelyat', kapitan. Disarm yourselves or I'll order them to shoot, captain."

I grit my teeth, fully intent on chancing a firefight until the voice in my head kicks up.

Do it. Now.

I only hesitate a second more before I make a show of putting my gun on the ground. I hear the rough growls from the others as they follow my lead. Damien smiles like he's won some kind of prize before waving a soldier forward to take our weapons off the ground. The next few to come at us bind our hands behind our backs, all the while I refuse to break eye contact with the snake eyed man. Once our hands are secure, Damien closes the distance between us, getting in my face to speak. "I am going to enjoy watching her play with you and the rest of your pathetic lot."

I take a breath, the being within speaking with me to create an otherworldly tone from my lips when I say "Ya budu naslazhdat'sya, smotrya, kak tvoy pozvonochnik otdelyaetsya ot spiny, kogda ya ego vyrvu. And I will enjoy watching your spine separate from your back when I pull it out."

The boys and I are pushed forward and all but dragged through the forest until we reach a clearing with another man waiting in between two tree trunks. This man is like a carbon copy of Damien, only he's missing the snake eyes, in their place are ice blue dead ones. Damien walks over to meet with who I am assuming is his twin, giving me the chance to communicate with my brothers behind me. I clear my throat, knowing without a doubt that they'll have their attention right where I need it. My fingers move quickly to give a short message. Hold Steady. Three different but distinct grunts meet my ears, letting me know that they understand just in time for us to be pushed forward once again, straight into an awaiting jump point invisible to the eye.

Walking through the other side, it's clear that we are still on the island, only now, we're completely surrounded by heavily armed candidates and criminals alike. I feel the boys press their backs to mine in an attempt to keep eyes on all sides. My eyes dart over the faces and features of everyone before me until I find exactly who I'm looking for. Sue and Dariah are drug forward, both girls have some bastard's hand in their hair clutched hard enough to make them both wince in pain. Silas is being held between two burley criminals in ragged clothes. He's jerking in their hold, visibly enraged and rightfully so judging by the swelling on his left eye.

The crowd opens, a woman walking through and I'm startled by her appearance. The woman looks like she could blow over with a strong enough breath, and she could use some sun but I'd be afraid she'd go up in flames with how pale she is. She walks on long, lanky legs until she stops a few feet off from us. Damien and his twin meet her there, the twin taking her hand and pressing his lips to the knuckles of her skeleton like appendage. I don't bother hiding the cringe on my face.

"I'll spare you the introductions, you won't be alive long enough for my name to be of any use to you." She speaks loud enough for everyone to hear, but it doesn't look as if she's straining as she leisurely walks toward us. I size her up, but it's hard to think with the growing growl at the back of my mind. I don't know this woman, but I hate her with a passion. Why do people keep saying that? Even as I think it, the twins chuckle like something is still funny about it. "It's unfortunate really. There you are, living your mundane life in a cell in the middle of nowhere. Set to rot like the garbage you are."

"Is she monologuing?" The eyeroll is audible in Max's tone of voice, but I know he hasn't turned to look. Instead they keep their eyes perfectly trained on their sides, their fingers working the ropes while the makeshift army surrounding us is distracted by the ghostly bitch.

"The sad part is that you don't even know why you're here. I mean, you would think that after all the candidates she's lost that she would've stopped her little shadow recruit operations by now. Instead she continues to send her little bunnies to the slaughter." Who is this woman talking about? "Ah well, I won't waste anymore of my time. Gordon!"

My eyes snap to the men holding the girls when Sue's goon starts dragging her forward by the hair. "I will offer you a trade, your captain for the little one and her girlfriend. The rest of you are small fish, just not big enough to really bite yet. As it stands, I will offer you the same thing I offered the rest. Turn in your captain, and take oath under me. You'll go-"

"Who the actual fu-" Vince whirls around, uncaring of the crowd around us until he stops on a surprised gasp. If I look at him, I'll laugh. Not what we need right now. Prompted by his pause, Marco whirls around, except he doesn't let the surprise stop him from opening his big ass mouth.

"Damn. You should see a doctor or something. Melanoma gotta be a bitch with that complexion. What do you use? SPF infinity?" I could actually kill him right now. Max's snicker let me know they all got a good look before I feel backs against mine again.

"Now," She tisks. I don't like the tone of her voice, even less the scent of bad intentions and the raunchy air of a bad fucking person. "That little mouth of yours is going to get you into a bit of trouble. See, I was going to let you live. Given the circumstances, I can't imagine you would actually be willing to follow a woman whose hands are just drenched in the lies she's woven. However, if you have her smart mouth, you must have her damned moral compass. I simply can't let you live knowing that."

Vince stiffens suddenly, glancing at me even as the smell of worry wafts from him. A million thoughts race through my head when I see the smile creep onto this woman's thin lips. Silas gets loose from his holders at that moment, landing a solid punch to the one on the right and dropping him fast before turning to attempt the same to the other. The ghostly woman removes something from her pocket, a light of some kind. Or at least, I think it is until she makes quick work of shooting Silas right in the chest. Time ceases when a beam of black light blasts at him, and before she even turns around the boy drops to the ground...lifeless. A wave of confusion crosses over the crowd of people, followed by the growing scents of fear and horror. I wait for him to move. Groan. Something....but he doesn't. Silas just lays there. A gasp to my right almost doesn't register, until I hear a struggle.

"Get up you sack of shit!" Marco screams. I can hear Vince holding Marco back, but he's not having it.

"I want everyone to see just how little power they have! Nobody is coming to save you." She starts closing the distance, pointing the strange weapon directly at me with an outstretched hand. The voice in my head isn't louder than my panic at this moment as I try to use my body to block the men I call my brothers. "Nobody is going to remember who you are, or what you were."

"I love you guys." I know Vince is struggling to shield Max and Marco with his hands still tied, and I can sense the fear coming from the three of them as if it were my own. If I die here, I will be with her. But they have to make it out. The woman stops so close I can see the clear silver of her eyes and the evil in them. Her smile is disgusting as she takes her aim at us.

"And the cycle will end the way it always does. With a dead bitch and her broken lap dog!" She yells like the heavens will hear her, but the sound that came from the weapon before never comes.

In fact, only the rippling sounds of gasps meet my ears, and the fading scent of excitement and iron pass before my nose. The ropes binding my hands drop to the ground and I slowly open my eyes to see the last thing I think any of us would've expected. The woman is still standing in front of me, nostrils flared and eyes wide. Horror written on her face where confusion should be. I mean, I would be pretty confused if my fucking arm was suddenly just gone. The woman begins to hyperventilate and panic, but I don't stop staring at the magically cauterized stump she's still pointing at me until the sound of someone sucking their teeth makes their way to us, breaking the spell.

A new face appears. Wild coils descend from the stranger's scalp, deep brown skin, and a lollipop between her painted lips. She is wearing tattered black camo short shorts, and what remains of a black shirt that she seems to have cut into a crop top adorned with the letter Z just above her right breast. A normal man would stare at the obviously nice looking woman, but I can't take my eyes away from a very pale arm, cut off at the very bloody elbow that she holds in her hand.

"Here," she says to the appendage before stabbing the elbow into the ground with a sickening squelch and what I can swear is a bone breaking. Then the unhinged woman places the stick of her candy between the dead fingers like a cigarette. "Hold this."

The surprise amputee finally lets loose a shrill cry of rage, but the panic she's feeling is very clear to my nose. I take the moment to lock eyes with Sue who for the first time through this ordeal has a subtle smile on her face that is also shadowed by relief. "KIARI YOU SNIVELING WHORE!? WHAT HAVE YOU DONE TO ME!?"

"Eu não preocuparia muito seu traseiro feio com o que fiz. I wouldn't worry your ugly ass too hard about what I did to you." Kiari breathes a chuckle through her nose. The heavy notes of her Brazilian accent prompt a low whistle from all three of the men who have taken place by my side. "Black, get your ass down here."

Some of the other candidates begin to stir, some even start to run away. Damien suddenly looks uncomfortable, like a kid about to get caught with his dick in his hand. The pale one's panic supersedes that of everyone else as she whips her head around to look to the sky while clutching her wounded arm to her chest. "NO! YOU'LL RUIN EVERYTHING!"

There is a sound getting closer, like the thap thap thap of a helicopter coming to a stop. Just then a speck appears in the sky, and while it looks like it could be a bird from afar it keeps getting closer. The sound gets louder as the figure gets bigger and faster, until I see exactly what, or rather who it is. Special Lieutenant Black lands with a hard thud and a final flap of his bright crystalline wings. Yes. Wings. While everyone is stunned, he clears his throat while giving us his profile before taking in a lung full of air. The voice that rips from this man's throat is his, but the volume is akin to a loudspeaker. His voice fills the open space of the island to the point that I can't be sure if it's audible from outside, or inside my head. "I have never in my days been so disgusted by a candidate pool before!"

"Black! You have no idea what you're doing!" The shrill woman closes in on Black, but he doesn't even look her way.

Two strides is as far as she gets before Iron bars shoot from the earth around her to instantaneously form a cage with winding bars. The woman is a mask of psychosis at this point when the one called Kiari speaks to seemingly no one, calling out over the screeching in a tone full of annoyance.

"Você está sempre atrasado, Kestien! You're always late, Kestien!" The events unfolding before our eyes have at least me awestruck. I haven't been able to look away to check for the reactions of the others or think about the fact that the army surrounding us hasn't moved a muscle. I watch carefully as Kiari leans her head back all the way, but what I'm not prepared for is the man that rolls out of her shadow like his back was pressed to hers the whole time. The male version of Kiari stands with his hands in his pockets, the same letter Z on the chest of his shirt. His hair is a personality, the curls tighter than his sisters just flopping off his head in a way that just sort of fits the man. Kestien smiles with perfect teeth on display until he unwittingly nudges the appendage still protruding from the ground between them. His disgust is quick, but the look he gives her is a clear *'Really?'*. She shrugs in reply, but doesn't need to meet his gaze to see the question. Twins for sure.

"Unfortunately, due to the current position we find ourselves in as a whole, this Choosing Game is officially over." Black begins to walk toward the now caged woman who has taken to seething and I take a quick look over the crowd. There's a feeling building quickly in my chest that I can't quite understand. A longing? An excitement? Maybe both. I look, and I know that the man sharing my mind is watching through my eyes with reverence. When Black comes to a stop just a step away from the enclosure, his wings snap once, enough to shove the unfortunate one right up against the bars with a heavy pang. "Narcissa Cox, you are a sad excuse for a soldier."

"I would rather be a sad excuse for a soldier than a disgraced angel." She spits. Black releases a dangerous laugh that sends chills through me, then once again his voice splits the air.

"Gordon Johnson and Nino Dover! You have till the count of three to release those women or you will be put down. Three. Two." Both men make the decision to pull their guns out at the same time, and their scent gives them away only to me. It all happens in the span of a finger snap. Before either of them can take the shot, or I can do anything but tense to take a step out of pure protective instinct, the eyes of both men go milky white and they both go rigid.

Their weapons slip from their fingers, making a home in the grass at their feet. In no less than a blink Dariah has a hold of Sue, and even faster is Marco right beside them. He doesn't ask permission before bringing the girls back to us in a rush of air and we all close ranks around them both.

"No!" Sue shrieks, quite childishly if I might add. "We want to watch!"

Vince slides out of the way a bit, but only enough for them to have a view of what's happening.

"Alright, whoever is out there in the audience that has the misfortune of willingly pledging their loyalty to Crapton Cox, do me a favor and just step forward. I'm jump lagged, I'm horny, and quite frankly, really pissed off." A new man has appeared from seemingly nowhere who looks like he might actually be able to go toe to toe with Vince. His eyes have the same milky white color to them, but it doesn't have the same effect on him as he closes the distance between himself and the curly haired twins. Instead of stopping in front of Kiari like I expect, he barrels straight into Kestien, scooping him up in one hand and planting a kiss on his lips that leaves no room for questions. When they break apart, they share a smile quickly before returning their attention back to the crowd. Like them, I check over the crowd, but now I see the real reason everyone is so still. Each person I see has the same faded white eyes. Everyone except the people within the circle. The new savior searches the crowd until his eyes fall on Silas' dead form on the ground. He looks at the body, then at the cage, then the body once more. His next words confuse me. "Alzati, regina del dramma! Get up you drama queen." Just like that, there is a rise to Silas' chest and a stir to his limbs. A groan later, he's standing. I half expect to see the milky white in his eyes, but instead I see red where I once saw blue. "Oh shut up, Milo. I'm nowhere near as dramatic as you. Vediamo se ti sparano al petto con un'aureola, poi potrai dirmi quanto sono drammatico. Let's see you get shot in the chest with a halo, then you can tell me how dramatic I'm being."

"What the hell is going on?" Narcissa screams, and I can practically taste her confusion and ire.

"What's going on, Narcissa, is that you are about to find out exactly how far up the losing side's ass you are." Black sneers in disgust. "I was informed of your treachery months ago, and I must say you are embarrassingly sloppy. Milo was able to confirm your involvement and plans about an hour ago. Every year the choosing game is held, there is a mole placed strategically within the candidate pool. This mole is meant to make sure there is no interference, and that all the candidates are playing by the rules. Usually, due to their aptitude for shadow work we like to employ the service of a Demon or Demon born Juggernaut. Like Silo the Saint Tracker here."

"Silo-" Narcissa's breath catches, the slightest fear bleeding into the air.

"I prefer Silas. Keeps me human." The red-eyed bastard winks in our direction, and Marco scoffs. He's impressed he just doesn't want Silas to know it.

All of a sudden the thunder clap sounds of trees falling breaks everyone's attention and all the clear eyed soldiers choose a direction to search with their eyes. Before anyone can spot anything, Narcissa starts a slow and maniacal cackle that forces me to drag my eyes away from a particular spot between the trees as the crashing sounds grow louder.

Uncaring of Narcissa as she begins to mutter in a psychotic way that makes me believe she's lost it, the three Z unit soldiers find their way over to us. "You leave me no choice. I did what I could to keep it under the radar. You people can never leave well enough alone."

"August." Marco growls low and I turn my head just in time to see him ready his stance. "We have incoming."

As he says it they start coming in from out of the shadows of the trees. Soldiers in full tactical gear, but the tactical gear they wear is lined with the same substance as Vince's brass knuckles. The men all carry modified Ak-47s and the number keeps growing as they file out and around us.

"Well then." Milo takes a deep breath before cocking his head to pop his neck. In an instance, all the white eyed candidates' heads loll forward and each and every one of them drops to the ground. The new soldiers continue to surround us and I see Black close the distance to us without turning around to face us. I assume he intends to stop with us, but instead he spreads his arm out and begins herding our whole group back, leaving Milo and the twins in front of us. None of them speaks, but in a full display of confidence they all start to stretch in place.

A ripple of visible energy begins to form beside them from nothing. It looks like its nothing, and could be misconstrued as a trick of the light. However, when the mirage dissipates, none other than Aurora stands where she most definitely was not before. They all exchange glances and greeting half nods before Aurora throws a wink at me over her shoulder and points to the sky. The strange feeling that has been building in my chest mounts, and the entity within me starts on a low whisper.

The Queen Lives.

The Queen Lives.

The Queen Lives.

A missile has a distinct whistle right before it hits, and I as well as the others brace for the impact our soldier instincts tell us is imminent. There's an impact, and it hits so hard the ground is overturned in a shockwave, sending everyone but our group flying back. With eyes wide we wait for the smoke to clear, and when it does I am robbed of the ability to breath. The cascade of long dark curls pulled back into a tight ponytail sends my heart into a speed that could be mistaken for still. My mouth dries at the sight of her body. I know it better than my own and no amount of time will make me forget a single inch. The tense flexing of her muscles as she drops her chin and drags her eyes over the soldiers who have now recovered and re-forming their circle. Everything else doesn't matter when she starts to turn on the balls of her feet until it finally happens. I finally see a confirmation of my existence. Reignited are the fires of my purpose as dark brown eyes with purple swirling in them settle on mine, and for a moment I consider that this damn well could be a dream. High cheekbones, caramel skin, and lips I've kissed a million times over.

"That's my fucking wife."

Chapter Twenty-Two

Kaila

Something doesn't feel right. An uneasiness settles in my chest as I go over the large file Milo sent to Kestien this morning. The General has been at work for far longer than we anticipated, given the evidence in front of me. I find no surprise in the photographs laid out in front of me on the floor of my bedroom. Government officials, Deadland council members, and ranked officers from all over shaking hands with not just the General, but other high ranking leaders of the Dead Army. Some I've seen, and some I have no recollection of. The colors surrounding me are a litany of exactly how I'm feeling, since no one is home, I feel okay letting them out and feeling them all. I've spent hours going over everything, and some things just aren't adding up. What do they want? Why are they meeting? Too many questions, and not enough patience for the answers.

A crash makes me snap my attention to my open bedroom door, the colorful smoke sucks into my body through my skin, waiting to be used as the weapon it is until Milo's panting form fills the doorframe. I trail my eyes over him, standing slowly as colors in tones I'm privy to bleed from him and into me. Versions of pink, yellow, green, and red. Pale, shock, murky, and crimson all setting me on high alert. The apologetic look on his face makes my heart race as he hangs up his phone, his hesitation palpable as the switch in my brain flips to captain mode. "Lay it on me, Mi'."

"Italy and Cairo bases have been infiltrated and compromised. I just got off the phone with Donnelo Vinelle whose family has been safely evacuated to safe point Seven. They came out of nowhere and they have the ability to dodge our radars completely." Milo begins, moving through the hallway and into our weapons room, knowing I'm hot on his heels. "When everything started to go south with the plans we were making, we started to suspect a mole, right?" He asks, changing his sneakers to steel toed boots.

"Right. We had a few names on the list but nothing we could confirm without alerting the wrong people." I confirm, grabbing my belt off the hook on the wall and securing my holsters. I watch Milo strap syringes to his ankles and around his belt, his weapon of choice.

"I'll give you one guess as to who I saw getting direct orders from Special General Mikhailov himself." Milo grumbles.

"Narcissa fucking Cox." I guess immediately. Milo nods once to confirm before he continues his debrief.

"Narcissa has been behind the loss of every single recruit we've had for the last four years, Kaila. She's been doing the inside work for The General for a long fucking time. I would've found more but I knew I needed to get back here for help. Something about your husband's Juggernaut is scaring the shit out of the bad guys and it's forced them to make a move."

"What move?" He hesitates to answer, but I need him to say it before anything happens. I just know it in my soul that what he is about to say is going to not only change the course of everything, but it's going to fuck up the plan I have worked for the entire time I've been here.

"The twins and Black have already made it to Galla. I called them first. There's an army waiting on that island on the order of that pale bitch and there's another closing in on the mountain on the order of Artur Mikailov. They plan to kill them, Kaila." That's his final word, and enough to send me directly into gear. Aurora appears, and I know he called her too by the fury in her eyes.

"All Jump point units have been ordered to stations." she says as she opens a doorway to the Island. With a nod Milo walks right through and it immediately closes. "On your lead."

I take three quick strides to a panel beside the television we never use and pull it open. The buttons and toggles all have different purposes but the one I'm looking for is a big, bright, red button that takes up the bottom row entirely. I press and hold, making sure to keep my voice as clear as possible. "Corporal code Zeta194. This is Special First Captain Kaila Petras enacting evacuation code 227. All Captains are to report to stations immediately. We have an unknown party incoming. It's about to get loud in here everybody. Engage if engaged only! Your first mission is to get all deadland civilians to their designated safehouses! Clear the mountain and wait for further orders!"

The moment my hand is off the button I turn to Aurora. We lock eyes and a rare smile that promises her ruthlessness spreads across her face. "Give 'em hell, Cap."

The window blasts open after a few intricate hand motions Aurora slashes into the air, turning it into a timed jump point. After training through countless contingency plans, this is one we never thought would actually be necessary, but times like this call for big moves. Aurora disappears through her own jump point on the other side of the room and I know Aurora has made her way to the Island. I back up, taking deep, lung filling breaths until my back is firmly against the wall. I allow myself five seconds to steady myself, to put all my anger and rage into a little box deep in the back of my mind. For four years I have slaved over every detail, every plan and shadow move to bring my family and I back together safely and now…everything is fucking ruined.

With a frustrated scream I launch myself through the portal just in time for it to close behind me. I instantly find myself in the clouds, a special entrance that took Aurora and I months to perfect. I reign in my panic and give the energy to rage, allowing the crimson smoke to envelope my body in a spiraling cocoon. I'm hurtling toward the earth like an atomic bomb seeking to level some shit. And I will be leveling some shit. I knew that bitch was involved, but I never thought she would have been stupid enough to come after what's mine. With the ground approaching quickly, I cross my arms over my chest and lock my legs straight with pointed toes. I feel nothing upon impact. I feel nothing when the dust clears, revealing the dirt field of upturned earth around me. Even as I see the hundreds of heavily geared up soldiers surrounding me, I settle into the lethal captain I had to become to survive here.

Until I feel him, igniting a moment I have feared for so long I instinctively brace myself. I allow my eyes to assess the situation around me, the immediate threat surrounding me and mine. No matter how bad my being is screaming to just look at him. To go to him. We have bigger problems. Big problems that hold no water to the real one. Which is what happens when I finally meet his eyes, and hear his voice for the first time in four years. "That's my fucking wife."

The force and pure will it takes for me to look away from this man is enough to be written in history as nothing less than a miracle. Instead, I turn to the bitch in Kestien's cage. A fitting place, and somewhere I hope to see her permanently when this is all over. "Well well well! If it isn't Kaila Jane Petras finally catching on."

"If it isn't Narcissist Cock, right where she belongs." The name dig is childish, but I'm struggling a little. I was a decorated Marine. I am a First Captain of the Dead Army. I have one of the deadliest Juggernaut abilities ever written. But my husband is *looking* at me. They both are. Hell, they all are and this isn't how this was supposed to go.

I push them from my thoughts and address the darkest aura of the wrong side. It doesn't take me long at all to find him, and it doesn't even surprise me that the snake himself decided to see this part through. The smile spreads, the one that makes my skin crawl as he makes his way out of his hiding spot. It's too late when I realize Artur Mikailov is not sending that look my way. No. Instead, as my skin lights on fire and the fibers of my being stitch together, I realize that he is in fact looking directly at my husband. Who is now standing right behind me. "Baby?"

"How cute. After all this time, you were brought together just to die together." Artur's feigned sympathy is grating on the ears. I can't bring myself to turn around, and it is not the time for this kind of distraction.

"Mi razon my reason, turn around." The insistence in his voice is like we aren't still surrounded and standing in front of a powerful man. I force myself to ignore my husband, hoping he catches the hint.

"Either you tell your men to vacate the island, or my team and I will be walking over their bodies." I warn. Artur's smile turns into one of amusement, prompting the thunder to roll over the sky as his Juggernaut begins to charge the air.

"Mi reina my queen." Augustine calls from deep in his chest. I know his final warning, and against my better judgment, I give my back to the enemy and what I see changes everything. Because for the first time since my Juggernaut awakening, when I look my husband in the eyes, in my mind there is suddenly silence.

No colors roll off of him, only a rainbow in his irises. The notion of it surprises me to the point I almost forget about the bastard behind me. Augustine stares at me like a man on the brink of dehydration coming to water. I can't breathe, but the air begins to ripple around us, breaking me of the focus of him. Augustine seems to feel the coming attack because like the man I married his arm snaps out to pull me behind him faster than I care to admit. A bolt of lighting blows the ground apart where I was just standing. My hand grips Augustine's shirt as I begin to back us up to convene with the others. "Whoever brings me the heads of everyone within the circle will be given the highest ranks within the Army of Halos."

My eyes lock with Black who has his arms locked around Vince like Milo has Marco and Kestien has Max. They're trying like hell to close the distance between us, and the tears in their eyes are like a jab to the chest. The look in Black's eyes though? That's enough to set the ball rolling. All the soldiers that had been waiting until now start closing in, and my team starts pulling their weapons out. Kiari hands my boys their weapons one after the other, but gives my husband's pistol to me. "Okay everybody, you're in my world now. I know you have questions and I have enough answers to make your head spin but I need all hands on deck."

"Tell me what you need and I'll see it done." I pull out the sister pistol I stole from my husband when all of this began and hand them both over by the barrels for August to take. I am once again grateful for Black's connections and knowledge. The bullets I've infused with my blood glow with my nearness and I see the subtle realization in August's eyes.

"Right between the eyes. We don't take prisoners." I say to him with finality in the moment we are both holding the weapons together. When I let go, I pull my sword hilts from their place at the small of my back and turn from him to the army tripping over themselves to get to us, most falling short with the help of Milo's life stealing juggernaut ability. With the release of my breath, violet smoke forms the blades that bleed from the dual hilts in my hands before I start barking orders. "Marco, take the girls and follow Kiari."

"I'm not-" Marco tries to protest, but it's Augustine who shuts him down.

"Go! Those girls are your responsibility." With a growl Milo helps Sue onto his back.

"I can help!" Dariah screams, and I can already feel her energy changing.

"No!" My team bellows. Milo's eyes go white with his Juggernaut's darker ability taking out another wave of soldiers. Kestien's back is pressed to Milo's while he waits for my signal, but I can hear the agonizing screams of the unfortunate souls being run through with the earth metal spikes that begin popping up throughout the battlefield at Kestien's will. I don't get the chance to see Dariah follow orders when I hear familiar gunshots go off. All hell breaks loose and I can no longer focus on holding myself back, nor can I focus on the others.

Splitting my focus for the moment only, I start cutting down anyone who gets close enough and every step I take, Augustine shadows. I wish I could watch him work as I hear the distinct shots from his dual wield pistols feeling every time a new bullet forms in the empty space of the guns. I feel the control each bullet gives as a piece of my ability takes hold in their intended targets. I focus on keeping the smoke red, filling every corner of the victim's body with pure unfiltered rage. My unfiltered rage. I don't have to watch the red encapsulate and sink into the bodies to know that this fight is not going to go the way Artur had originally intended, so it is no surprise to me at all when I feel his panic and hateful anger fade from the island itself until it disappears entirely, letting me know that he's left all these people to die for his cause.

My blades slam through two soldiers who managed to get in on my right and left, but I risk the glance to find Narcissa's cage empty, snarling at the sight. Augustine's arm suddenly blocks my vision and I have just enough sense to lean away from the eardrum shattering pop. I lock eyes with him over my shoulder, and his look says more than I am able to feel from him. I don't like that at all. I've never been unable to feel and see the emotions from anyone.

"Mikailov took the bitch and ran! There's another jump point opening up too close for comfort." Aurora calls from somewhere behind me. She and I lock eyes, having a quick but silent conversation that has her nodding her understanding even as she slams a dagger through the underside of a female soldier's jaw.

"Kes', cover her!" I bark. The soldiers are coming in faster, and it no longer feels like the group is thinning as more join.

The ability Kestien has is not one that can be duplicated. His ability works by forcing the natural metals of the earth to bend to his will, making iron bars is easy work for him and the iron spikes skewering the bad guys left and right have been crucial in more than one fight before now. Making a solid dome requires focus that means he has to be protected for a few minutes. Pulling my swords from another dead man I take the step away from Augustine to run and cover Kestien, but my husband steps in front of me with his guns still aimed behind me over my shoulders.

"Vince, cover him!" he yells out as he shoots with his eyes locked on mine. "Worry about you."

I grit my teeth and duck under his arms to get behind him. It's like a dance between us at this point.

Slash. Pop. Step.

Stab. Slap. Step.

Slice. Clap. Step.

"Clear!" Aurora's voice cuts through the sounds of slaughter right before another wave makes it to us.

"Everybody go!" I call out. Pulling my focus quickly I let purple tendrils run their way through my hair. This particular trick I learned for emergency purposes, but I need them all out of my way.

Max and Silas jump through first, followed by Black and a reluctant Vince. Aurora does her best to keep the soldiers off of her but she's going to have to close it fast. I turn to Augustine to urge him to follow. "Go with-"

"Don't even try it." Augustine cuts me off before he turns to Aurora, sending shot after shot at anyone coming with practiced precision. "Respectfully, wait a few minutes and open it again on the east side of the Island. Hold it and we'll get there."

For some reason, Aurora does as directed, and it's just the two of us in a sea of shit eaters. The tendrils in my hair form a braid, but it isn't a fashion statement. My annoyance with my husband's indignation has reached its peak when I let the roar into my voice. "Augustine I need-"

"To realize that your time of making decisions alone is over!" His anguish and finality is so clear that I simply begin to growl, gathering each color I can because I can't stop it once I start.

"You have to get out of here, Augustine." I beg him, panic rising within me at the nearness of him to the danger that is me. I take two steps, turning my back on him to put distance between us and calling out to Kestien over the com in my ear. "Drop it and get him out of here, Kes'."

I don't see his hand snap out to grab my purple coated braid and wrap it around his hand, but I do feel him pull my back against his chest hard. And I do feel the collar drop from my neck. The world drops into slow motion as two things happen at the same time absolute fear and realization hit me. The emotions of everyone on the Island are sucked into my body in an array of visible colors that were only visible to me until a second ago, and Augustine's growl from deep in his chest sounds directly into my ear. "Woman, you are never leaving my fucking sight again."

My control snaps and I can't hold it back anymore. Instead I can only watch in horror as a shockwave of colors and emotions blast from me. I watch it tear through flesh and bone of every soldier in my sight path, tearing each and every one apart and painting the earth around me until a shower of blood and sinew falls from the sky like rain. The fight is over. I know it is. Yet even as the darkness tries to grip me I manage to find the strength to push it away. The rushing of blood in my ears as I become painfully aware of the lack of pressure on my hair, even now that I know the purple has released the strands.

I turn slowly, the sound of the dirt under my boots the only thing filling the sudden silence. I can't decide between closing my eyes or keeping them open, but I need to see. When I do an extremely unattractive sob rips from my chest at the sight of my husband standing unharmed just a step from me. Awe in his eyes where there should be nothing at all but soullessness. I don't remember the last time I truly cried, or even allowed myself to feel some form of relief. But as this beautiful man closes the distance and takes me in his arms with a firmness backed by desperation, I release the control.

I let go of the strength. I give the reins over to the ether when his lips touch mine and whispers "I've missed you so fucking much."

There's a gentle whisper at the back of my mind, echoed by something deeper speaking from the bottom of my soul. A voice so ancient and familiar it should startle me, but nothing in the world except the unconsciousness about to take me under could break me from this man's lips on mine.

Finally, my love.

Chapter Twenty-Three
Marco

Kiari leads us through a waiting jump point to a brand new place. The silence of it is one thing, but the homey feeling that immediately envelopes me is something I am not expecting. I desperately want to give my undivided attention to the absolute goddess that led me here, but I know I can't. I can't even address the elephant in the room yet, but I plan on doing that in just a moment anyway. I place Sue on one of the couches next to Dariah who immediately starts checking Sue over for injuries. I quickly give them both a once over before I round on Kiari, intent on getting answers. Kiari stands with her arms crossed and waiting for me before she walks away into the kitchen the moment my mouth opens to start asking the litany of questions in my brain. "You girl's okay?"

"We're fine, Marco. Go get your answers." Sue says softly with a knowing look in her shifting eyes.

When I reach the kitchen where Kiari is waiting for me, three sets of four coffee mugs on the counter catch my attention, drawing me closer as Kiari watches and waits beside them. For a moment I start to wonder whose house this is until Kiari takes a deep breath right beside me. She brings her finger up to point at the set of four closest to the sink, moving down the line as she speaks. "X. Y. Z."

I look closer at the center group, seeing the newness of each cup, telling of their non-use. The rest are worn, but these have the slightest bit of dust covering them. Like they were placed here and left alone. I also realize now that these are the only four that are turned over, and Kiari reaches for them one at a time to turn them upright. "Augustine. Vince. Max. Marco."

She glances at me, making sure I look up at her before leaning her head to signal that I follow her again. Already stunned silent, I keep a few steps of respectful distance between us as she leads me up a winding staircase that opens up into a long hallway of doors.

"These are our personal rooms." She keeps speaking softly, relaying to me little bits of information meant to calm my mind. Kiari stops in front of a door in the middle. "This is your room."

She steps back, allowing me the space to open the door. When I step through, it isn't what I expect at all. The room on the mountain had a practicality to it, a simplicity I liked but wasn't comfortable in. This room was made with me in mind entirely. A flight simulation computer in the corner with my favorite program running softly. A down comforter on the king-sized bed, something I prefer to any other material. There is soft lighting and a balcony outside of a floor-to-ceiling window. On the walls, there are photographs I didn't even know existed. Accomplishments and surveillance images of me and the boys. Childhood pictures of my sister and I at different stages of life. A sob catches in my throat, and no matter how many times I try, I just can't clear it.

I hear a crash and a commotion from downstairs, and I'm grateful for the reprieve from my emotions right now. In a blink, Kiari is out of the room, and I follow slowly. By the time I make it to the bottom of the steps, I'm not even surprised to see Kiari standing between Max and Vince trying to keep them apart.

"Esto es lo que has estado ocultando!? Ni una sola vez en nuestras vidas nos hemos guardado secretos el uno al otro. Ni una sola vez, ¡y ésta! This is what you've been hiding!? Not once in our lives have we kept secrets from each other. Not once, and this!" Max roars. I should stop them, it's my first reaction usually, but I can't bring myself to do it. Max is right, and I'm too raw to play peacekeeper.

"No crees que esto me ha estado matando!? Ella vino a verme y me dijo que era importante no decir nada. Ella me hizo prometer. Don't you think this has been killing me!? She came to see me and told me that it was important not to say anything. She made me promise." Vince's hand in his hair is enough to signal to me of the fact that he's spiraling hard, but Max is ignoring the signs completely. The rest have broken up into pairs, and I can see Milo making his way around, checking wounds while he listens to our family drama unfold. We know everyone is listening, but there are too many chaotic emotions and adrenaline between us to give a shit.

"Entiendo poder ocultármelo. Por muy cabreado que esté, puedo entenderlo. Pero Marco? I understand being able to hide it from me. As pissed off as I am, I can understand it. But Marco?" Max throws his hand out to point to me, tears in his eyes. Vince is a mess, and I'm sprung into action by the blood on his shoulder dripping down his arm. When I get to him and pull his arm straight so I can see it better, Milo puts a hand on my shoulder with a deep sympathy in his eyes.

"I got it. I'm a medic, and this conversation is a family thing." The way he says it so softly is like he's letting me know I can pay attention to the situation at hand. I do my best to give him a grateful look, but my face is frozen with the influx of puzzle pieces falling together. They continue to argue when the air shifts around us, a jump point opening up in the middle of the room for a split second to spit out two women. One is a face I've never seen, but the other is the nurse that Max said was named Sophia.

Aurora clears the distance in three heavy strides taking a hand of each woman in hers. "You girls alright?"

"We cleared the mountain just in time for them to hit us. All units are in the wind. The druids have taken the civilians as refugees and scattered them as well. No casualties, but we have some unfortunate news." Sophia speaks in pants, doing her best to calm her breathing as she is led to a seat at the breakfast bar. Aurora takes her face in her hands, a sisterly gesture. "None of the units that hit us are dead soldiers. Nobody registered within ranks. That's what took us so long to get here, we had to check. I brought Kestien the master disk for the surveillance on the mountain."

"You girls did amazing. Wait for Kaila, we all have a lot to debrief." The praise earns her a smile. It dawns on me how much time has passed since I arrived, and the knowledge makes me antsy.

"Where are they?" I say, speaking up for the first time in a broken voice. Max and Vince's attention snapped to Milo and the twins. I watch Milo and Kiari look at Kestien, who nods once in answer to a silent conversation that passes between the three.

"They should be here soon." Kestien replies, his tone meant to placate.

That's it. That's the answer that sets me off.

I walk over, drowning in the onslaught of realizations and emotions. Max and Vince haven't stopped arguing for more than a few seconds, their snarls at one another sound so far away in the midst of the blood rushing in my ears.

"Podrías habérnoslo dicho! ¡Tendrías que habérnoslo dicho! You could have told us! You should have told us!" Max bellows.

"Y ponerla a ella y a todos nosotros en riesgo? ¡Ella dejó claro que necesitaba que lo mantuviera en secreto hasta que pudiera reunirnos! And put her and all of us at risk? She made it clear that I needed to keep it quiet until she could bring us together!" Vince shouts.

" Dale tus excusas de mierda a alguien que no la haya extrañado tanto como tú! Make your bullshit excuses to someone who hasn't missed her as much as you have!" Max spits, turning his back on Vince.

"Confié en mi hermana! I trusted my sister!" Vince's shout makes the floor shake, but when Max rounds on him with a face contorted in rage and pain, the house vibrates with the intensity of his next words.

"ELLA TAMBIÉN ES NUESTRA HERMANA! SHE'S OUR SISTER TOO!"

Dariah is fussing over Sue on the couch. Aurora and her girls are on one side of the breakfast bar, conferring with each other while simultaneously trying to look like they aren't watching my brothers fall apart. Milo and the twins are whispering to one another in harsh tones. Milo's whispered words barely reach my ears when he speaks softly in Italian. "Pensi che sappiamo che possiamo capirli? Do you think they know we can understand them?"

"Não seja insensível, Milo. Se fôssemos eles, também não nos importaríamos. Don't be insensitive Milo. If we were them we wouldn't care either." Kestien whispers back, scolding in Portuguese.

As the question and dots connect in my mind, more just take their place.

"Where are they?" I ask again, my voice clogged with emotion. Nobody is paying attention, everybody so wrapped up in the disaster show my brothers are having that nobody even notices my silent spiral. I bring myself to stand in front of the four freshly upturned coffee mugs on the counter beside the kitchen sink and look at them for a second like they somehow hold all the answers. Everything fades away but the anger rising in my chest, spreading through my body to the tips of my limbs and appendages before I take the cup Kiari pointed out as mine. I realize the weight these cups hold. What they are meant to represent.

She made us a way.

She built us a home.

And she did it on her own.

The anger hits a breaking point, and I lob the cup as hard as I possibly can against the wall separating the living room from the kitchen. The silence that comes after the crash is sudden and absolute when all attention snaps to me with wide eyes of surprise.

"Where. The. *Fuck*. Is. My. Sister." I bellow. There is only breathing for a few heartbeats before Aurora points to the corner of the room beside the shattered dish, where a clear ripple takes the form of a door. I hold my breath until I lock eyes with Augustine, who's covered in blood, cradling my sister's unconscious body in his arms. His eyes should be more of a concern to me right now, but I can't take my eyes off of her. There are more scars on her body than I can count, but she looks even better than the last time I saw her. Her hair has grown so much longer, and she isn't nearly as thin as we used to poke fun at her for.

In an instant the room erupts into movement. The twins move from their spots, Kiari gathering supplies while Kestien disappears up the stairs. Milo makes an attempt to take Kaila's unconscious body from Augustine's arms, and I don't make it to tell him how bad of an idea that is right now. A heavy rumble penetrates the air around us, originating from Augustine's chest. Milo puts his hands up, palms out in surrender. There's no fear on Milo's face when he speaks like he's trying to calm an animal. "I need to check her over. I would never dream of hurting her. I just need to do my job."

Sue comes from the living room to put a hand under August's arm, pulling him into the living room and down onto the couch. I'm across the room fast, Max and Vince hot on my heels as if we're drawn to her by a magnet. Max grabs a small pillow and props it against August's thigh when Vince takes her from a reluctant August and gently lays her down across the rest of the couch. I adjust her legs and make quick work of taking off her boots as gently as I can before getting comfortable on the armrest at her feet. Vince pulls a chair up for himself and one for Max, setting up as close as they can without getting in Milo's way, their fight on pause for now. We all watch in reverent silence while he works. He checks her vitals with a stethoscope and blood pressure cuff, grunting and muttering to himself while scribbling in a notepad that looks a little worse for wear. Milo removes the cuff from Kaila's arm, tossing it aside and putting a pulse oximeter in her finger, scribbling the results on the paper with the others. He checks her temperature last, sucking his teeth at what he sees before putting all his tools down and hovering his palms from the top of her head slowly down to her toes. It looks strange, but there's a faint glow of white in his eyes as he does it that lets me know there's a juggernaut ability at play.

Kiari hesitantly walks up to Augustine, and he stops stroking Kaila's hair to look up. Kiari hands him a bowl of water and a rag.

"In five minutes, her fever will spike." Kiari turns to give Vince and I a meaningful look before she continues, sympathy bleeding into her tone. "Roughly ten minutes after that, she'll seize. You'll have to hold her down or she'll hurt herself."

August wrings the towel out and starts patting around her face and neck, but after a short few minutes the sweat on her body starts coming faster and her breathing shallows. I touch her ankle in curious concern to feel her skin slick with perspiration and immediately latch onto each ankle with my hands. "Augustine, she's on fucking fire."

Milo comes back with a defibrillator cart and flips the switch to turn it on. He crouches down, spreading a blanket on the hardwood floor. "Get her on the floor and hold her down."

I hold her ankles firmly, and with August and Vince's help, we get her to the ground just before the convulsions start. Fear hasn't let me go, and it sinks its claws deeper as I struggle to hold her legs. My sister, who even after all this time is half my size is causing four grown men to grunt and struggle. The tension in my brothers' faces as they help hold her feels wrong. All of this feels wrong, but eventually Kaila collapses into a sedated state. Everyone in the room releases a collective breath of relief and Milo moves in to check her vitals again. The whirring of the defibrillator is the only sound in the room for a moment until Milo speaks once again. "She's stable for now. You can put her back on the couch. She won't wake up for at least a couple of hours. Until then we have to get ready."

"I'm not leaving her alone." August says in a gravel tone.

"Trust me when I say that there isn't a single person in this room who would ask you to do that. I need you four to stay with her while the rest of us do what we have to do." Milo is still calm when he hands me a bag. "It's best if you all change now, she'll want us to go as soon as she wakes up."

"Where are we going? I don't understand anything anymore!" I spit through gritted teeth. Kiari comes to my side, placing her hand gently on my shoulder.

"If we try to explain it all, it won't make any sense. I can vouch for how long she's been preparing for you guys to hear everything she has to say. The burden I've had to watch my captain carry from the moment I met her is so heavy we can't even help her carry it."

"But we're hoping that at the very least, you can." Kestien sends Augustine a look that tells me that particular hope rests in him. Not surprising to me at all. Without another word, everyone disburses. Aurora takes Sue and Dariah, while the others disappear with Silas and Black deeper into the house. We get comfortable around Kaila after we return her to the couch, but the way Augustine is watching Vince makes me feel bad for my big brother.

"Augustine, I-" Vince doesn't get the chance to finish the sentence.

Chapter Twenty-Four

Max

The tension in the room sends electricity over my skin. Vince fucked up, and now that August knows it, he's in for it. Augustine holds up a hand to stop Vince from speaking, planting a delicate kiss on Kaila's forehead and then carefully moving out from beneath her head. Vince braces, but it isn't enough to stop him before August decides to barrel straight at him. Vince's back slams against the wall on the far side of the living room while Marco and I watch. August keeps his growls low, but we all hear him as he speaks. "You knew about this."

"August-" Vince makes the attempt to explain, but Cap' ain't asking questions.

"You kept her from me. This whole time?" His voice rises slightly and Marco and I glance over to check on Kaila. She remains unmoving except for the steady rise and fall of her chest. I'm having a hard time believing she's real, and I can no longer stop myself from reaching over to take her hand just to be sure of it. I run my thumb over the back of her hand in a soothing motion the way she did the night I came to stay with them.

I remember the fear, the loneliness I felt when I sat down in a car full of a family that asked no questions. The way she reached over to steady my trembling hands, offering me the kindest smile I had ever seen until that age. Vince, Marco, and Kaila folded me so seamlessly into their siblinghood that I never had to question if I belonged. After the beginning of my time in this existence was less than ideal, having them teach me what it means to be loved...to know loyalty? It made my life worth holding on to. It's the same thing that makes the vile rage bubble in my gut knowing that this woman who would hold my hand through night terrors and anxiety attacks growing up has been here, alone and alive. It's clear she's made friends, something that has always come so easily to her that it isn't surprising in the least. If she trusts these people, then it's because they can be trusted without fail, but it wasn't us. Not Vince to shield her, not Marco to make her laugh, not me for her to confide in, and specifically without Augustine to love her.

August slams Vince back one more time, drawing me from my thought spiral before Sue and Dariah stand from the other couch. Sue's hand comes to land on Augustine's back gently, and the far away look that seems to live in her eyes is steady.

"She didn't give him a choice, Augustine." There is an absolution in her voice that seems to be there a lot. I assume it's because of her ability to see things differently from the rest of us. August hesitates, probably trying to decide if he's going to beat the shit out of Vince regardless. Instead Augustine releases Vince with a final snarl and takes his place as Kaila's pillow once again as if it's physically painful for him to be too far from her. I, for one, have no doubt that it probably is. If missing her these four years caused me this much pain? Augustine will be feeling the epitome of agony right about now.

Sue and Dariah bring a couple of chairs to sit with us and we all fall into a seemingly comfortable silence. It stretches on for a longer time than I am aware, because my mind is busy trying to imagine what could have possibly marred her skin so terribly. I see cuts, tears, burns, and the bite marks of what looks like a couple different creatures. It makes me sick but I can't look away for fear that if I do, she'll disappear again.

I barely notice when the others in the house start to trickle back into the living room to wait for Kaila to wake, and within the silence, tensions rise and rise. After two hours, I almost can't stand it. The silence is uncomfortably weighted, too much tension, too much…human. My nervous ticks causing me irritation that has me standing to my full height so fast I knock the chair over. "Somebody needs to explain what the fuck is going on before I lose my fucking mind. What the hell happened to her? Why is she so…so…"

I don't get the opportunity to finish before the front door opens, drawing everyone's attention like a snap. Special lieutenant Andrew fucking Black steps inside before holding the door open and ushering in the nurse from the clinic where we took The Battery.

"Helena, my dear." Black says with a bow as she walks passed him. Marco reaches over to grasp my belt while Vince uprights my chair. Marco forces me back down into it before taking my hand and holding it without looking away from Black.

"I'll make tea." Helena says after her eyes assess the room full of soldiers surrounding Kaila and Augustine. "My darling, I think it's time."

Helena doesn't meet Black's eyes but I can tell that's who she's talking to because he nods even as he watches her disappear into the kitchen. Kiari stands, irritation in her face as she speaks. "You know she wants to be the one to explain. It isn't your story to tell."

"Sit down, Kiari." Black snarls. "I know damn well what I can and cannot share. But there are things that even you three don't know about what the hell is going on here."

"What the hell is that supposed to mean?" Milo grumbles, pulling Kestien from the chair and into his lap.

"It means that it's time I filled you in on my backstory and how I came to know the woman who has the loyalties of everyone in this room." Black says as he sinks down into an empty armchair, resting his elbows on his knees. "I'm not a juggernaut like the rest of you. I'm what's known as a celestial. An angel, to be more specific."

Kiari takes the seat Kestien just vacated, the room falling dead silent as we listen to Black dive into his explanation. "The story of my origin isn't important, so I won't get into it now. The story of my purpose, however, is. I know Miss Sue has filled you boys in on the story of Ryn and Kyn, the bedtime story that's been watered down over the millennia. Everyone in this room knows the tale for what it really is. A history, not a fairytale."

"I was tasked to watch over Kyn when Ryn finally met her fate, the task given to me by the same goddess that tested them." Black is cut off by a puff of grey smoke that suddenly appears to reveal a red eyed Silas, perched right in the chair Kiari first sat in, the one right next to Marco.

"What'd I miss?" He winks at Marco who snarls, but I don't miss the slight coloring in his cheeks. Curious, and something I'll watch out for.

"Shut up, Silas." Milo sighs, urging Black to continue.

"As I was saying, The goddess, who I know as Calissa bestowed very unique and special gifts upon the lovers before Ryn died. The sorcerer who cursed Ryn gave her what we know as the madness. It basically takes the mind and twists it up until it eventually makes it bleed. The madness is a brutal and explicitly forbidden curse for the cruelty of the way it kills its host. Once bestowed, it cannot be undone. Which is why, Calissa decided to gift Ryn the power of emotion, turning Ryn into the most powerful empath ever created. Kyn, was given the gift of the hunt which gave him all the senses and attributes of an apex predator while keeping him in a human form. Much like a shifter, he could run faster, hit harder, and heal almost instantly-but there was more to his senses. The way Kyn explained it, it was like he could sense the emotions and intentions from others through his sense of smell." Marco, Vince, and I shoot Augustine a knowing look, watching his eyes narrow on Black. "Now, as the story goes, Calissa's husband-a god named Darcin- gifted the couple what my people know as tied immortal reincarnation."

"That's cruel." Silas gasps.

"It was that. But it was also a blessing." Black agrees.

"What does it mean?" Marco and I ask simultaneously. Helena chooses that moment to walk into the room holding a large tray full of cups steaming with the liquid inside of them. Black jumps up instantly, taking it from her and offering her a scathing look. I realize then that they might actually be together.

"It means that Darcin tied their life cycles together and bonded them. When they died, they would reincarnate, meet, fall in love, and repeat. Forever." Helena answers softly, taking a seat.

"Only what the story doesn't tell you is that there was another god at play. A god by the name of Draxin, Darcin's brother." Black sighs. "When Draxin heard what Calissa and Darcin had done for the lovers, he was outraged for reasons still unclear to this day. So, he decided to grant the same fate to the king and the sorcerer who cursed Ryn and Kyn. Every cycle, every single lifetime, Kyn and I had to watch Ryn lose her life in some way or another. Almost always to the madness that somehow reincarnated with her. Each time, they met, fell in love, and he lost her in the most brutal ways until they did it again. I would wait for them to reincarnate, find Kyn, and we would spend that lifetime trying to find ways to stop the madness before it took her. Each time we failed."

Helena puts her hand gently on Black's arm to soothe the defeat in his demeanor. Black clears his throat as if he's reliving the anguish as he tells us all this horrible story. "This lifetime, something changed…everything changed. Because this time, I met Ryn first."

Black's eyes settle on Kaila's unconscious body and it's as if the entire room is robbed of the air to breathe. Vince speaks up first, being the first one to put words to the realization we all seem to be having at once. "And you think our sister is the reincarnation of Ryn?"

"That can't be possible." Kiari say's breathlessly.

"I know it to be true." Black replies without an ounce of doubt. "You can't tell because you have only gotten a glimpse of the power your sister has. The colors you saw on Galla? The colors in Augustine's bullets? They're all physical manifestations of the emotions she is able to control. This state that she's in? Is a direct result of the madness. Ryn had fainting spells, seizures. There is no other person on the planet who has an ability like her."

"No. Absolutely not." August snarls, shaking his head like it will make it any less true.

"You can deny it all you want. Tell me you don't have the hunt. Make your denials but I can guarantee this for fact. Kaila Petras is the reincarnation of Ryn and you, Augustine, are the reincarnation of Kyn. I know it. Look around this room and tell me everyone here doesn't know it too." Black argues.

"I just got her back!" August rages, clutching Kaila just a little closer. "You mean to tell me that I'm just going to fucking lose her again?"

"I said this time was different. Not just because I met her first, but because of who you both are in this lifetime. In the lifetime before this one, Kyn's reincarnation and I found something, an ancient and unknown magic that we tried because we were both desperate. At the time, we figured it was just another dead end, another failure because a few weeks after that, she ended up dying again. I'm starting to think that wasn't the case."

"Why?" Milo interjects before Augustine can argue more.

"Because neither Ryn nor any of her reincarnations were able to use the emotions as a weapon. Manifesting emotions into physical forces? No. That's all her." He says, pointing to Kaila. "And then there's you. A man who not only has all the attributes of the hunt, but you're different, too."

"Different how?" August growls, rubbing at his temple.

"Because you can hear him...can't you?" Black says, confusing us. "You can hear Kyn in your head. You've met him?"

August doesn't say anything, he doesn't get the chance, because right before he opens his mouth in confirmation or denial I double over, clutching my head as what I can only describe as howling wolves split my mind apart. The temperature in my body seems to rise fast, and all I can feel is discomfort, pain, and my sweat starting to accumulate all over. Time seems lost all of a sudden. I sense more than hear a commotion around me before Dariah's voice speaks.

"Max?" she says my name so tentatively I almost miss it through the rushing in my ears. "Max, can you tell me what you're feeling right now?"

My head is beginning to pound with a rising force as the howling gets louder, and my mouth is drier than sandpaper making it impossible to swallow the bile rising in my throat. If this is an anxiety attack then it's the worst I've ever had in my life, but even so I try my best to explain. "Head hurts…hot. Howling…make it stop."

I can barely understand what I'm saying, the words coming out in a slurry mess. I don't get to see the commotion around me but I can hear it like I'm stuck in some kind of filter or under water. While my eyes are closed tight, the world shifting, Dariah starts giving frantic orders. "Get his shirt off and help me get him to a shower."

"Come on, kid." Black's voice comes in on a grunt when I'm hoisted out of my chair. I can't get my legs to work. My body feels limp. "You gonna help me out here?"

"Can't." I managed to say. Someone else's hands offer more support, and when I start to hear the faint echo in the room, I know we've made it to the bathroom somewhere. I feel someone pull my shirt away from my body and hear the tearing of fabric. The clink of a belt and the slide of my cargo pants being removed lets a draft of cool air hit my skin and for a second I can't even be embarrassed by the fact that I am very much so in my briefs and socks as they grunt to lift and put me in the tub. The cold water doesn't really register all that much, but it does allow for a small relief in temperature.

"What the hell is going on?" Marco asks, the worry in his voice audible even in the state I'm in.

"Do you know who his parents are? Anything about his bloodline?" Dariah gives the question but I can't answer her.

"His parents died of an overdose. He's never known anything about his family otherwise. They abandoned him before he was born." Vince answers for me from my left side. He's holding me up in the water with Black on the other side. I can't really feel my body anymore, and the feeling of not feeling anything is a trip all its own.

"What about his blood type?" Dariah asks, followed by the sounds of cabinets opening and closing. Rummaging stops short when Milo pipes up.

"Woah woah woah! That's a sedative!" Panic envelopes me and I do my best to thrash.

"No needles!" My brothers shout together.

"I have to sedate him!" Dariah screams.

"I can sedate him, but I won't do that without knowing why, Dariah." I just know it's Milo's hands on me, and irrational fear takes over. I somehow find the strength to thrash harder than before.

"If you come any closer to him with that shit I will put you through the floor, Doc'." Vince warns.

"What am I supposed to do! If his temperature rises any higher he's gonna start-" Milo's words are suddenly cut off when the room goes silent outside of the screaming in my mind.

The room stops but the feeling of calm somehow settles around us. My heart rate starts to slow, and while the heat doesn't subside, the panic does. "Put him down, guys."

I got to hear that voice grow up, so it's a privilege to know it even with my eyes still shut. It's older now. Stronger in a way only she could be after everything she's probably gone through. I feel myself being lowered until the water is cascading over my face, and slowly but surely the water goes from room temperature to ice cold. The unadulterated relief is one that forces a moan through my teeth, and the pounding in my head lessens exponentially.

"Is everything ready to go?" Kaila asks, her voice weak with exhaustion.

"Just waiting for you to wake up." Kiari's voice comes from a distance, but a gentle hand rests on my face even as the water falls right on me. In a rush I feel exhaustion, the weakness in my body making it hard to hold my head up. I hear the shower turn off and then I'm being carried again, my body laid down on something solid. I feel something being laid across my chest and ankles, and a click secures them there.

"Where are we going?" Marco asks again, no longer standing close to me. I hear Kaila take a deep breath before diving in to answer. Like she's gearing up to give bad news.

"When Aurora is finished opening the jump point here in the next few minutes we'll all head to New Zealand."

"New Zealand? Why?" Vince asks.

"Because with everything going on in the Deadlands, the Pack Beta will be out for blood unless we bring his daughter back alive. The Pack doctor will be able to help Max when we get there." Kaila pauses, but I hear the shuffle of movement as she walks away from my side. "Dariah was sent here on the word of her Alpha because a seer told him that his son and true Alpha heir has been alive since his kidnapping. Along the way, she found Sue and was pulled into a deeper purpose that brought her to us."

"I've just sent confirmation over mind link that we've found him, the doctor will be waiting for us at the border with the Alpha." Dariah sounds like she's about to cry, but she clears her throat.

"Pack? Please, tell me we aren't adding wolves into the mix of shit we didn't know actually existed!" Marco says, incredulously.

"Everything exists, little brother. All of this is real. I'll go more into detail when we get there and have a chance to breathe but for right now you're going to have to be okay with the quick notes version. Four years and seven months ago I was kidnapped by a cartel. I was held captive for six months before Black and his unit found me and brought me to the deadlands. For four years, I've learned everything and anything I could about anything and everything that is kept hidden from regular human knowledge. As soon as I became a ranked soldier with a unit I could trust, I started plotting and planning to bring my family together. You guys want answers? Fine. I have them for you in spades and they're all yours but we cannot stay here for me to give them to you freely. All you need to know right now is the following and then we need to get our asses out of here. I am really alive. We all really have supernatural abilities we don't fucking understand. And Maxwell St. James is really the long lost son of the last living alpha of the Still Breath Pack. The strongest and longest reigning shifter clan in the history of the hidden world of Joelynn."

"The minute we're safe, you better explain." Vince growls.

"As soon as we're safe, I'll fill you in on everything I know." Kaila agrees. "Augustine…"

"I will follow you anywhere." He growls, and I'm assuming he's right in her face when he does it. "I will follow you, but make no mistake, amor love. You will tell me *everything* that happened from the moment they took you from me. You will tell me the origin of every scar, every mark. You will tell me *everything*."

There is complete silence, my mind fading quickly into unconsciousness as only the shuffling of boots and what I think are backpacks fade into the background. The last thing I'm able to hear before I drift off against my will is Kaila as I'm jostled a bit like we're moving, remaining on my back in a parallel position.

"Stay close and do not engage unless you absolutely need to. The rules where we're going aren't like they are everywhere else. Just try not to kill anyone."

I know when we enter the jump point, but that's all I know before my world goes utterly and completely dark.

Until something meets me in the darkness.

About The Author

Maribel Navarrete was born in Chicago and raised in Nebraska, where she grew up with a love for books, music, and storytelling. She works as a Registered Behavioral Technician and finds joy in supporting others and making a difference wherever she can.

When she's not reading (usually a book a day), you'll find her rolling dice in a Dungeons & Dragons campaign or listening to music that fits her mood. She's also a proud mom, a loyal friend, and someone who believes in fairness, kindness, and staying curious.